Hen Party

ALOHA CHICKEN MYSTERIES: BOOK 2

Josi Avari

Quill
Canyon
Press

Want to know about new releases, free books, and fabulous prizes? Sign up for my newsletter!
josiavari.com
and connect with me on facebook

Also by Josi Avari

AND INTRODUCING TWO NEW COZY MYSTERY SERIES!

The Desperate Strangers Travel Club Mysteries

Stranger on the Seine (Book 1)

Hen Party

First edition. March 8, 2019.

Copyright © 2019 Josi Avari.

Written by Josi Avari.

Cover art and illustrations by Richard Lance Russell

See more at richardrussellart.com

Chapter One

Saffron hefted the chicken in her arms, trying to settle Tikka's protests. Tikka was not a car chicken. She did not enjoy car rides, and though the Empress insisted that a chicken could be trained to like civilized living, Saffron was not seeing much evidence of that with Tikka.

She carried the black and orange hen up the expansive

steps of the Empress' estate house, juggling it in one arm and a package in the other. In the paper-wrapped package was a gift for the Empress, a large fish called a kūmū. Saffron had bought it from Oke, the fisherman who showed up sometimes along the shoreline with his deep-bottomed canoe filled with fish. Saffron was always happy to see him, as his fish were fresh and delicious. Today she'd picked up some for herself and some to take to the Empress.

The Empress' home was an old plantation house built into the side of the mountain behind the little Hawaiian town of Maika'i, which Saffron had called home for several months now. She knocked and turned to take in the rugged palms that surrounded the estate, and beyond them, the gleam of the teal ocean striped with whitecaps.

The colors of Hawaii dazzled Saffron. The rich greens and bright floral accents, the golden sun and sand, the crystalline blue water, all of it fed her in a way she'd never experienced.

Saffron knew color differently than other people did. Color was a special experience for her. She seemed to see color more intensely and to see more colors than anyone else. When she looked at a red hibiscus blossom, for example, it was not just red. It was red with soft yellow hues, with the palest of blue cast over the curved surface of each petal. She had stopped trying to explain this to people, since to them a red flower was a red flower.

Today, the pale pink of the plantation house was shaded with yellow reflections from the brilliant sunlight, making it a cheery peach color. The subtlety was not something Saffron often thought of, but occasionally, when something stood out, she wondered about the strange ability.

She also had a perfect memory for color. In her mind was an extensive catalog of every color she'd ever seen, and the information her eyes sent her brain was constantly being cross-checked against that catalog. For example, the bronze sheen on the doorknob was exactly the color of the drawer pulls on the oak cabinets in the shabby Washington DC apartment where she'd grown up and the perfect match to the arms of a park bench in the U.S. National Arboretum. She toyed with the shade in her mind as the door swung open.

Carlo, one of the two strong middle-aged men employed by the Empress, opened the door, invited her in, and took the fish to the kitchen.

Coming here always felt like going back in time. The interior was decorated with lavish wood antiques from Europe, gilded mirrors, and Renaissance paintings. It smelled cool and dusty, and the crystal chandeliers were kept dim. Carlo returned to show Saffron through the vast entry and back into the drawing room.

The Empress sat, as always, at the window, gazing out at the immaculate garden and stroking Princess, her pet chicken. The Empress carried her everywhere on special pillows or lap quilts. Princess was a silkie, a breed of chicken known for its soft, fluffy feathers, blue earlobes, and devotion to its owners.

The third trait was evident now, as the little bird's eyelids drooped in contentment at the Empress' attentions.

"Saffron!" the Empress exclaimed, and Princess jumped at the sound of her voice. Rex, the assistant behind the Empress, moved without command to turn the Empress' chair and wheeled her over to greet her guest.

The Empress was a vast woman, colossal in friendliness as well as size. She enveloped the room with her genuine interest in and affection for all living things within it. Her warm skin was the color of sable orchids, and the silver hair piled atop her head was secured with carved koa wood combs. She spoke with the soft accent of her first language—Samoan—draped over each English word. Saffron smiled as the Empress exclaimed over Tikka.

"What a beauty! What a regal beauty you are!" Tikka

arched her neck in response, and Saffron could almost believe that she knew what the Empress was saying.

The Empress waved a hand, and Carlo swept Princess from her lap and held the chicken. The Empress waved Saffron closer and gathered Tikka out of her grasp. Tikka was much larger than Princess, but the difference was slight on the Empress' ample lap. Saffron tensed. Tikka generally spent her days out in the pen with the other hens, laying an egg nearly every day, scratching for bugs, and bathing in the sand. She was not a house chicken like Princess. Saffron wasn't entirely sure what Tikka would do. One look at the vases, rugs, and delicate carvings surrounding them brought an image of Tikka flapping and scratching her way around the pristine drawing room.

But the Empress' warm personality seemed to have the same effect on chickens as it did on people. As she stroked Tikka's head, the chicken stilled, then settled, lying down with her soft underfeathers spread around her like a skirt. She gazed placidly over at Saffron, who breathed a sigh of relief.

"This is a very special chicken," the Empress gushed. Saffron shrugged. She thought so, too, as Tikka had been her first friend when she'd moved here and taken over her late uncle's egg farm last fall, but she wasn't quite as demonstrative about her sentiments. The Empress went on, "she is a Wyandotte. Gold-laced, see?" she indicated Tikka's brassy feathers, each outlined in with a sharp black point, "they are very docile, generally, and make wonderful mothers." Here, the Empress' eyes flicked up to the clock and rested a moment on a silver frame on the marble mantel over the fireplace. She turned to Rex, "Check the window, will you? He should be here any time."

Saffron raised her eyebrows in an unspoken question.

"Oh, my dear, when I asked you over, I didn't know that my boy—my Davis—was coming to visit me today! He's in the

Navy, you know, and I don't always know when he is near his home port. But he is coming, and I can't wait to see him. I didn't call off our playdate because Princess is so looking forward to spending time with Tikka, and because—who knows?—you and my Davis may find something in common."

Saffron tried not to smile. So that was it. Since she'd moved here, everyone in town who had an eligible bachelor relative from 21 to 50 had been subtly and not subtly trying to set her up. She didn't mind, but she had been spending a lot of time with her favorite bachelor—Keahi Kekoa—lately, and he might mind her being set up with someone else.

Rex came back into the room and shook his head. "No one yet, ma'am."

The Empress waved a dismissive hand, "Thank you, Rex. Never mind." To Saffron, she said, "Oh, but that's not really why you're here. Let's go out to the garden so the children can play."

Again, Rex moved without instruction to wheel her toward the tall glass doors, and Carlo, cradling Princess in one arm, threw them open to let her pass.

Outside, Carlo put Princess down in "the chicken garden," a sunny spot where Saffron had seen her play before. It had been planted with chicken-friendly shrubs and sported a feeder, a small pond, and a nice sandy stretch for dirtbathing. Princess immediately set to work pecking at bugs in the grass below her. The Empress waved to Rex, and he gathered Tikka and set her down on the lawn next to Princess. Again Saffron tensed. She had seen displays of dominance in her flock at home, and she'd tried to talk the Empress out of the idea of this hen party, but the Empress had insisted that Princess was lonely for her kind and must have a visitor. Saffron had chosen Tikka to bring along because she was the most docile of the flock at Hau'oli ka Moa Egg Farm, and because she had recently raised several chicks, so she was more tolerant than many of the other hens.

Princess went immediately to the newcomer, watching her with one eye. Tikka didn't seem to notice the little ball of fluff. Saffron could only assume that because of the silkie's strange appearance, Tikka didn't realize Princess was another chicken, and so didn't feel threatened by her. Princess mimicked Tikka's movements and followed her around contentedly as they both scratched for bugs and pecked at seeds on the bushes nearby.

The Empress watched for a while, a look of pure satisfaction on her face. "This is what she has been needing. They are flock animals, you know?"

Saffron nodded.

"Humans need each other," the Empress stated, "and so do other creatures."

"I think you may be right," Saffron said, watching the birds as they dipped their beaks and raised their heads, drinking from the pond. She had struggled with loneliness herself, back in Washington DC, before she came here. Since arriving in the islands, she had learned to value friends.

In the still of the moment, a loud call broke the heavy Hawaiian spring air. It was half battlecry, half victory whoop, and it made the Empress' head swivel, and her hands flutter. Rex and Carlo scrambled to spin her around just as a handsome sailor strode out of the house.

"Mama!" His resonant voice filled the backyard, and he crossed the garden in three steps to throw himself to his knees beside the Empress' wheelchair. He wrapped his arms around her, and Saffron looked away as the Empress buried her face in his short black hair, tears streaming down her cheeks.

"Six months is too long for me to not see you!" she said, her voice soft with tenderness.

"Too long for me, too," he smiled.

The Empress seemed to suddenly remember Saffron.

"Oh, my Davis!" she said as he stood, "I have got a girl for you to meet! This is Saffron. She's come all the way from Washington DC to take over Beau's old egg farm!"

Davis smiled, a grin full of warmth and humor. Saffron saw in his eyes that his mother had also set him up plenty of times, "Nice to meet you," he said, "Mama's sent me lots of interesting tidbits about you while I was at sea."

Saffron felt her cheeks flush. Davis smiled and turned back to his mother.

"Guess what?"

"What?" The Empress' tone was light and playful.

"*I've* got a girl for *you* to meet."

Saffron felt a rush of both relief and disappointment.

Davis turned toward the house, and Saffron looked up to see a willowy girl with light brown hair drifting out the doors like a petal on the wind.

"My fiancé!" Davis' impossibly wide grin grew even more expansive. The girl slipped up to him and settled into the curve of his uniformed arm.

The Empress squealed like she was on a roller coaster. "What? My baby's getting married? When? How? Why haven't I heard of this lovely girl? What's her name? Davis! Introduce me to my new daughter-in-law this instant!"

Saffron squirmed. A confirmed neat freak, she did not like for things to be out of place, and that's exactly what she was now. This was an intimate moment between the Empress and her son, and Saffron felt conspicuous and awkward being there. She glanced at Carlo and Rex, both of whom stood calm and detached. They seemed more a part of the garden than part of the event: two stately topiaries whose only movement was the flick of an eye in the general direction of the now-forgotten chickens.

Saffron was glad to have the chickens to direct her attention to as she heard Davis say, "Mama, this is Lyza Carelli."

"Where in the world did you meet her? Was it in a port of

call? Did you see each other across a crowded marketplace?" The Empress had an affinity for exotic historical romance novels, and it was showing now.

"No, nothing so exciting as that," Lyza said, her voice soft and musical. Saffron couldn't help but glance back at the striking couple.

"We met through my bunkmate, Logan Prentice. He's another seaman from Lyza's hometown. She was vacationing in Spain when we came into port at Rota. She came to visit him in port, and she and I hit it off. Logan was on duty, so I took her to dinner."

"The rest is history," Lyza chimed in.

"And last night, when we came into port, she met me here and I asked her to marry me," Davis' face was shining, his eyes dancing with the news.

That's what it looks like to be in love, Saffron thought. Watching them together, she felt a stab of jealousy for the first time in a long time.

"Well, this is just the most exciting news!" The Empress beckoned the couple closer. "When's the big day?"

Davis laughed, "We haven't decided yet. But you'll be the first to know. I just wanted to bring her here, to introduce her to you, and show her where I grew up."

"Ah," the Empress said, "you're going to love it here, and my grandchildren will be close to me," She gazed lovingly at Davis and Lyza. Saffron noticed that it was their turn to squirm. No wonder, they had just gotten engaged, and now there was talk of grandchildren.

The Empress looked suddenly upset, "But you don't take her to the diving rock!"

Davis waved her away, "Aw, Mama, the accident was twenty-five years ago, and I can swim now! I'm a sailor!"

Lyza's blue eyes were wide, "What happened?"

"I was seven, a little too brave for my own good. We used

to hike from the beach up to the top of this cliff and look down on the diving rock and the bay. We were up there, and I saw people jumping off the diving rock, so I decided I needed to do it, too. Us boys went back down, and as soon as we got there, I climbed the diving rock like the teenagers were doing and threw myself off. Of course, I didn't know how to hit the water, and I belly-flopped. Got the air knocked out of me, that's all."

The Empress' eyes were closed, "He sank like a stone. I couldn't get to him. I was screaming and screaming for someone to get him out of the water."

"When I could kick, I pulled in a big lungful of water," he was shaking his head, "If Uncle Mano hadn't been there, I would have drowned. He dived right in and hauled me up, pumped the water out of me on the beach. Saved my life."

"You know Mano?" Saffron blurted. The three of them looked at her as if they'd just remembered she was there.

"Oh, yeah. His grandson and I hung around a lot."

"Keahi?" Saffron still couldn't say the name without smiling.

"That's right. You've met him?" Davis shook his head, "Of course. I forgot he was back around here." Speaking to Lyza, he said, "You'll have to meet him. He's a great guy."

"And his grandfather saved your life. I'll have to thank him for that," Lyza gave Davis a squeeze and smiled up at him.

"That was a terrible day," the Empress said. "Terrible. I still have nightmares about it." A little shiver ran through her voice on the word *nightmares*.

Davis reached for his mother's hand, "Mama, I told you, I can swim now. I'm on the water all the time."

The Empress' hand trembled as she gripped her son's, "That's not the problem, atali'i, you mustn't go to the bay because the manōs have returned." Her voice was low.

"Your friend's grandfather?" Lyza asked.

"No, though that is his name, too," the Empress said patiently, "manōs are sharks."

"Sharks?" Lyza's blue eyes were bright with alarm.

"She's from Massachusetts," Davis said, as if this explained her reaction, "don't worry, baby. They're just coming in to feed and mate."

"Ch," The Empress chided Davis, "You simplify. These are not just sea animals doing animal things. They are ʻaumakua. And they have gathered for a purpose. They sense something. They have not been to Maikaʻi all together like this for many years," the Empress said, "Of course, they individually have visited their families, but not as a group. The researchers, they say that the manōs have not been gathering because of currents or tourists or because there is not enough food, but we know. They have not all been needed at once. But they are needed now. Something is coming, and they need to protect their families from it."

Saffron had not been in Hawaii long, but the time she had spent with Keahi, and his grandfather had taught her that there were deep traditions here that she respected and was continually trying to better understand.

Lyza blinked rapidly, tipping her head up at Davis in a question. Saffron could see a struggle in him, between, she supposed, his traditions and his modern life, his mother and his fiancé. Finally, he closed his eyes and nodded, "Many families here have deities in the form of animals that watch over them and protect their families."

The empress smiled warmly as she explained further, "these are our ancestors, their spirits return in the form of these animals to warn us or protect us. Some families have ancestors that appear as honu—sea turtles. Others have geckos or eels or birds like the pueo—the owl." The Empress' words were reverent. "We know our own ʻaumakua, and we take care of them."

"Oh," was all Lyza said. Saffron thought she could be more enthusiastic. It was a powerful and beautiful belief.

Davis went on, "For many families, their 'aumakua is a shark, and there's a legend—"

"An account," the Empress corrected crisply, and she went on from there, "of a gathering of 'aumakua: sharks that came to the beach at the diving rock and waited. Their families knew them, and they went and fed them. And when a huge jellyfish bloom came, the sharks stood guard and turned the tides and fed on the jellyfish to keep them away from the beach, and no one here was stung. The towns around Maika'i suffered, but no one in Maika'i was hurt because the 'aumakua protected their families."

There was a long pause, and Lyza cleared her throat, "that's amazing," she managed.

"And now they have returned, and they have work to do," the Empress chided, "so don't bother them at the diving rock."

"And if it keeps me away from there, then the 'aumakua are doing you a favor, too, huh, Mama?" Davis was teasing, but there was a gentle reverence in his voice.

"I give them an offering now and again," the Empress returned. "And they've kept you safe at sea, haven't they?"

Davis looked closely at his mother, "Hey, speaking of offerings to the sharks, where is Princess?"

The Empress' hands flew to her lap in a burst of momentary panic before she spied the two hens curled together, resting in the shade of an oleander bush. "We're having a little hen party, aren't we, manamea?" She used a Samoan term of endearment, a word that Saffron had gathered meant something like *sweetheart*. Princess looked up at her. "Come here, come here, then and see your big brother." She reached into a bag hanging from her wheelchair arm and extracted a small can, which she shook. The rattling made Princess leap to her feet and lumber over in an awkward canter to flap her way into the Empress' arms.

Tikka, disturbed from her nap, also stood, shook her feathers, and meandered over. The Empress rewarded each of them with a few golden treats of dried grains from the can.

Saffron reached down and collected Tikka.

"I'd really better be on my way," she said, grateful that a smooth segue had presented itself, "I've got customers coming for eggs soon."

The Empress bade her a cheerful goodbye, and Carlo saw her out. Saffron left the Empress and her guests cooing over Princess.

Chapter Two

The next afternoon, Saffron was waiting under the monkeypod tree that stretched over the lanai when Keahi's steel-gray SUV came rolling up the drive. She'd finished her egg deliveries and dealt with the Tuesday pickup customers that came each morning before their own work to pick up a dozen eggs for the week.

She called it the egg line because they lined up in their cars down the driveway and stopped at the yard, where Saffron handed them eggs through the windows of their vehicles.

Keahi swung out of the car with the natural grace that

always surprised her. He was a head taller than her, with powerful arms and a quick smile. He'd been a surgeon on the mainland until he lost a 6-year-old patient and came back home. Saffron didn't know the whole story, but she knew him well enough to know the trauma of the loss was still fresh. Now, he worked at the Laki Luau, performing dances and songs from his native Hawaiian culture.

Keahi pulled her into his arms for a hello kiss. She laced her fingers through the cropped curls on the back of his head. Keahi laid his cheek alongside hers and inhaled, which Saffron had learned from his grandpa, her friend Mano, was an intimate greeting. She inhaled, too, and the warm scent of koa wood and orange filled her mind.

Keahi's kisses were not frequent, so Saffron lingered as long as she could in the moment.

"What are we doing today?" she asked as he stepped back and walked to the car.

"I've got a special place to show you."

It was a fifteen-minute drive before Keahi pulled the SUV off the highway, stopping in front of an ornate iron gate. He hopped out and punched a code into the keypad on the gate, then they drove up a driveway with foliage so dense that Saffron didn't see the house until they were upon it.

It was magnificent: a wood-sided two-story perched out on a jutting black cliff. Keahi led her inside, where they were greeted by Mano.

"You kids have come to appreciate my work," he said, waving a hand at the ornately carved cabinets he had just finished polishing. Mano was a master carver.

"The people who own this house have hired Tutu," Keahi used the Hawaiian word as he referred to his grandfather, "to do all the woodwork."

"And it's all complete, finally," Mano said, waving a hand.

Saffron walked through the house, studying his intricate

carvings on the doors, the window frames, the broad, curving banister that led up to the second-floor balcony over the greatroom.

It was the greatroom that took her breath away. Glass walls offered an unimpeded view of the panoramic ocean and the hazy islands in the distance. On either side of the room, the cliff fell away so sharply that you couldn't see the black rock that supported the house. It gave the effect of the house floating in midair fifty feet above the blue water.

"This place is spectacular," she said, "who owns it?" It was tastefully furnished but lacked any personal touches: family photos, knick-knacks, or the general clutter of living, like unopened mail or empty grocery bags.

"Keahi's friend from medical school," Mano said.

Keahi held up a hand, "not exactly my friend," he said, shaking his head, "he was the Chief of Vascular Surgery at one of the hospitals where I interned. He's retired, and he bought this land, then had the house built. He had all the work inside done by local craftsmen."

"Mostly by me," Mano laughed. Saffron loved hearing the musical sound of it. The old man had lost his best friend when she first got here, and it was good to see him happy again, "Hiwa lani," he addressed his grandson. Saffron had learned that the phrase meant *beloved or favorite child*, and she liked hearing Mano say it, "I need to borrow your car while you picnic. I have several more final pieces to bring and install this afternoon. Then the place will be finished."

"Sure," Keahi handed him the keys, and Mano left them alone. He'd been scheming to get them together ever since Saffron met him in the hardware store, and he wasn't letting up.

Keahi smiled at her. They both knew Mano's ulterior motives, and she thought it a good sign that neither of them minded the old man's matchmaking.

Keahi took her hand. "If you think the view's great from in here, you should see outside."

Together they left the house and walked through the brisk breeze onto a wide side yard set back from the tip of the point. There, Keahi had spread a picnic blanket. She saw one of the Oceanside Cafe's famous "Beachy Baskets," packed meals that patrons could pick up and take along for outdoor dining. All they had to do was return the basket. Saffron tried to imagine what was inside, but when Keahi opened it and pulled out the contents, she was still surprised.

A full tray of glazed shrimp lined up on skewers brought a tantalizing sweet and savory scent. Keahi lifted out a bowl of coconut sticky rice next, and a mango, pineapple, strawberry, guava, and kiwi salad was last. Saffron had eaten it at the Oceanside cafe before—the honey ginger poppyseed dressing set off the fruit flavors perfectly. She waited impatiently as Keahi piled two paper plates high with the bounty.

Saffron pulled a shrimp off its bamboo skewer with her teeth, wondering if she'd ever felt so content as she did now. The light wind tossed her strawberry hair across her field of vision, and she tucked it back behind her ear. Somewhere below the lip of the cliff, she could hear seabirds crying. Occasionally, one would peak in its flight just a foot or two above the edge of the cliff. They always seemed surprised to see Saffron and Keahi casually lunching at such a great height.

The unusual thing about the Hawaiian shoreline, Saffron had found, was how varied it was. In some places, like her farm, the golden sand ran in a gentle slope up to the stubbly grasses where the house sat. Here, the sea had worn away all traces of sand and left only these rocky cliffs and a steep plunge down to the water.

The breeze picked up and lifted Saffron's napkin from her lap, sending it scudding just a few feet away on the lawn. Both she and Keahi jumped up to grab it, and both chased it a dozen feet before pulling back as it sailed on a wind current up and over the edge.

"I think we'll let it go," she said. She stepped back from the cliff.

"We should." He said. "But you should still take a look over the edge. It's beautiful."

Saffron's heart pounded. "That's okay."

"Listen, I've been coming up here my whole life. Over there," Keahi pointed across the lawn, to where the dense trees and bushes began, "is a path that goes all the way down to the beach by the diving rock. My friends and I used to climb up here and let the wind blow in our hair and watch people jump off the diving rock. None of us ever fell, and we were careless thirteen-year-old boys. You'll be all right."

Saffron shook her head. The only experience she'd had with heights was from inside elevators. Even then, she wasn't crazy about the thought of how far away the ground was.

Keahi must have recognized her discomfort. "It's okay. I'll hold you." He took her hand.

She wanted to show him she could do it, and she wanted to keep holding his hand. She edged forward.

He was right. Looking down into the crystalline water below, she could barely breathe. It was like flying with the whole ocean stretched out below you.

Keahi slid his arms around her, and she leaned back into his strong presence, but she didn't take her eyes off the water.

Directly below them was a deep bay, where the cliff fell off into the sea. Slightly to the right, about halfway down the cliff, was a conspicuous jutting rock and, beyond it, on the far right of Saffron's view, was a beach that ran off casually around the next gentle curve of the island.

"Want to go diving?" Keahi said.

"Diving? From here? No."

He laughed. "From the diving rock down there. It has a perfect trail up and a great little drop."

"This is enough of a thrill for me," Saffron said, sure she could never willingly jump into the sea. The birds set up a noisy protest. They wheeled high in the air and swept up above Saffron and Keahi's heads, winging away toward the mountains behind them. Saffron looked down at the clear water again and grasped at Keahi's arms, tightening them around her. "Keahi! Look!"

The azure water below them was alive with dark shadows: perfect silhouettes of enormous sharks. They glided, weaving together and around each other, turning as one and sliding under the water, back around the dark shape of the diving rock together, until the last one had disappeared. Saffron and Keahi watched in stunned silence until the group returned and repeated their maneuver.

Keahi's arms had tensed. Saffron turned to look at him. "How many do you think there were?"

"Twenty or more," he said, his voice filled with awe.

"A group of sharks is called a frenzy," Saffron said, the fact skimming through her mind like the shapes of the big animals below.

"Hmmm," Keahi replied.

"What kind are they?"

"I can't tell for sure, but I think tigers."

Tiger sharks. Saffron felt a chill run up her spine. She'd watched for sharks ever since coming to Hawaii, but these were the first she'd actually seen. Their graceful shapes in the water mesmerized her. The sharks came back around the point of the rock, patrolling the bay. They didn't all swim in the same direction, some looped back past and under or over the others, but as a body, they moved together. She thought about what the Empress had said, that the sharks were gathering to protect against some unseen threat. The way they moved, Saffron could almost believe that's what they were doing.

Watching them made her understand power and majesty in a whole new way.

"I need to make a phone call," Keahi said, stepping back from the cliff's edge. Saffron heard him over her shoulder, talking to Mano on the phone, telling him about the tiger sharks in the bay. His voice was low, and Saffron could tell that there was significance in the gathering of the sharks.

She wondered if Keahi's family had a shark 'aumakua. She let herself consider for a moment that one of those powerful creatures may be an ancestor of Keahi's.

She jumped as her own phone rang. It was the Empress. Saffron braced for another playdate invitation, but that wasn't what the call was about.

"My Davis has decided to get married this weekend!" the Empress' voice shook with excitement.

"This weekend?" Today was Tuesday.

"Yes. Right here in Maika'i so that his mother can be there. Lyza was just insistent that she didn't need anything big, she just wanted to do it now. They've already called friends and family, and I've talked to the kahu about marrying them. But we need you to put together the party!"

Saffron tried to find words. "In four days?"

"I heard all about your magical open house when you were going to sell Hau'oli ka Moa. I know you can do it!"

"I don't know—I haven't planned anything here, really, I haven't got any contacts."

"Well, it's time you start making some. I'll send you some names."

Saffron tried to breathe. "Four days?"

"Four days," the Empress said, "I know that's a rush, so we'll pay extra for the extra work." She named a figure. Saffron gulped. That was more money than she'd made on three weddings back in DC. She took the job.

Keahi was standing at her elbow when she hung up.

"Planning a wedding?" he asked, smiling.

Saffron nodded numbly. "In four days."

"*This* Saturday?"

"This Saturday."

"Wow. Where at?"

"I don't know," Saffron snapped, "I still have to plan the whole thing!"

"Okay," Keahi's voice was even. He was good at being calm when Saffron was feeling tense.

"Where am I even going to hold it? At the Oceanside Cafe?" Saffron paced. This would be her first paid event in Maika'i, and it was for the Empress. She wanted it to be wonderful. "No, it needs to be grand and impressive."

Keahi laid a hand on her arm, and she stopped pacing.

"How about here?" he said, waving his other arm wide. "This is pretty grand and impressive."

Saffron pressed her lips together, picturing the kahu—the Hawaiian pastor, along with the bride and groom standing in front of those glorious windows in the house. "That could work," she said slowly.

"Do you want me to check with Dr. Evans? I'm sure he wouldn't mind. He's said they'd like it to be useful to the community. They designed it to withstand storms so people could shelter here. He gave the codes to the local police and emergency people. And he's said they'd like to even have parties out here."

Saffron began to imagine it, "Would you check with him?" she asked tentatively.

Keahi pulled out his phone. Dr. Evans was, apparently, a jovial person, because there was a lot of laughter and promises to get together. Saffron was relatively sure that the answer was yes, and by the time Keahi hung up, she was already envisioning a navy and mustard color scheme.

"He says go ahead," Keahi smiled, "and he said you can have it all weekend, in case you want to do a rehearsal dinner or reception or anything in addition to the ceremony."

Saffron stopped, took a deep breath, and smiled at him. "Thanks." Keahi was always good at finding solutions.

Another voice answered from behind her, "Thanks for what?" Mano was walking across the lawn toward them.

Keahi didn't answer him, just stepped forward to intercept him and led him quickly to the cliff's edge, where they stood talking in low, earnest tones for a long time.

When they turned back to Saffron, Mano's eyes were joyful.

"My namesake is in town," he said. "Come on, kids."

Together, they piled into the SUV and started off. Ten minutes later, they were pulling off the road in front of a ragged little house just steps from the beach.

Mano waved the two after him, and they went in without knocking. It was dim inside. There were various types of art everywhere: woven wall hangings, carvings, tikis, and paintings. She looked a long moment at a short wooden oar carved with just the kind of sharks she'd seen from the cliff.

"Who lives here?" Saffron asked, her eyes running over the artifacts.

"Uncle Akoni," Keahi answered.

"He has a lot of . . . things," Saffron said, not quite sure what word to use.

"He's a kahuna," Keahi said, then, as he was getting very good at doing, defined, "sort of a spiritual guide and teacher. He's also a great friend of my grandfather's."

Mano called out as they entered, "Hey, Akoni, howzit?"

A shout came from the back of the house, and they walked

through the living room and the kitchen, out onto a small lanai
where an old man was gutting an enormous fish.

Mano waved Saffron and Keahe on past them, and they
stepped off the lanai into the amber sand of the beach. Saffron
could see where the water came, at high tide, nearly to the
worn boards. Now, the waves lapped ten feet away, across the
beautiful sand.

Akoni's house was not isolated. It was one of many little
old beach houses in various states of repair in a line along the
shore.

Saffron heard the men talking, though she was trying not to
listen. They were talking about the sharks.

"We need to find what has brought them here. They must
sense something is coming."

"That bad-luck boy is back in town," Akoni said, "maybe
he's the reason."

"Davis *had* bad luck, braddah, he didn't *bring* it."

"You say."

"I do."

"It wasn't until we got rid of him to the Navy that things
started turning around here. We get rid of him again, maybe
the 'aumakua are satisfied."

They were talking about Davis. Saffron wondered what
made Akoni say that he was bad luck.

Keahi was ahead of her, at the edge of the water, looking
out over the vast reef. He was reliable and handsome, solid
and dependable, and Saffron couldn't help but want to be
near him. Just as she reached his side, though, Mano called to
them. Saffron turned to see him holding a huge chunk of the
fish Akoni had been working on. Mano jerked his head
toward the house, and Saffron could see a boat propped up
against the worn siding. It was long and narrow and had a
support float jutting out from its side. Keahi jogged up the
beach and across the porch. Saffron followed, and he shot her

a smile as she helped him lift the boat and carry it to the water.

Mano and Akoni were waiting for them. They stepped up with big chunks of the raw fish and settled them into a square wooden chamber in the center of the canoe. It looked almost like a lidless cooler. On either side of it, toward each end, were two narrow boards that made up four seats in all. As soon as the canoe was set into the water, the old men climbed in the back and settled into the two rear seats. The boat seemed perilously unbalanced. Saffron stood watching.

"Come on!" Akoni waved to her and Keahi.

Saffron eyed the canoe. It looked like it barely fit Mano and Akoni. She didn't see how it would float with two more people. But the men had obviously left the front for the two of them, and when Keahi climbed in and stretched a hand toward her, she followed.

She settled on the bench seat right in front of Keahi, and he slid an arm around her waist and pulled her back against his chest as the canoe began to move out into the water, rowed by Akoni and Mano.

Saffron saw the golden sand dropping away below them as they went farther from the shore. In some places, jagged coral jutted up near the water's surface, but Akoni and Mano seemed to know just where these hidden dangers lurked and avoided them expertly. Saffron gazed across the water, watching it stretch toward the horizon, an unbroken ribbon of blue.

"Is that a boat?" Saffron pointed to a triangle of white bobbing far out in the water, and Keahi put his cheek next to hers and looked where she was indicating.

"I think so," he said.

Mano answered, too. "That's right. It's Oke Cooper's canoe."

Saffron squinted and thought she could just make out the

shape of the wiry man she'd bought the kūmū fish from yesterday. She'd eaten hers last night, steamed with a little lemon,
just like Keahi had taught her. She'd become quite the cook in
her last few months here. She thought about Oke as she
watched the sail of his boat bob up and down far on the
horizon.

Oke was not an old man, but he looked old. His face was
heavily pocked, his hands and arms scarred from years of net
fishing and working with his catch. He was thin and sun-worn
and rarely smiled. The most remarkable thing Saffron had
learned about him was that he lived on his boat, night and day,
sleeping in the hull at night and filling it with fish in the day.
He sailed all around the island fishing and selling his catch on
the beaches. He showed up irregularly in Maika'i, and people
flocked to him when he did.

Saffron liked being on the water, liked the sound of the
waves lapping the canoe, liked the splash of the paddles behind
them. Impulsively, she turned her head and kissed Keahi on
the jaw. He looked down into her eyes and kissed her back
quickly.

"Hey!" Akoni barked, "Get to work up there!"

Mano chuckled, "They are just getting close to centralize
the weight, brah. It's good for balance."

Akoni made a grunt and Keahi smiled as he let her go and
picked up a paddle. Saffron felt the speed of the canoe increase
as Keahi put his powerful arms to the task of slicing through
the waves.

She could hear the old men talking behind them, laughing
at having a young man aboard. At one point, she looked back,
and they were both leaning back with their sandaled feet on
the edge of the boat and their hands clasped behind their
heads, making a jovial picture of relaxation.

"We're just like the tourists. Strong bruddah rowing us out
to see the sharks," Mano said.

"Sharks?" Saffron curled involuntarily into the center of her seat. This did not look like the kind of vessel one took to see sharks. Desperately, she tried to think where they had driven. They had come down off the point and back up the coast. She looked around and saw, to her horror, the big black diving rock looming in front of them. Above it, on the point, she could see the big house with the beautiful view. They were heading directly to the bay where they'd seen the sharks.

Chapter Three

She saw the dorsal fins from thirty feet away. Just as she'd always imagined them, cutting through the water like saber tips, sliding past each other in an endless dance. They rose and fell in the waves, peaking and slipping back under the water, a constant reminder that below the surface lay another world.

Saffron looked at Keahi. His strong face was expressionless, his amber eyes calm.

"Move around that way," Mano said. He was no longer lighthearted. His always-smiling face was now composed and serious. "Keep our shadow behind us."

The canoe jolted softly sideways as a thirteen-foot shark bumped it with his side as he sailed by. Saffron saw the dark shadow of his body below the water, and her heart stopped beating.

"Yes, we have these for you," Mano reached into the center part of the canoe and lifted a flat slice of fish. Saffron pressed her lips together as Mano leaned over the side of the boat and laid the fish in the water. The surface of the sea played around his wrist, and all she could think of was whether he would pull back a hand or not.

She watched, wordlessly, as the big tiger shark turned and cut through the water back toward them. Saffron could see, now, his smooth skin, light gray with dark blotches that looked like stripes. This one had a peculiar marking—a particularly dark patch, like a jagged slash—just in front and to the left of his dorsal fin.

Mano was murmuring in Hawaiian to the shark as it approached. Soft words that Saffron didn't know, but still understood. It was a greeting, gratitude, almost a prayer. She waited for the shark to lunge, to come gaping and snapping out of the water as she had seen on countless movies. Instead, it swam gently forward, mouth open, and Mano floated the fish past its rows of jagged teeth.

Saffron had never seen a shark this close before. She found that she was holding her breath.

The shark reached eagerly for another treat, but Mano gently pushed its nose to the side, "Don't be greedy," he said softly. Saffron waited for the shark to lunge, to take his hand off if he wouldn't offer another slab of fish, but the shark didn't. Its head twitched to the side, and it skimmed off along the top of the water before diving down into the crystalline blue.

She glanced back to see that Akoni was now offering a slab of fish to another, smaller tiger on the other side of the boat. It, too, approached, took the offering, and went on.

There were dorsal fins all around the boat now, but other than the occasional jostling from a shark cutting slightly too close, they didn't touch the boat.

"Keahi," Mano said under his breath. He jerked his head toward the water. Saffron saw the big shark with the prominent stripe returning.

Keahi nodded and twisted around to the box of fish pieces behind him. He lifted another and, like Mano, held it under the surface of the water.

"No," Saffron didn't mean to let the word escape, but she knew how strong and gentle those hands were, she couldn't bear the thought of the shark that was now moving toward them.

Keahi shot her a reassuring smile. "It's okay," he said, "this one is our 'aumakua. Our great-grandfather, who has been granted the power to return to us in this form. He knows us. We know him." He turned his attention back to the approaching animal, and he, too, murmured something in Hawaiian that sounded reverent and pleading.

The shark was even closer now. Saffron could see its glistening onyx eyes, the white countershading that ran up its belly and to the tip of its nose. It was the shark Mano had first fed, the one with the jagged slash. He was so close she could even see black freckles around the creature's nostrils. It opened its mouth, peeling back its lips in a grim smile as it anticipated the fish. She found herself not breathing again.

Keahi waited, then slid the fish forward just as the shark's jaws opened. Saffron saw the gleam of its white teeth and the pink gums stretched tight between and around each jagged point. It gulped the fish, reaching up again with a twist of its robust body, asking for more. Keahi did the same thing his grandfather had done, bumping the shark's nose with a playful hand. The shark turned and stretched itself the length of the canoe as it glided away.

"Breathe," Keahi said, his wide smile pulling Saffron back to the present.

She did, and her words came out in a hiss, "What are you doing?"

Keahi, characteristically, seemed undisturbed by her disbelief. "'Aumakua are protectors. They're helpers."

"They are *predators*." Saffron tried to keep her voice low. The old men were still feeding other tigers that approached the boat.

Keahi's eyes were patient. "I know it seems strange, but it's no different than the mainland idea of guardian angels, and I saw plenty of evidence for those when I was practicing medicine."

Saffron opened her mouth to debate but realized that he was right. It was also hard to ignore the great calm exuding from the big sharks. They didn't seem like a frenzy to her.

"Everyone needs their ancestors," Keahi said softly, "to help, to guide, to protect. They have wisdom we don't have, and perspective. Tutu has taught me a lot about them."

"It's not always sharks, though?" She remembered what the Empress had said.

"No," Keahi said, "There are other animals, too. Our family has another 'aumakua that is a honu—a sea turtle—she's from Tutu's mother's side. This one is from his father's side. It's where he got his name."

The box of fish was nearly empty. Mano reached down and picked up the last slab. He held it out toward Saffron in the front of the boat. She shook her head.

"You feed them, Ipo. You need protection, too. And you're part of our ohana." The crinkles around Mano's eyes folded kindly as he said the Hawaiian word for family. His silver beard framed his gentle smile. Saffron couldn't refuse him. She reached past Keahi and took the fish. It was cool and firm in her hands.

Keahi slid his hands on either side of her waist, making her feel, as always, secure.

"Just be steady," he said, "and push the fish toward him as he opens his mouth. Don't reach in past the teeth."

Saffron wanted to say something about how ridiculous that was, but her stomach was much too tight for her to speak. The big shark was coming again, the one with the slash. Its eyes seemed to have more feeling than she'd noticed before, more emotion in their glassy depths. She lowered the fish, feeling the warm Hawaiian water cover her fingers, her knuckles, her wrists. She was leaning out over the water as she'd seen them do, and she tried not to think of falling in and flailing in the center of the swirling frenzy of sharks.

The tiger was nearly there. He opened his mouth in anticipation.

The others had smoothly floated the fish to the sharks. Saffron's delivery was much less graceful. As the big teeth reached forward, she shoved the fish toward the gaping maw, against the weight of the water, and snatched her hands back. She fell backward from the momentum of the action, and Keahi pulled her to him as the boat bobbed crazily to the side. The float counteracted her motion, though, and the canoe stayed upright. None of the others seemed concerned. Saffron peered over the edge and saw the big shark dive and gobble the slab of fish just as he moved underneath the boat.

A rush of new understanding came to Saffron. The shark wasn't after her, it wasn't trying to get in the boat. It was happy with the offering. Saffron closed her eyes and melted into Keahi's embrace.

Mano was jubilant. "Maika'i loa!" he said—*very good!*—from the back of the boat.

Saffron opened her eyes and twisted to give him a small smile. Akoni glared past Mano at her. She could see he wasn't as impressed by her effort.

"That's all," Mano said to a passing tiger as Keahi released Saffron and picked up his paddle. "We're out of fish." The boat began to move away, and soon the slicing dorsal fins were just distant shapes among the waves.

FRIDAY CAME QUICKLY. Saffron had spent the week getting flowers from the flower shop in Maika'i, arranging catering, and booking one of the town's bed and breakfasts for a posse of friends and family flying in last-minute for the wedding.

The cliff house was decorated with hints of Davis and Lyza's love story. Among them, embossed anchors and window boxes of red geraniums reminiscent of the flowers Davis had picked for Lyza as they walked the white-walled streets of Rota, Spain, on their first date.

Saffron was at the cliff house gobbling a malasada from Juno's Bakery. Keahi had introduced her to the custard-filled Hawaiian donuts. This one was giving her just the boost of energy she needed to get this marathon event underway. Arranging and pulling off a wedding had been a lot easier with her two assistants when she ran Every Detail Events back in Washington DC. She finished the treat and went into the great-room to set up the last of the chairs for the ceremony. The combined bachelorette and bachelor party would start in less than an hour, and the guests were already arriving.

Saffron glanced up to see Lyza enter with an entourage. Her parents, several girls, and another handsome Navy man walked with her.

"See," Lyza was saying, "that's going to be the backdrop for the ceremony."

The sailor whistled. "Wow. That's some view."

Saffron crossed to them.

"Saffron," Lyza said, her liquid blue eyes bright, "I want to introduce you to everyone." She tapped the girl closest to her. "This is my little sister Myra." The girl was twenty or so, with long eyelashes and the same blue eyes as Lyza. Saffron's color memory matched that shade with the ocean off the south side of the island, at a particular spot where a reef nudged up from the ocean floor, and the sun hit directly on the water. The bride pointed to the two girls to her left, "and my friends from college: Rachel Adams," who was short and square and smiling, "and Sylvia Deluna," Saffron recognized the name as the friend Lyza had been visiting in Spain. Lyza went on. "My cousins, Tiff Johnson," Tiff was plain and nondescript, while the other cousin, "Evelyn Harris," was just the opposite. Striking, delicate and lithe, Evelyn had sweeping, jet black hair, skin the color of seafoam, and piercing blue eyes. She was fit and graceful. Saffron doubted she'd ever eaten a donut in her life. There was something off-putting about the flawless persona she exuded. Still, Saffron chided herself, the girl had a pleasant expression and seemed supportive of her cousin. Lyza was wrapping up the introductions as she waved at the young man, "and my best friend, Logan Prentice."

"Ah," Saffron said, snapping back to the moment, "the man of honor."

He laughed. "Is that what we're calling it?"

Saffron was relieved to see that he seemed right at home in the bridal party. When Lyza had asked if she could have a male maid of honor, Saffron had wondered how he would feel about the arrangement. She'd also worried about how that would affect the procession down the aisle, having one extra man, but the groom, Davis, had solved that problem by choosing, from his friends, a best woman who would walk with Logan.

"And this is my mom and dad. Byron and Cyndi Carelli," Lyza went on. Cyndi, a small woman with wispy brown hair the color of old moss, stepped forward and thanked Saffron for all her hard work.

"This place is just beautiful! We don't have anything like this view back in Winchester."

"Winchester?" Saffron asked politely.

"Winchester, Massachusetts," Cyndi nodded, "That's where we're from. No palm trees or golden beaches there, I can promise you. And none of these lovely exotic flowers!" She waved a hand toward the flowers on the table, "it's beautiful. I can't believe you pulled it together in such a short time. We're just amazed, aren't we, Byron?"

Saffron flinched as the bride's father evaluated her with cold eyes, "Amazed at the bill for this farce, is more like it," he said. "Eight hours on a plane to get to a sweaty, steamy island in the middle of the ocean. We already got three thousand dollars sunk into this thing just to fly in on such short notice. How much is all this going to cost me?" He waved an erratic arm.

"Daddy!" Lyza's voice was sharp. Saffron didn't interrupt to say that she'd dealt with plenty of cranky fathers of the bride in her wedding-planning career. She also didn't give him the satisfaction of knowing that the Empress was footing the bill for Saffron's services. "Be nice," Lyza begged.

"I'm done being nice," he said, turning his cold gaze on his daughter. Saffron felt the tension rising as if someone were cranking a thermostat. The bridesmaids froze and glanced at each other uncomfortably as he went on, "I was too nice, I guess when you brought that kid around last month. If I hadn't been so nice maybe we wouldn't be here, and maybe you wouldn't be making the biggest mistake of your life."

"It's not a mistake!" Lyza cried. Her eyes were brimming with tears under the tirade, "Davis is the best man I've ever known, and he loves me, and we're doing this. It's happening tomorrow, and there's nothing you can do to stop it!"

Byron's jaw tightened. Saffron saw the strain in his clenched fists, his narrowed eyes, his squared shoulders. He opened his mouth, but Logan stepped up and threw an arm around his shoulders before he could speak.

"It's gonna be alright," he said soothingly, then, turning the father ever so slightly away from his glaring daughter, he said, "come and look at this view."

Byron allowed himself to be led to the window, although the tension remained. The rest of the bridal party stood awkwardly while Myra patted her sister's shoulder and tears dripped onto Lyza's pale purple shirt.

Saffron jumped when Davis' voice rang through the big room, "Who's ready for a hen party?"

Saffron turned to see him enter pushing his mother's wheelchair. He looked dashing in his Navy whites, the "crackerjack" uniform that perfectly meshed with the wedding decor. It consisted of bell-bottomed pants and a white jumper, with navy blue piping and a black neckerchief. He wore a perfect white sailor's hat that Saffron had heard him refer to as a "dixie cup" to complete the uniform.

Davis had two crackerjack uniforms—this one, in white, and another, dark blue. Saffron had requested his whites for the prenuptial activities, and his dark blue crackerjack uniform for the ceremony tomorrow, and she had coordinated the accent pieces—the flowers and the centerpieces—for the two different occasions with the two different outfits.

Another splash of white drew Saffron's attention. Princess rode regally on her doting owner's lap as Davis wheeled them in. They were followed by the groomsmen: Adam, Tyrone, Sione, and Carl were all local boys who had grown up with Davis. Keahi was in the group, too, and so was the best woman, Natalie Crofts.

She was vivacious, a blonde with a short, ragged haircut and a relaxed style that revealed her youth in Hawaii. She and Davis had been close in high school and had joined the Navy together, and she, too, was wearing her white crackerjack uniform.

Byron moved away from Logan, stepping between his daughter and her approaching fiancé.

It was impossible to tell whether the Empress knew what he was doing or not. Either way, she played it as if the man were coming to greet her and held out an enormous hand. Byron hesitated, then took it awkwardly. Though it wasn't how Saffron had imagined the moment, there was no denying that the party had now begun.

Saffron tried to salvage the ambiance by keeping up cheerful chatter as she ushered the group through a wide archway into the dining room.

It was, like the rest of the house, made for entertaining. The temperature was just right—the air conditioning had done its job, and happy island light bounced in from high windows and a skylight overhead. A large koa wood table filled the center of the room, and granite-topped buffet counters lined each wall. They were filled with the catered dinner Saffron had just finished arranging.

Saffron had recently met the Ionas, a local family that catered out of their own kitchen, and she had called upon them to help her with the recreation of the meal that Lyza and Davis had shared on their first date. It was to be an elaborate tapas bar with a variety of small breads crested by both Spanish and Hawaiian-inspired toppings. She'd never seen anything exactly like it before, but it looked sensational. From what Saffron could tell, Iona Catering could cook anything.

She had picked up the food from them, and now she was relieved she had gotten the tapas bar set up first because most of the guests had just flown in and driven straight up from Honolulu. They swarmed the food like a flock of seagulls.

She glanced around for the bride and groom and saw them in an alcove under the stairs, Davis wiping a gentle hand across Lyza's face and tossing an angry glare at her father, who was sneering at the offerings on the long granite counter from where he sat at the table.

Otherwise, it was a pretty standard gathering. The bride's cousin was flirting with the local boys, the seamen were laughing loudly as they got their food, and the man of honor was carrying a drink to the best woman.

It was planned as a casual affair, with tapas for everyone at the beginning, then glow-in-the-dark touch football out on the lawn for the guys and karaoke in the media room for the girls. Saffron had offered to do a formal rehearsal dinner, but Davis and Lyza had waved it off, insisting that they just wanted their guests to have a good time.

Most of them were doing just that, but Byron still seemed pretty sour. Saffron tried to give him a wide berth as he stood from his seat at the far end of the table and headed toward the counter with the food. There was a clatter as something heavy and metal fell from his pocket onto the wood floor. He didn't seem to notice, so Saffron moved over to the chair and picked it up. A small, rectangular business card case, it had "B. Carelli" etched into its shining silver lid.

"Sir?" she said, and he swung around to glare at her intrusion.

He saw the case she was holding out to him and gave her a grudging, "Thanks, the stupid thing's always slipping out," as he took it. Saffron retreated from him, thinking how unpleasant he was. This was the eve of his daughter's wedding, and even though it was expensive, he was in paradise. How could he not be enjoying it?

Byron was now preparing a plate of tapas for his wife. As the bride and groom passed Saffron on their way back into the celebration, Lyza looked at her father and patted Saffron on the arm.

"Oh, he's settling down now," she said. "See him taking care of Mom? He'd do anything for her. That's how you are, Davis."

Davis smiled, obviously relieved that his fiancé was cheering up. "I would. I'd do anything for you." They went to the buffet together.

Saffron noticed that Byron didn't sit next to his wife, who was chatting animatedly with the Empress. Instead, he left her plate for her and sat alone at the far end of the table, his anger radiating out in a palpable sphere around him. Saffron thought she might approach him to let him know that the Empress had paid for the entire wedding in advance, that there was no further financial obligation he needed to worry about, but his seething face kept her away.

Saffron glanced around to find Keahi. The sight of him usually reassured her. This time, though, she saw the raven-haired Evelyn Harris standing close to him with a hand on his arm. The two were talking in quiet tones.

Saffron was walking across the room before she realized it. Evelyn looked up, surprised when Saffron said her name, and Keahi stepped back from the girl as if he'd been bitten. Saffron realized that there was a strange urgency in her voice and tried to sound more relaxed.

"Evelyn, did you try the artichoke hearts? They are delicious."

"Oh, I don't eat things with oil," Evelyn said. "It's not good for your heart, right, Doc?" Evelyn reached up and touched Keahi's chest.

Doc?

Keahi, for the first time since Saffron had known him,

stumbled over his words. "It's okay, it's just, I mean, some oils, are good . . ." He trailed off, obviously flustered.

Evelyn turned a sharp eye on Saffron. "Oh," Evelyn said slowly. "I see."

Saffron made her eyes wide, trying to look unconcerned, "Pardon?"

"Well, you should probably introduce us, Doc," Evelyn said, a sharp edge underlying her cheery tone.

Again, Saffron could barely stand to hear the usually confident Keahi's halting words. "Well, you know, Saffron, this is Evelyn Fairbanks. Evelyn, Saffron." He didn't contextualize: *Saffron, my girlfriend,* and Saffron realized that they had never really defined their relationship, although she had assumed certain things about it. Keahi's eyes held an apology, but Saffron didn't know what it was for.

"That much we know," Evelyn broke in, batting a playful hand at him, "Let's be a little more specific. Keahi and I dated two years ago back in Boston."

It felt like the floor was falling out of the room, "Boston?" Saffron heard herself asking. She knew that Keahi had been a surgeon there before coming back to the island, but he'd never mentioned any relationships.

"We were pretty serious, huh, Doc?"

Saffron wanted to tell her to stop calling him that. It suggested a level of intimacy that even Saffron didn't feel with him. The looks he and Evelyn were passing between them cemented the impression.

"I—uh, yeah," his awkward reply made Saffron's head hurt.

"Until Doc didn't show up for a date and I got a call two weeks later from area code 808."

"I'm sorry," Keahi said. It was becoming more apparent to Saffron now. When Keahi had lost his young patient, he'd fled Boston, his practice, everything. And apparently, he'd left

Evelyn in his wake. Saffron took a deep breath and centered herself. She'd been an event planner long enough to have seen plenty of awkward guest encounters. This was no different.

"So, Evelyn, you are Lyza's cousin? And you didn't know Keahi knew the groom?"

"No idea." Evelyn tossed back. "It's a nice surprise, though, huh, Doc?"

Keahi was regaining some of his composure. "Yeah. It's great to see you."

"Too bad it will be such a busy weekend," Saffron said, a little too loudly. "You two will hardly have time to catch up at all!"

A tight smile appeared under Evelyn's narrowed eyes, "Well, luckily, I planned extra time. I'm here for two whole weeks!"

Chapter Four

Dinner was over. The men were outside in the dark playing glow football, and their shouts rang through the air and bounced into the dining room, where Saffron was cleaning up the remains of the tapas bar.

Saffron had secured a hard plastic football with LED lights inside it just for this night. The boys had complained about its hard plastic being too rough on their hands, but it looked so cool streaking through the dark that they came to appreciate it. She'd put together a scoreboard that used glowsticks for tally marks.

The bridesmaids and best woman were belting out a stirring rendition of an upbeat love anthem in the media room. Saffron put a hand to her head as they howled out the lyrics.

She cringed, trying not to hear Evelyn's perfect pitch in the lead part.

"I love you!"

Saffron slid a half-eaten plate of tapas off the table into the trash can.

"You're the only one!"

Saffron left the cleanup and walked to the side door. She

stepped out onto the lanai. She thought that the closing door would dampen their enthusiastic harmonies, but open windows around the house let the sound spill out into the night. The bass from the state-of-the-art media room felt like it was shaking the whole island. She took a deep breath and leaned over the railing. A warm wind was blowing, and it caught her hair. The glow from the windows made bright squares on the shaded lanai.

She could hear the voices of the men as they shouted and played on the lawn around the other side of the house. She'd better check that they were keeping it touch football instead of tackle. Those dress whites would be awful to get grass stains out of. Slowly, she walked over and peered at them around the corner of the house. She picked out Keahi immediately. He was right in the middle of the fray. She looked for the groom, but couldn't make him out in the darkness. The glow-in-the-dark football whizzed back and forth, and there were shouts as the two sides grappled for victory.

Behind the singing, Saffron heard something else—a low growling voice. She continued around the lanai and walked down off the steps onto the grass. As she came down, she heard a voice under the lanai, by the side of the house.

"She's too young and too trusting," it was Byron, the father of the bride, "You'd better not go through with it. I'm warning you."

The voice that responded was easily recognizable as well. It was Davis. He spoke with characteristic military deference to authority, "I understand your concerns, sir."

"No, you don't. You don't have any idea what you're going to do to that girl's life. She won't finish college. You'll drag her around from port to port, where she doesn't have any friends or family, and then you'll be out on your ship while she's all alone in some strange place."

Davis was quiet.

"Didn't think of that, did you?"

"No, sir. Not like that. I guess I looked at it more as we would have each other."

Byron made a scoffing noise, "The stupidity of youth. That's not enough."

"I'm sorry, sir, but I can't break her heart. And I don't want to be without her."

"She's not marrying someone from far away. I've told her that her whole life. That's why she's sprung this whole thing on me out of the blue. She doesn't want us to have any chance to stop it."

"Well, really, we just decided because I have leave the next few days, and we wanted to—"

Byron's voice was steely, "If you think that I'm allowing it to happen, tomorrow or ever, you're dumber than I thought."

"Saffron!" A voice called from behind her. Saffron snapped out of her focus on the ominous conversation and spun around to see a dark form coming forward from the game. At her feet was the glowing football. "Little help?" She recognized Logan as he drew closer.

Saffron was embarrassed that she'd been listening. She scooped up the football. It was hard and heavier than she expected. She covered the distance between herself and Logan quickly, getting away from the lanai in case Byron and Davis emerged from beneath it. She tossed Logan the ball, and he caught it with practiced ease.

"Thanks!" he said warmly.

Saffron forced a smile, trying to drive Byron's gruff voice and bad attitude out of her mind, "No problem. Who's winning?"

"Groom's side is killing us," Logan shrugged, waving toward the glow sticks on the scoreboard that clearly indicated he was right, "but we're down a man."

"Oh?" Saffron thought she did an excellent job of seeming surprised.

"Yeah," Logan shrugged as he turned back to the game, "Byron wandered off somewhere a couple minutes ago. And Davis went to find him. If he doesn't get back soon, we'll get slaughtered." Logan fired the ball back into the group, and one of the local boys made a grunt as he caught it.

"Easy there, Rocket," called his teammate, "this isn't the NFL. Catching your passes makes my hands hurt."

"Davis says Logan's a superstar quarterback," Keahi called. "Is that right?"

The sound of Byron's voice behind her made Saffron jump. "He had the fastest, most targeted passes in the country, according to Highschool Hotshot Magazine his senior year." There were pride and affection in Byron's voice, a stark contrast to the menacing tone he'd used with Davis.

Logan waved them off, "Aww. That was a long time ago."

Byron and Logan moved back into the field of play. Davis still hadn't come out from under the lanai.

Squinting, Saffron could see the shape of Keahi standing at the edge of his team. He threw her a wave, and she kept her expression neutral as she waved back, even though it was dark and he probably couldn't see her very well either.

The game resumed, and Saffron watched a couple of plays, keeping an eye on the bright, glowing ball as it flew from one player to another. It was an unbalanced game, she could tell, with Keahi dominating the field and backed up by several of the local boys. They'd probably played together in high school. Logan and Byron's team had some of the locals, too, but even with Logan's skill, they were struggling to keep up.

Keahi must have realized they were winning too easily. Saffron saw him beginning to hang back on plays, a dark shape at the edge of the field. Logan's team began to regain some

ground, and the glow sticks on their side of the scoreboard
started to multiply.

Her heart beat harder as Keahi started toward her.

Saffron realized she had been over-sensitive. She had no
reason to think that Keahi's blossoming feelings for her had
changed since Evelyn had appeared. So he was flustered. So
what? It would rattle anyone to run into their ex without
warning.

She saw his teeth flashing white in the dark night as he
approached and she anticipated taking his hand.

She loved the way their hands fit together. Saffron was not
a small girl, and she loved that Keahi's hands were big enough
to make hers seem dainty. She loved the combination of their
skin tones: like seafoam and warm sand, perfectly complemen-
tary according to Saffron's color sense, and most of all, she
loved the way holding his hand always made her feel safe and
wanted and welcome.

Above her on the lanai, Saffron heard the music come
spilling out into the night. She looked up, and the girls were
spilling out, too.

The media room had a retractable wall that opened out
onto the lanai. It was powered by a button inside, and it made
for a modern, flexible space that offered endless entertainment
possibilities. The bridesmaids were opening it, and their party
suddenly expanded into the outdoor space as well.

The tell-tale opening strains of the Surfer Boys' "Be
Mine" splashed down onto the yard. Someone snapped on
the outside lights, and the football game sprang into sharp
focus and screeched to a halt as the players rubbed the light
blindness out of their eyes. Evelyn called down from the
lanai.

"Hey, Doc!" Evelyn's voice cut through the night. "Come
on! We need the boys to sing this one!" She was waving a
frantic arm as she and the other girls came pouring down the

steps onto the lawn. They were holding wireless mics, which they held out to the football players.

Evelyn walked directly between Saffron and where Keahi had frozen when the light hit him. Saffron could only watch as Evelyn positioned herself on the other side of Keahi and slid an arm through his.

The musical intro came to its end and Natalie, standing beside Logan, nudged him into singing the high opening bars of the song.

Keahi smiled sheepishly as he followed Logan's lead with a smooth, deep, background harmony. Saffron was annoyed to see that he didn't pull away from Evelyn.

"Davis!" Lyza cried, standing in the middle of the lawn by herself, "Hurry!"

Davis emerged from under the lanai, jogging toward her and arriving just in time to burst out with the first line of the chorus.

Byron slunk out from the shadows and positioned himself on the stairs, leaning against the rail, watching with a look of skepticism. Saffron admired Davis' ability to shake off his future father-in-law's disapproval and throw himself into singing. She tried to hang onto her own irritation with Keahi, but as the boys took the microphones and drew away from the girls, back together into the center of the lawn, taking parts expertly, the bouncy tempo filled the night and made it impossible to be annoyed.

She didn't know if it was the girls watching, the mothers clapping from up on the lanai, or the warm island breeze, but the men synced perfectly and threw all their energy into the performance. They even did some impromptu choreography.

Keahi was smiling at her as he sang backup on the line, "Every kiss is heaven to me." Saffron felt herself smiling back. At the end, he broke into the harmony with the others, and Davis ended up on one knee in front of Lyza, grinning up with that same look of adoration Saffron had seen in the Empress' garden days ago.

The Empress and Lyza's mother applauded heartily from their vantage point on the lanai.

"Wonderful!" the Empress said. "Even Princess loved it!" The chicken punctuated the remark with a trill.

Saffron wondered if they'd sing again, but the next song that started was definitely for a girls' group. As it began Evelyn and the college friends all started in on it. With the rest of the bridesmaids hanging all over the groomsmen, it looked like the football game was over.

The girls danced around on the lanai. When the next song started, they passed a microphone off to the Empress, who belted out "Happiness in the Chapel," with the bride and bridesmaids for backup.

Saffron couldn't help but laugh as the Empress substituted "cliffhouse" for "chapel" throughout the song.

It was a new, lighthearted Empress that Saffron had never seen before, and her pleasure over her son's wedding was obvious.

In the breathless quiet that followed the song, the sound of an engine whining up the driveway drew their attention. Headlights washed over the lawn, and the party grouped instinctively together, squinting at the approaching vehicle. It was an old range rover, and from it sprang a small man. Saffron recognized Akoni.

"Stop!" he yelled, waving a hand as the next karaoke song began to blast out into the yard.

Keahi stepped forward, "Uncle," he said, a question in his voice.

"Turn it off! Turn the music off! You're making them crazy!" the old man shouted.

The whole group moved forward, straining to hear the man over the music. Saffron had lost track of Keahi in the crush of people. She turned to run up the steps and turn off the music and was grateful to see that Byron was no longer blocking them. As she reached the top, the music stopped abruptly, and the lights switched off, plunging the whole yard into darkness.

Only the rover lights remained, capturing the group in a single cone of light with Akoni at its point. Logan emerged from the media room and passed Saffron with a grim look. She followed him down the stairs.

Saffron saw Lyza standing at the edge of the crowd, looking frightened. She crossed and took the girl's arm.

"It's okay," she said, "Keahi will learn what it's about."

It turned out that everyone learned. Akoni's voice was loud.

"Your noise is upsetting the 'aumakua," he said, his words like barbs.

"I'm sorry," Keahi said, "we didn't know it would bother them."

"You want them to leave?" Akoni directed this at the whole group. The local boys looked down, taking the chiding to heart, but the mainlanders still stared at the strange visitor with puzzled expressions.

"The lights upset them, too," Akoni said gruffly, "the bay should be dark and quiet at night."

"I'm sorry, Uncle. We're almost done anyway. We have a big day tomorrow, right, Dave?" Keahi turned to address the groom, but Davis wasn't there. Saffron looked around, scanning each face. He wasn't in the group at all. Maybe he'd gone up to stand with his mother on the lanai? But when Saffron looked up, she didn't see him there, either. She couldn't remember seeing him since the big finale of "Be Mine."

"Davis?" Akoni looked around. "Where is that bad luck boy? It's him that's causing all this. You need to get him out of here. He can't be in Maika'i, especially while the 'aumakua are here. He upsets them. He has to go." Akoni said.

From up on the lanai came the authoritative voice of the Empress. "My boy is not bad luck!"

Akoni didn't let her finish before he was speaking again, "You should know best what bad luck he is! You could walk before he came!"

The Empress swelled in her wheelchair, becoming even more imposing. "Don't you tell me what I know, you crazy old—"

Keahi spoke again, his voice covering the Empress' final word, "Auntie, Uncle, don't fight. We'll keep it down." He said, edging Akoni toward his car. Saffron was, not for the first time, grateful for Keahi's commanding presence.

Akoni blinked, his whole lined face folding with the action. He looked back toward the sea where, in the darkness, the cliff fell away to the bay the 'aumakua had chosen. "See that you do. The 'aumakua must be respected. You don't need to be disturbing them at night. They're feeding."

"Yes, Uncle." Keahi gave a repentant smile. Saffron liked the respectful way he treated people. It was especially apparent with older people.

Akoni made a grunt and turned back to his rover. Climbing in, he backed the vehicle up and retreated down the driveway toward the road. The group trudged back up the stairs, much of their enthusiasm gone.

They gathered back in the dining room.

There was some quiet talk among the guests. Saffron stood to the side, not sure how to restore the festive atmosphere. She was relieved when the guests started talking more freely and even laughing quietly on their own. Soon the boys stood and moved to the buffet, loading plates of tapas leftovers. Keahi joined them, and Saffron was relieved to see that Evelyn hadn't made a beeline to stand beside him. She glanced around. Evelyn wasn't anywhere, actually, and there were other conspicuous absences, too: The bride and the groom, Byron, Natalie, and Logan were all missing as well.

She noticed the olive tray was empty and went to fill it.

She got out several jars of olives, each soaking in a different marinade, and filled the platter.

Passing by the media room on her way back to the dining room, she glanced in and saw Natalie and Logan locked in an embrace. Saffron glanced away quickly. It wasn't the first time she'd seen the principal attendants hook up at a wedding. In some circles, it was almost expected.

As Saffron entered the dining room, Lyza bolted in from the side door, screaming for her father.

Logan pushed past Saffron, who had frozen in the doorway. Natalie came in, too, wiping a delicate finger across her mouth and running her hands through her short hair.

Logan was at Lyza's side, "Lyze, Lyze, what's wrong?"

She clung to him. "He's gone. He's—I think he fell!"

Saffron thought of the cliffs outside and felt suddenly sick.

"Who?" Logan bent, trying to peer into Lyza's downturned face.

"Da—" she stopped, a sob shaking her. The word was small when she managed to get it out: "Davis."

Logan's jaw tensed, "Show me where," he said. Cyndi, Lyza's mother, was at her daughter's other side, grasping her hand, and she walked with them out through the side door. The rest of the party followed them around the side of the house and down the steps off the lanai.

Keahi appeared beside Saffron with a strong flashlight. Its beam cut sharply through the night air.

"I don't know where. I went out to look for him, and I heard him—" Lyza choked, "I heard him call out. When I went toward the sound, I almost fell myself. There's a dropoff," she was pointing into the darkness ahead, "there."

Saffron tried not to think of the jagged black cliff, of the water breaking on the rocks below, of the sharks in that water. She tried instead to remember how gently the big creatures had skimmed alongside the boat, how playful and serene they were.

"What's going on?" Byron came striding across the lawn toward the group, emerging from the darkness like a specter.

"I can't find Davis," Lyza dropped her mother's arm and clutched her father's shirt. "Help me find him, Daddy."

Byron's expression didn't change. He reached out and snatched the flashlight from Keahi. Sweeping it in an arc in front of him, he strode to the front of the group and walked ahead, as if he were putting himself between Lyza and Davis for the second time that night.

Keahi and Saffron matched his pace, outrunning the rest of the group slightly. As they neared the edge, Saffron saw something small and shining on the ground between Byron and the cliff. She was about to call out to warn Byron not to step on it when she saw him look deliberately down at it and then, in a single, swift motion, kick the object over the edge.

Saffron's mouth hung open. She looked at Keahi. "Did you see that?"

Keahi nodded.

"What was it?"

"I couldn't tell."

"Mr. Carelli, be careful so close to the edge!" Saffron called. He glanced back, surprised to see them.

"Don't come close," he said, but neither Keahi nor Saffron slowed.

"What did you kick over?" Saffron asked as she approached.

His answer was quick and harsh, "A rock."

Saffron couldn't say for sure that the object hadn't been a rock. She tried to calm her spinning thoughts.

Byron was leaning out, looking over the edge. "You don't want to look down there," he said, his voice hard.

He was right. Saffron didn't want to look. But she couldn't bear not to, either. She peered over the edge. In the bright white beam of the flashlight, she saw what she'd been dreading: Davis' white crackerjack jumper, snagged on the rough lava rock thirty feet below, stained with red and snapping like a flag in the wind.

Chapter Five

S affron's home was the Hau'oli ka Moa egg farm. Driving up to it that night, she saw the headlights slide across the house, the three little cottages in the back, and the dark foliage obscuring the path that led to the egg house where more than 12 dozen hens lived in spacious indoor/outdoor pens and laid eggs for Saffron to sell each week. She mostly used the money to buy them more chicken feed. The house was a rectangular blue bungalow with a wide wraparound lanai and big windows. It was quiet when Saffron walked inside. The time was well after midnight now, and she'd spent the last hour scrubbing the cliff house. She'd left the decorations and all the chairs set up, and it broke her heart to think that there would be no ceremony for Davis and Lyza tomorrow.

After the grisly discovery, the jovial evening had ended quickly. The guests had gone to their homes and their rooms at the bed and breakfast to await any news of Davis from the search and rescue team. Saffron had seen them all off, trying to make sure they were all okay. But nobody was really okay. The horror of the accident had left them all gutted. Saffron had called Rex and Carlo to come and get the Empress, whose tight lips and the jerky, compulsive way she was petting Princess were the only evidence of her anxiety. She didn't cry, didn't wail. Just asked in a controlled tone for Saffron to please let her know any news.

Lyza's parents had driven away in their car, Cyndi riding in the back with the weeping bride. Rachel and Sylvia had left together, and cousin Tiff had taken Lyza's sister Myra back to the bed and breakfast. The local boys had dissipated quickly, and Saffron was sure that Maika'i was abuzz with the news already.

Saffron took a ginger ale from the fridge and walked through the quiet night down to the egg house. Night sounds rustled in the trees, and she breathed in the island air, carrying with her the weight of the accident. She used a black light to check for scorpions. Seeing none of the pests, she switched her torch to a regular beam and shone it around.

Last week, before the Empress had called her to arrange the wedding, she'd had a predator break-in. She'd come just in time to scare it away—although she'd only caught a brief glimpse of its long, furry body and wasn't entirely sure what it was—and none of the flock had been hurt. But she hadn't expected it—it had slipped in during the night when she was least expecting it. She thought about how tragedy often struck without warning and gulped air to stop her eyes from burning with tears. She shone the beam of her light around so she could look at her flock.

There was something calming about chickens. Something about their predictable reactions, like the disapproving clucks they gave her as she entered.

They were all on the perches in their pens, blinking sleepily at her as she entered.

Saffron shook her head, trying not to think about the jumper flapping in the wind or the dizzying height of the cliff. She had kept the boundaries of the football game well back from it, but she hadn't thought about people wandering on their own. Guilt draped around her like a blanket. She tried to hold on to some hope that the rescuers would find Davis, that they would call and tell her he was hurt, but alive.

But she'd seen the cliff in the daytime. She knew the chances were slim.

She tried to think of something else, of Keahi. But when she thought of him, all she could see was that moment Keahi had told her, with that apology in his eyes again, that Evelyn needed a ride home. Evelyn, apparently, had ridden to the event with her aunt and uncle, but now she wanted to give them space to comfort the bride.

What should Saffron have said? She could have offered to take Evelyn herself, but the cliff house had to be sorted. She had to clean up after the party, close the sliding wall in the media room, shut down the karaoke system, put everything back in order. Well, at least everything she could put back in order.

And then there was Natalie. Natalie, in her white cracker-jack uniform, standing like a statue in the middle of the lawn atop the cliff, waiting.

Waiting for what, Saffron didn't know, but the girl would not be moved. No amount of reasoning or pleading could get her to budge. She couldn't speak without her voice cracking in a sob, and Saffron finally left her outside in the wind to deal with her grief. It was upon entering the cliff house that she noticed Logan hadn't gone yet, either. He was still inside, standing at the window, watching Natalie out on the cliff.

Saffron had smiled at him as she came in. It was a small, sad smile. "She says she's staying out there until the rescuers come," Saffron told him.

The only local police officer, Bradley, had already come and gone. One look over the cliff and he'd whistled and called for a rescue team from Laie on his radio. They wouldn't be able to rappel down until the morning brought the light back. Nobody was giving Davis much of a chance anyway.

Logan had nodded. "They were good friends. Grew up together here, I think. Like Lyza and me. They were thrilled to have this last deployment together. That's where I met them."

"Do you think Lyza will be okay?"

Logan's eyes closed for a moment, and Saffron could tell he was worried about his friend. His reply was choppy and disjointed, and Saffron couldn't blame him. It had been an awful shock. "I hope so. They haven't known each other that long; I guess she'll bounce back. I don't know."

A particularly strong gust of wind howled around the cliff-house, and both Saffron and Logan looked out at Natalie. The sailor stood squarely, her feet wide apart and her hands behind her back.

"She looks so determined," Saffron said.

Logan shook his head, and there was admiration as well as

pity in his voice. "She's standing at perfect parade rest. Collins would be proud." There was bitterness in his voice.

"Collins?"

"Yeah. He's an officer on our ship. Tough. Always cussing us out if we're not in perfect form. He's especially hard on Davis, er, he was." The past tense hung heavy between them.

"Why was he so hard on Davis?"

Logan shrugged. "It's like that sometimes. You just don't get along with some people, like any job, only it's tougher in the military because they control everything about your life." Logan sighed heavily. "Collins sure pitched a fit about us all asking for liberty at the same time."

This piqued Saffron's interest. "Liberty?"

"Leave. Time off."

"Oh. And Collins was unhappy?"

"Well," Logan conceded, "we went over his head because we knew he wouldn't let us off. We'll pay for it when we get back." He was thoughtful for a moment, "In retrospect, maybe we shouldn't have pushed so hard."

Saffron felt a stab of guilt. If she hadn't planned the events here, if she had been more cautious about that cliff, maybe this wouldn't have happened.

"Will she stay out there all night?" Saffron asked. "I told her she could come in and spend the night here."

"She's standing watch," Logan said, "I don't think she'll leave."

"I hate to leave her out there."

Logan pulled his dixie cup hat from his back pocket and put it on his head. "I'll stand with her," he had said.

Saffron thought of them now, two white figures in the night, standing over their fallen friend. Finally, in the egg house by herself, with the calming night sounds of the flock around her, Saffron cried too.

THE NIGHT HAD PASSED SLOWLY. Saffron hadn't slept much, and she was back at the cliff at daybreak. The rescuers were there, too, and they had gone over as soon as there was enough light.

The morning sun shone on the broad lawn as Saffron, Keahi, and Natalie sat waiting for them to climb back up. Logan had gone to check on Lyza as soon as Saffron had arrived, and Keahi had shown up not long afterward. Natalie was still and quiet now. Her uniform was rumpled from the night out in the damp, and an air of deep sadness had settled over her. Saffron wondered, briefly, if Logan's presence had offered her any comfort.

Officer Bradley had returned, too. He not only had to process the accident scene, but he also had to interview everyone from the party. Saffron flinched as she thought of Lyza having to relive the event. Even if Bradley had been good at dealing with people, discussing your fiancé's death would be hard. Saffron didn't envy Bradley's task.

He paced at the top of the cliff. The team had rappelled down the cliff this morning, hoping to recover Davis' body. They had been very clear that there was little hope of his survival, and the rescue was complicated by the frenzy of sharks that still patrolled the bay below.

After what seemed an eternity, Saffron saw the first gloved hand reach up and over the edge of the cliff, and saw the rescue workers at the top of the cliff assist the first rescuer to return from below. Saffron stood and walked over to them, followed by Keahi. She noticed that Natalie stayed where she was.

"A lot of blood down there on the rocks," the man was saying, "those sharks are still stirred up."

"Do you think they . . ." Even the weathered rescue worker couldn't say it. "The sharks I mean?"

The climber glanced back toward the edge, and Saffron saw a shiver run through him. "Yeah. Looks like."

Bradley strode to his car and returned with a clear plastic evidence bag. The climber unclipped from his ropes and met Bradley several steps from the edge. He carried a big loose canvas bag, and Saffron was transfixed as he began to empty it. He pulled out the jumper, torn and ragged. The stains on it had darkened to a disarming wine color. It was followed by one black shoe, also crusted with blood, and the plastic football, its neon orange garish in the morning light. Saffron looked away, only to see another climber cresting the cliff.

This one was young, maybe twenty. He stood unclipping his ropes.

"Anything for evidence?" The first climber called.

"Just a couple things," the young climber said. The bag on his belt was much smaller than the first rescuer's. As he came toward Bradley, he reached inside. Slowly, he extracted a knotted black neckerchief.

"This," he said, dropping the neckerchief into the evidence bag. Then he reached in again. "And I found one other thing."

Bradley paused in sealing the bag. "Does it need to go in here?"

"I don't think so." The young rescuer said. "No blood on this one." From the bag, he drew out Davis' dixie cup hat, its bright white fabric marred by scuffs and dirt and water stains. Behind them, Natalie let out a little cry and buried her face in her arms.

Bradley took the item awkwardly, holding the evidence bag in one hand and the hat in the other. "I'll have to tell his mom," he said.

"Tell her it probably wasn't painful. Looks like he probably hit his head on the way down. Probably was knocked out before he fell as far as the ocean." The climber didn't mention the sharks, but they all knew what a mercy it was if Davis was unconscious when he hit the water.

Saffron imagined the gruff Bradley standing on the steps of the Empress' estate, the cap in his hand. Suddenly, she couldn't stand it. "We'll do it," she said, "we'll tell her. Keahi and I will go." She held out a hand expectantly.

Slowly, Bradley handed the hat to her. "Well, you know her better than I do," he said. Relief showed on his face.

THERE WAS heavy silence in the drawing room as the Empress caressed the folds of Davis' hat. The ever-present Princess had been whisked away by Rex as they'd presented it to the Empress. Saffron couldn't help but notice that the old woman stroked the hat in just the same rhythmic way that she always petted her chicken.

"I told him to stay away from the edge," she said. "I always told him."

Keahi and Saffron exchanged a look. It wasn't clear if the Empress was talking to them or not.

"He wasn't bad luck, you know," the Empress said, looking directly at Saffron. "He was the best thing that ever happened to me."

Saffron nodded and let the old woman continue.

"They said he was bad luck because when he was born, I had complications that put me in this chair. And they blamed his father's death on him, too. My late husband, Nelson, died at a beach barbeque three months after Davis was born. Nelson was swimming and got caught in a riptide. Akoni spread the lie about my Davis being bad luck because he felt guilty that he wasn't paying attention and didn't go out to save Nelson.

"That's why you didn't want Davis swimming?" Saffron asked.

"I couldn't save him, could I? If he was on the land, at least I could crawl to him if I had to." The Empress' voice cracked. "I always knew I'd lose him. I have been warding off the spirits from him for years, but I couldn't keep him here forever."

She was crying now, and Saffron left the couch and crossed the drawing room, crouching beside her friend's wheelchair and putting her arms around the old woman.

"I'm sorry," she said, and she meant that she was sorry for Davis' loss, for the old woman's pain, and for planning the wedding in the first place.

KEAHI TRIED to take her hand as they walked down the wide steps. She pulled it away. As hard as she tried, she couldn't shake the image of Evelyn's perfect face smiling up at him. It was one more bitter memory from this already difficult weekend.

He stopped in the middle of the stairs.

"Saffron?"

She didn't want to look at him, but she did. She knew her eyes were cold and her face was drawn.

"Saffron, are you upset about Davis?" He seemed genuinely confused.

Suddenly, she felt ashamed. Davis was dead, and her mind was consumed, not only with grief but also with jealousy. She couldn't tell Keahi that she was mad at him because he'd driven his old girlfriend home. Not in the face of real pain like they'd just witnessed in the Empress. It seemed childish and petty. She didn't want him to think that was who she was—she didn't want to be that person in the first place.

"It's been a long week," she said, and then, because she

couldn't think of anything else to say, she turned to go to her car.

"Wait," he called, "can I see you later? Let's go to dinner. I'll pick you up?"

Dinnertime was four hours away. Maybe by then, she'd be feeling better. "Okay," she called back before slipping into the car and driving away.

She was going to go home, but instead, she found herself driving back to the cliff house. The rescuers were gone, and a deep quiet permeated the place as she entered the code and let herself in the front door.

The smell of garlic lingered from the tapas last night. The decorations stood ready in the greatroom, and the pile of unopened gifts sat on a table in the dining room. Saffron walked to the front of the great room and looked out at the sea.

Life changed so quickly. One moment was joy and anticipation, the next grief and regret. The vast sea outside made her feel small and insignificant. Accidents always seemed to suck the sense of order out of life. Why? Why had this happened? When Davis and Lyza were on the eve of the happiest day of their lives? Saffron was a planner, good at it because she craved order and worked to put everything in its place, but in one second the world could shatter, and there was no way to put back all the pieces.

Saffron wondered how Lyza was doing today. She wondered if Bradley had interviewed her yet.

Saffron sat in the front row of chairs. She couldn't help but feel more acutely the height of the cliffhouse, its precarious position on the rock. It seemed less secure now, though the house felt no different around her than it had before.

There was a knock on the door, and Saffron jumped, even though she knew it would be Officer Bradley. He'd called to ask for a short interview, and she'd told him where she was. She went through the great room and the entry then opened it. Bradley stood on the step, looking haggard.

"Do you have time now for a few questions?" he asked.

"Sure," Saffron waved him in and led him to the dining room, where they sat across from each other at the big wooden table.

"You were here last night at the time of the accident?" Bradley asked.

"Yes." She said, "I'm the one who planned the party."

"And when was the last time you saw the deceased?"

Saffron tried to remember. She could picture him kneeling in front of Lyza, but not after that.

"I guess after he and the boys sang karaoke. I don't recall where he went after that."

"Seems to be a common theme," Bradley said. "Would you say there was adequate lighting outside to see the dropoff?"

Saffron thought back to the lawn, flooded with lights, and the stark edge of the cliff.

"I do," she said, but as she spoke, she remembered Akoni's visit and amended. "Well, not when the boys were playing football, and not after Akoni came. Someone turned off the lights then, and it was pretty dark. Only Akoni's headlights were out there."

"Why was Mr. Kale here at all? Was he invited?" It took Saffron a moment to realize that the word Bradley was using, which sounded like Kah-leh, was Akoni's last name.

"He was upset. He didn't want us bothering the sharks with the lights and the music."

"Was there anyone Mr. Kale directed his anger at particularly?"

Saffron saw where this was going, but there was no other answer, "Yes. He particularly mentioned Davis. He thought Davis was bad luck."

Bradley nodded and made a note. "And after Mr. Kale left? Did you see him again?"

Saffron shook her head. "No, I assumed he went home."

Bradley leaned over his notebook on the table. "He didn't."

"At all?"

"Apparently not. His Range Rover was parked a couple hundred yards down the road, and nobody reports having seen him after that last night."

"It's still there?"

Bradley nodded. "Nothing incriminating inside, but the bride's father is adamant that we find Akoni and question him."

Saffron was only half-listening. Why wouldn't Akoni have left last night? Where was he now?

"Akoni has strong beliefs," Bradley said. "And a history of taking the law into his own hands."

"Oh?"

"Sure," Bradley was conversational now, and Saffron could see he was glad to talk about something other than the current case. "A couple years ago, he stole thirty pigs from his neighbor's field."

"What?"

"Right. Because of some superstition. Stole every one of them and let them go on some mountain."

"He admitted it?"

"Yep, and paid for them, too. There wasn't much else we could do."

"Still," Saffron said, "it's a long way from stealing a pig to killing a person."

"Not as long as you might think," Bradley said. He jotted something down in his notebook. "Were there any other uncomfortable situations at the party last night?"

Saffron immediately thought of Evelyn and Keahi, but that

wasn't, she was sure, what Bradley meant. "Well, Lyza's father yelled at Davis when he arrived."

"Oh? They weren't getting along?"

For the first time since she'd heard it, the conversation between the two men under the lanai popped into Saffron's head. That was definitely what Bradley meant, "no, in fact, I heard Byron telling Davis that he wasn't going to stand by and let Lyza marry him."

At this, Bradley scratched furiously in the notebook, then looked up with an expectant expression. Saffron recounted what she'd heard as well as she could remember, ending with "I'm warning you."

"Sounds like a threat when you say it that way," Bradley said.

"Sounded like one when he said it, too," Saffron replied simply.

"He didn't like the idea of her marrying someone who wasn't from nearby her hometown?" Bradley clarified.

"Right. He thought she'd be too far away, and that she'd be lonely."

"Hmmm," Bradley said.

"What?"

He looked around. "I probably shouldn't say," Saffron knew that was a good sign. Bradley only said that when he was about to actually say something he probably shouldn't say. "But his wife said something about that, too, when I interviewed her this morning. She said, 'At least now I know my baby won't be halfway across the world.' Which seemed too much looking on the bright side to me."

Saffron nodded. She could see how Cyndi's thoughts would go there, but in connection with what her husband had said last night, it seemed suspicious.

"He said he wouldn't let the wedding happen," Saffron added. "Something about 'not tomorrow, not ever.'"

Bradley turned abruptly and stood, walking to the window as he pulled out his radio. "Mary," he said to the dispatcher, "you've got all those contact numbers for the witnesses, right?"

Mary's nasal voice came from the speaker, "Yep."

"I'd like you to send out a request that nobody leaves the island just yet. I think we may not have an accident on our hands."

"What do you mean?" Mary asked.

"I think Davis might have been murdered."

Chapter Six

When Keahi pulled into the egg farm, Saffron was ready for him. She'd spent the afternoon stewing about what Lyza's father had said to Davis under the lanai, and she kept thinking she should have said something to someone—that he was dangerous. She was ready to think about something else. What she wasn't prepared for was seeing Evelyn in the front seat of Keahi's SUV.

The two of them climbed out, and Saffron noted that Evelyn was overdressed for the Oceanside Cafe. The girl's dark hair was pulled up in a neat bun, and she wore a fitted navy sheath with a spray of embroidered flowers. Saffron glanced at her own flowing blouse and capris as Keahi bounced onto the lanai.

"Hey!" he said. He was wearing a boxy button-up with two sleek vertical stripes down either side, slacks, and wingtips. Saffron could see his days as a Boston surgeon in the outfit. They made a striking couple.

"You're dressed up," was all Saffron could manage.

"Change in plans. I thought we'd show Evie something more than just little old Maika'i."

Little old Maika'i had been enough for Keahi's dates with Saffron, but she didn't mention that. "Where are we going?"

"There's a great jazz club in Honolulu called *Chromatic*. I haven't been there in a while."

In at least six months, Saffron thought. He'd never mentioned *Chromatic* before, or even jazz for that matter. Still, what was she going to do, send them off together?

"I'll have to change," she said.

"You look great," Keahi smiled. Saffron glanced at Evelyn, who had wandered across the lawn past the house and was eyeing the path that led to the egg house. Keahi's compliment boosted her opinion of the evening. A jazz club could be fun, and she desperately needed a break from thinking about Davis and his ominous almost-in-laws.

"Thanks. I'm going to change anyway," Saffron said, "something more appropriate."

She slipped back into the house just as Evelyn called to Keahi and he started across the lawn after her.

Saffron thought fast. Keahi liked her long strawberry hair. He'd said so, and when they sat together, he entwined his fingers in it. She'd leave it down. She scrambled to her closet. When she'd first come to Hawaii, she'd only brought a few outfits, but she'd returned to DC when she sold her business there, and she'd brought her best clothes back with her. Now she looked desperately through the closet for something that would compete with Keahi's blast from the past.

"Am I competing?" She said out loud. She didn't like the taste of the words in her mouth, but she still felt the truth of them in her mind. She wanted, more than anything, to outshine Evelyn tonight, and there was only one dress for that.

Saffron pulled it from its hanging cover. It was a feminine flared dress in white and deep teal. She knew how it looked on her. She decided to accessorize with her best island jewelry: a set of carved wooden bangle bracelets that Mano had given her, a large shell necklace carved to look like plumeria blossoms that had been a gift from Keahi, and the enormous pearl ring that had belonged to her late Aunt Ila.

She slipped on a pair of heels, wondering when she'd worn them last. They didn't lend themselves to sandy adventures on the beach or hiking the mountains. Still, she felt ready when she stepped back onto the lanai to face whatever Evelyn had in mind.

Her companions were nowhere to be seen. Saffron carefully descended the stairs and followed the path to the Egg House. Keahi was showing it off, demonstrating how the automatic feeding system lifted a bag of feed up to a bin where it was poured in, then how the turn of a crank sent feed rattling down pipes into the pens in the various feeders.

Evelyn looked amazed. "I had no idea you were such a *country girl*," she said smugly.

Saffron felt her defenses rise. "I wasn't," she said, "until I moved here."

The chickens were loudly protesting Saffron's lack of attention to them. She unconsciously unscrewed the top of a container on the counter and dipped her hand into the golden grains before scattering them out into the nearest pen. The hens fell on them and snatched up the tasty treats. Two of them, a big round Buff Orpington that Saffron called Sunshine and a scrappy little black and white Plymouth Rock named Stripes, began a loud quarrel over the best one.

Evelyn was looking at her hand. "Wow," she said, "That's some ring."

"Thanks," Saffron held it out to her.

"And your bracelets!" Evelyn reached out a manicured finger to tap them. Her fingernails weren't long, but they were groomed. Before Saffron could explain, a slow smile crept across Evelyn's face. "And I'll bet I know where you got that necklace." She turned a sly glance to Keahi, whose eyes widened suddenly.

"We should go," he said, moving toward the door.

But Evelyn didn't stop talking as she moved to follow him. The tone of her words exactly matched the sound of the hens' squabble behind them, "Keahi gave me one of those, too!"

Saffron couldn't help but slam the egg house door as she left and followed them up the path.

Inexplicably, Saffron ended up in the back of the SUV.

"This is Evelyn's first trip to Hawaii," Keahi explained as they rocketed down the highway toward Honolulu. Saffron leaned back and tried to fight the urge to take the necklace off. She supposed it was just comeuppance for her own smugness about wearing the tangible symbol of Keahi's affection tonight. But it was hard to hang onto what she'd thought they had in the face of he and Evelyn's extensive past. Harder still since they wouldn't stop talking about it.

"Remember that time when you were in your residency, and we were in a staff meeting, and the attending physician was giving that big lecture on not dating other members of the staff?"

Keahi laughed, his face alight with the memory, "I barely kept it together."

"I know. I was biting the inside of my lip, and Carrie was beside me, and she knew we were dating, and she kept kicking me in the ankle."

"And *you* kept kicking *me* in the ankle?" he said.

None of that seemed to Saffron adequate justification for the amount of laughing they were doing.

"That wasn't the only time, though. We got caught when we were out to dinner by Doctor Evans." Evelyn said. "Remember? He was so stern, but I don't think his heart was in it."

"How could it be? He *married* his operating room nurse."

They laughed again, and Saffron had that same out-of-place feeling she'd had in the garden with the Empress. But she had been in many strange situations since coming to Hawaii. She could handle an evening in awkward company without falling to pieces. She spoke up.

"Is that the Doctor Evans that built the cliffhouse?" She asked.

"That's right," Keahi said. Mention of the cliffhouse took some of the jocularity from his voice. "I had to call him earlier and tell him what happened."

Saffron knew that must have been a hard call.

"What exactly *did* happen?" Evelyn's direct demeanor cut through the creeping melancholy. "I went to my car to get an allergy pill, and when I headed back, everyone was pouring outside."

Saffron considered that, "Did you see anyone when you went to your car?"

"Like I told the local law, I saw that old man that came and yelled at us. He was walking off into the trees from the driveway."

Saffron's head was spinning. "What? Akoni was back there?"

"I guess. I didn't see his car, though."

"You know what I can't figure out?" Keahi said, "Why was the football down there? Did they throw it too far? When did we lose it?"

Saffron had no memory of the football from the time it was whizzing between teams to the time she saw it brought up from the cliff.

"Evelyn," Saffron said suddenly, "your Uncle Byron, is he an—angry man?"

Evelyn seemed to tense in the front seat. "I suppose," she said.

"Why?"

"My mom always said it was because he never got the son he wanted," Evelyn said. "But that sounds pretty old-fashioned."

"Just the two daughters?" Saffron asked, "Lyza and Myra?"

"Right. You've noticed my family has a thing for y's. All but Tiff's family," she shrugged. "Anyway, he's always been kind of prickly, ever since I've known him."

"And he didn't like Davis," Saffron stated it as a fact instead of a question. The lychee trees and mango trees, broken up by the occasional giant albizia trees, whizzed by the window.

"I don't think it was Davis, particularly. I think he just had . . . Other plans for Lyza."

"Other plans?" Saffron prodded.

"Oh, you know, he wanted her to marry Logan. *Everybody* wanted her to marry Logan. They were the Great American Couple."

"How did Logan and Lyza feel about it?" Saffron asked.

"I think they thought of it when they were younger when they were in high school probably. But then she moved on, and they just became great friends. I think Uncle Byron just never could let go of that possibility. And then when Lyza brought Davis around it was only for like a day and a half. They didn't really have time to get to know him. Then, a couple weeks later they get a call that Lyza is marrying him in four days." Evelyn kept talking as Saffron watched the road outside the window. "Naturally, they were shaken. I was surprised at Uncle Byron the other day, though, because I thought it was mostly Aunt Cyndi who was upset about the wedding."

"Your aunt?" Saffron knew her voice held incredulity. "She seemed all for it."

"She did all her crying on the plane over here," Evelyn said. "I should know. I sat by her. She just knew that Lyza would live far away and she'd never see her. Plus," Evelyn glanced over her shoulder and gave Saffron a pointed look,

"She didn't get to be in on any of the planning for the wedding, which you can understand she's been looking forward to for my cousin's entire life."

Saffron felt another vague stab of regret. She hadn't thought about any of that. Now she had a vaguely unsettled feeling. What if Cyndi hadn't wanted the marriage to go through? What had Lyza said about her father? That he would do anything for his wife. She wondered what, exactly, that included.

The lush greenery of the highway soon gave way to the dense architecture of Honolulu. Houses and apartment buildings, schools and warehouses filled every street. Keahi seemed to know where he was going, though and parked easily before opening both passenger doors with a flourish. Saffron and Evelyn both stepped out simultaneously. Keahi moved naturally between them.

"I'm a lucky guy tonight," he said breezily. Saffron stopped herself from punching him in his lucky arm.

Chromatic was a medium-sized place with a bar, a stage, several small tables, and a whole section of comfy modern couches and chairs. Though the furniture, walls, and counters were all shades of gray, everything was underlit with bright colored lights: blues and reds and yellows, greens, and purples. Some of the lights were connected to the bass amplifier and pulsed with the deepest notes for an immersive sound experience.

"Wow," Saffron breathed.

"Pick a table," Keahi said.

Saffron was torn. She shifted her gaze from one to another. "That one's beautiful," she said, "with the orangey-yellow light. And that one, with the almost purple."

Evelyn made an annoyed sound and began pulling them toward the closest table. Keahi planted himself to stop her from going there and looked at Saffron. "You get to choose," he said.

Evelyn didn't like being impeded. "Almost purple isn't a color," she said, her voice like scraping metal.

Saffron felt the sting of it. She'd always seen colors differently. Besides her art teacher, others had commented on it throughout her life. They'd call something blue, she'd call it purple. They'd see red, she'd see orange.

Keahi was looking at her with interest, "What do you mean by 'almost purple?'"

Saffron sighed. She didn't want to have to explain it right now, but she waved a hand. "What colors do you see?"

"Rainbow," he said, "red, orange, yellow, blue, green, purple."

"Okay, and which are purple?"

Keahi pointed out three tables and a couch.

"Only they're not all the same, and they're not all purple. That one is the truest purple—" Saffron pointed to the table in the center, "the one on the far left is more red, the couch is so red-purple that it's almost fuchsia, and the last table is just slightly on the blue side of purple." She looked deliberately at Evelyn, "*almost* purple."

Keahi was gazing at her with fascination. "Saffron. That kind of color sensitivity is amazing."

"It sounds more like obsessive to me," Evelyn was blunt.

"No," Keahi was quick to contradict her, "no, it's not psychological. It's probably physiological."

This intrigued Saffron. "What do you mean?"

"You might be a tetrachromat," he said, and he seemed genuinely delighted, "some women have four types of cones in their eyes that process way more color information than us regular trichromats who only have three."

Saffron felt herself gripping Keahi's arm. "Really? Because I've always just thought I was crazy."

"Really. You may have superhuman color recognition."

Evelyn was obviously bored with the topic. "Can we just sit down? Any color of table is fine."

Keahi looked at Saffron, "You pick."

Saffron ran her eye over the room. There was a bright, brilliant blue coming from under one booth. She pointed at that one.

Saffron liked the club in spite of the circumstances. She pushed away the thought of how much fun it would have been if she and Keahi were here alone.

They slid into the round booth. It had a high back that caught the sound and held it close to them. Their table glowed that pure blue and the light caught in Keahi's shining eyes.

"Saffron, what if you *are* a functional tetrachromat?" Keahi asked. Saffron saw a rare glimpse of his scientific side, the one he didn't show very often. She liked the spark of excitement in his voice, and she liked that he was still thinking about it. "That would be amazing," he went on, "It would explain so much about your ability to design with color and your sensitivity to color in your environment."

Evelyn broke in. "The club seems pretty great," she said, apparently trying to change the subject.

It worked. "I love this place," Keahi said. His gaze left Saffron and wandered around the room.

"I didn't even know it was here," Saffron tried not to let the bitterness echo in her voice, and she must have succeeded because Keahi glanced over and smiled at her.

A server came around, and Keahi ordered some shrimp and sliders, then a veggie platter for Evelyn. Saffron didn't like that he knew just what the other girl would want. Evelyn laughed when he also requested a water and two raspberry ginger ales.

"Still not going for the hard stuff, huh, Doc?"

"No use being a doctor if you ignore all that schooling," he said. "After all the evidence in the research about what the stuff does to your insides, I don't touch it, and neither should anyone else."

"You've never been afraid to tell people that. I remember some awkward dinner parties," Evelyn laughed.

"I didn't go to med school so I could tell people what they want to hear," Keahi said. It was strange to Saffron to see him like this: so confident in his role as a physician. Mostly he'd kept it to himself ever since she'd met him. Evelyn's influence was undeniable.

"You either?" Evelyn asked Saffron, waving at her soda. Saffron shook her head. He'd seen what it did to people on the inside. She'd seen what it did on the outside. "I'm amazed you've found someone else that shares your dislike of alcohol," Evelyn said. She leaned around Keahi to catch Saffron's eye. "I always thought that's why we were such a good match," she said, "I don't drink, and Keahi is a soda guy. I never thought he would find someone else like me."

Saffron wasn't sure she liked the direct comparison. "You and I aren't exactly alike," she said as the server set down a plate of shrimp scampi swimming in fragrant olive oil and a plate of plain sliced veggies.

Their conversation dropped off dramatically as a young quartet took the stage and started in on a thrilling set. It was jazz with a distinctly unique Hawaiian flavor, with a saxophone, bass, drums, and a ukulele. The uke held its own, and the smoky voice of the lead singer added a warm quality that mesmerized Saffron.

For the next forty minutes, nothing else intruded. Saffron was caught up in the music and enjoying every moment. Keahi slid his hand over hers on the seat between them, and she moved close to him, secure for the first time since Evelyn had appeared at the party yesterday.

When Saffron's phone buzzed, she had no intention of

answering, but a glance at the screen showed her a picture of Princess—it was the Empress. Saffron showed the phone to Keahi and slipped out onto the thrumming Honolulu street to talk.

"Saffron! It's not right!" the Empress' voice was shaking. "The Walking Wonders—they came by. They brought things. It can't be! Why would they do that?"

Saffron cupped a hand around the phone. The Walking Wonders were a local group of older women who'd formed a walking club. They walked the beach every morning. It would make sense for them to visit the Empress in her grief with offerings of home-cooked food, but why would that upset her so much?

"What did they bring?" Saffron managed to slip the question in between the Empress' sobs.

"They brought Davis' things. They found them washed up on the beach south of town. Far from where he fell. One of his shoes. His wallet."

Saffron imagined her in the big drawing room with these things spread on the gold velvet sofa.

"But why would they do it?"

"The Wonders?"

"No, the manōs! His wallet has manō's teeth marks in it."

Saffron closed her eyes against the image.

"I thought they were 'aumakua. Why would they do this? Is it my fault? Should I have gone down to take care of the 'aumakua before this happened?" The Empress' voice trailed off, and all Saffron could hear were sobs.

She didn't know what to say. Quickly, she covered the phone and strode back into the club.

Keahi was leaning close to Evelyn, who was speaking in a low, animated voice.

"I need you," Saffron said. To her relief, Keahi stood immediately and followed her outside. "The Wonders found more of Davis' things," she said, "only, they'd been torn up by the sharks. Maybe we should have told her that's what they suspected had happened to him. Now she's hysterical, and I don't know what to say to her." She laid a hand on his arm. "She feels like it's her fault because she didn't feed the 'aumakua."

Keahi closed his eyes for a moment, then held his hand out for the phone. Saffron laid it in his strong palm.

"Auntie," he said, "this is Keahi. It was an accident. You can't blame yourself."

There was a long pause while he listened to her. Saffron thought of the delicate line he was walking. It was an age-old question, and one she herself had asked: why would deities allow bad things to happen if they had the power to stop them? Saffron also knew enough to know that the answers to those questions came in their own way. She had asked those questions when her mother had died. But then she hadn't known that her Uncle Beau would feel sorry she was alone, hadn't known that he would leave her the egg farm, and hadn't known that he would bring beautiful Hawaii into her life as a result. Maybe someday the Empress would see why this had happened, but not today, amid all this pain.

Keahi was talking again, speaking low and calmly. She imagined that he'd had to give a lot of bad news to people in his career. When he hung up and handed the phone back to her, he shook his head sadly.

"I don't know," he said. "She's pretty broken up."

"I wish they hadn't found anything," Saffron said. "And she'd never have to think about something that horrible happening to him."

"Me, too," said Keahi.

He held her hand as they walked back into the club. This time, Saffron didn't pull away.

Chapter Seven

S affron threw herself into egg gathering the next morning. She needed the work to get her mind off the morning phone call she'd received from Rex, the Empress' steadfast helper. There would be a memorial service for Davis tomorrow, out on a boat leaving from Maika'i harbor. The Empress would take great comfort in having her there.

Saffron would go, of course, and she had offered her help to the other invited guests by going out early and taking their clothes to Sandwashed, the dry cleaners' shop in town. She'd have to pick them up tomorrow morning before the service and get them back to their owners.

The eggs were carried to the work areas at the front of the egg house by hand-cranked conveyor belts that ran behind the nest boxes. The hens laid their eggs in the nest boxes, the eggs rolled out onto the conveyors, and then all Saffron had to do was turn the crank and the belts brought the day's crop of henfruit to her.

She took them off and put them through the egg washer, then arranged them in cartons and stacked the containers on her rolling cart. That went up to the lanai, where an avocado green fridge had been placed to hold the eggs. It was self-serve, and Saffron kept a can inside where people dropped off their checks and cash if she wasn't home when they picked up their eggs. On days she didn't do the egg line, people could still come and get what they needed.

She was keeping ahead of demand, but only just. She could imagine a day when she had to fill the last few pens in the egg house to keep up with the appetites of Maika'i. Her biggest customers were the Oceanside Cafe and the Paradise Market. Though the Paradise was under new ownership, she got on well with the friendly couple who'd bought it, and they took several dozen a week to sell. As she arranged the cartons in the fridge, she glanced up to see a black car kicking up dust from her long driveway.

It wasn't a local car—those she knew. This one stood out because of its tinted windows and detailing that was so nondescript that it was conspicuous. Most cars had a chrome stripe or make and model name, a badge on the grill. This one had nothing. Someone lost, she suspected, looking for directions.

Saffron stood and walked to the edge of the lanai as the car pulled into the yard. Out of it stepped a tall, rectangular man in a khaki uniform and a sharp white hat. A gold badge gleamed above the nametag on his chest that said COLLINS. This was the commanding officer that Logan had mentioned.

A small man in gray camouflage attire climbed out of the passenger's side door. He reached back in for a clipboard and followed the officer to the lanai.

"Ma'am," Collins said. "Are you the event planner that was in charge of the Howard and Carelli wedding?"

"I am," she responded.

"I'm here to investigate the death of one of my sailors. I understand you were there the night Davis Howard was killed?"

Saffron nodded.

"Did you see him fall?"

"No, sir." Something about the way he asked questions made her answer in a military style.

"May we talk with you more extensively?" Collins asked.

Saffron made a sweeping gesture toward the door. "Please," she said, "come on in."

The men accepted a cold drink, then Saffron told them briefly about the catastrophic night.

"You say there were sharks in this bay?" Collins clarified.

"Yes. Tiger sharks."

"You could tell they were tiger sharks from that height?"

"No, I saw them from closer up earlier this week. I went with some friends in a boat out to see them."

"And were the animals aggressive at that time?"

Saffron was used to looking at details. For example, she could tell by the mirror shine on his badge and the reflection from his spotless black shoes that Collins was very serious about his work. She could also see that his young assistant was less concerned about it. His boots were slightly scuffed at the toes. Such powers of observation were both a gift and a curse, though. Saffron could also see from Collins' perfectly calm demeanor that he was the type who was in control of any situation, on or off his ship. This made her more nervous than she liked to admit.

"No, they weren't aggressive," she said.

"But they're sharks, right?" the assistant broke in. He was young, maybe twenty-two or –three, and Saffron could see that he wanted to please his boss and that he was enjoying the investigation from a voyeuristic standpoint. "They can go into a feeding frenzy at any moment."

She hoped he wouldn't talk like this when they were interviewing Davis' mother.

"I've got some paperwork from a local officer here," Collins held out a hand and Marks whipped some papers off the back of the stack on his clipboard and passed them over to Collins. "They detail a couple of arguments you overheard the night of Davis Howard's death," he handed her the papers, and she read Bradley's recounting of her information on Byron's annoyance with his future son-in-law and Akoni's visit to the cliffhouse. "Is that accurate?" He asked.

"It appears to be," she said.

"Do you think either of those people could have killed the sailor?" He asked, "either on purpose or inadvertently?"

Saffron answered as honestly as she could, "I don't know."

The interrogation went on for several more minutes, but Saffron found that she had more questions than she had answers. After a while, she sensed the interview was wrapping up. That sense was confirmed when Collins stood abruptly.

"Could I use your head?" Collins asked, standing, "er, your facilities."

Saffron knew what head meant. It was the term for the bathroom on a ship. "Sure." She pointed him in that direction, then came back to sit with Marks. She didn't believe for a moment that Collins needed the facilities. He was getting a better picture of her, she was sure. She didn't blame him. She would have done the same.

Marks went on, conversationally chatting. She wondered for a moment how he'd ended up in the Navy. He didn't seem the type. "I wonder if my boss saw the sharks when he was here before."

Saffron's eyes narrowed. She pounced on the information. "Collins has visited Maika'i?"

Marks answered casually, "Sure. He came up the day of the accident to check up on those sailors. They said they were going to a wedding, but he was suspicious. He's always suspicious. That's what makes him a good Master-at-Arms."

"What does he do, exactly?"

"MAs are kind of like police," Marks shrugged, "he keeps order."

Saffron understood that. She understood how it was a necessary skill to have, and also how it could become an obsession. "What did he find when he came here?"

"I don't know. He hasn't written up a report for me to file yet."

"He hasn't given you any hints?"

"Collins doesn't give out a lot of information. He's better at gathering it."

Saffron watched the young man carefully. He was thin, with big glasses and a ready smile. He seemed an odd match for Collins. She imagined it was difficult for Marks to keep his chipper attitude when he was always dealing with the stern Collins.

Saffron jumped as the Master-at-Arms strode back into the room and said her name. "I understand that you have access to the scene of the incident?"

Saffron nodded. Dr. Evans had asked both her and Keahi to be in charge of the cliffhouse, to be the local caretakers. Though he had someone else in town for maintenance and lawn care, he wanted the cliffhouse to be a welcoming spot for the locals, so he wanted locals in charge of access.

"Would you please come with us? We need to investigate the scene."

"Bradley and the local rescue personnel have access, too," she said. Her shoulders tensed up. She found herself reluctant to return to the cliffhouse.

"But I want someone who was there. Who can walk us through the events while we're in the space."

It made sense. And Saffron wanted to help. Maybe it would take away some of the guilt she felt about the party going so wrong. She agreed and was soon riding in the back of the black car.

"We have a few interviews to do on the way," Collins said. "I'd like you to sit in. The people know you and might be more forthcoming."

Saffron cringed. "They don't know me that well," she said, "Most of them I've only met once." Still, she sensed that she didn't have a choice, that what the MA wanted, he got.

He brushed her protest aside, and silence settled in the car. She leaned back against the leather seats as the palms flashed by the windows and the surf played beside the road. Collins cursed as traffic ahead of them caused a slowdown, and they crept along on the narrow road. Saffron wondered what was holding up the line of cars.

A sudden flash at the window made her jump. An owl had dipped suddenly down and was now winging its way into a nearby tree. It was a compact bird, dark brown and stocky, with creamy underwings. It landed and sat blinking. Saffron was surprised to see another just a few trees over.

As they proceeded, Saffron felt a tingle up her spine. Owls could be family deities as well. Was this another gathering of 'aumakua? Like the sharks?

There were several more owls, and Saffron soon saw the cause of the slowdown. At one spot, several local cars were parked along the side of the narrow road. Their owners were in various stages of positioning and filling some T-shaped stands. About hip-high, the stands were placed near the trees, and Saffron could see that the people were putting something on them. Their movements, their expressions, told her immediately what this was. They were, like Mano and Akoni, feeding their ʻaumakua.

Collins muttered as they passed, and picked up speed as the road opened up again.

The bed and breakfast Saffron had booked was called the Felicity Inn. Saffron had made friends with the couple who owned it—the Ashwoods—several months ago when they'd come to buy eggs. They were regular Egg Line customers now, and they offered the use of the sun-drenched parlor for the interviews. Collins excused Saffron while he interviewed the Ashwoods about their guests.

Saffron wanted to warn Lyza that they were here, anyway. She went looking for the bride, who the owners said was upstairs in room number 3.

The bed and breakfast was a Craftsman-style building with lots of woodwork, including a wide central staircase that went up to a wide landing and then turned back. As Saffron climbed it, she saw two figures in the upstairs lounge, their backs to her as they looked out the open French doors. She caught the deep tones of Logan's voice as he comforted Natalie. Both were in civvies rather than the uniforms they'd been wearing when Saffron had last seen them. Natalie's tee and skirt gave her a distinctly feminine appearance that threw Saffron off for a moment. She looked like a completely different person.

"It will be okay," she heard Logan saying. He laid a hand on Natalie's arm.

"It won't be okay," Natalie's earlier despair had turned to anger.

"*You'll* be okay," Logan revised and slid an arm around her waist. Saffron wondered if they'd been involved with each other before they'd been called upon for their bridal party roles. Just as Saffron was good at event details, she was also good at reading the details of people, and there was a closeness between them, an intimacy, that she couldn't quite define. She supposed it might come from serving on the same ship together, but it seemed to go even deeper than that.

Logan must have sensed Saffron's presence because he turned his head as she reached the top stair and gave a tight smile that didn't reach his eyes.

"Hi, Saffron," he said. Natalie turned, too, her eyes wide.

"Hi," Saffron said, "I wanted to let you both know that Collins, from your ship, is downstairs."

Neither of them seemed surprised, "He's the one doing the investigation, then," Logan said to Natalie. They seemed to have been speculating about that sometime before.

"Figures," she said, the edge of bitterness still in her voice.

"I'm supposed to bring everyone down to the tree room," Saffron said.

Logan nodded and slipped his hand around Natalie's. "Come on," he said, "Collins doesn't like to be kept waiting."

Collins had finished with the Ashwoods, and he waved Saffron into the tree room behind a subdued Lyza. It was a bright parlor, with French doors, a wall of windows, and as the name suggested, dozens of potted trees reflecting the array of trees outside the windows. Saffron sat down in an inconspicuous corner.

"Miss Carelli," the MA began, "I'm sorry for your loss." He said it like a person trying to speak a foreign language. The words were right, but the tone was off.

Lyza nodded.

"Can you tell me a bit about the last time you saw the victim?" Collins cut straight to the point.

Lyza seemed to straighten, gathering her courage, Saffron guessed. She would have already had to relive the experience for her parents and Bradley, but it didn't look like it got any easier with the retelling. "The last time I saw him was at the end of his song." She said. "He sang," here her voice broke, and she took a moment to regain her calmness, "he sang to me, and we kissed, and then he went to gather up the football stuff. And that old man came, and I didn't see him again."

"But in Bradley's notes, some of the others said you came in shouting that he had fallen."

"I did. I said I didn't *see* him again. I just," she took a ragged breath, "I just heard him. When we went back upstairs, we were supposed to open the presents, and he wasn't there. I went looking for him."

"Did you find him?"

"Not," a sob slipped out between Lyza's words, "in time." She was twisting her hands together, and Saffron thought it looked rather painful. "I thought he might be out by the cars, but I didn't see him there, and I went over to the lawn, but it was really dark—there was only the scoreboard—and I thought I heard something over by the cliff, so I started walking that direction." Lyza's eyes were closed now, "and then I heard him shout, and I ran forward, but there was nobody there."

"What did he say?"

"He said, 'No!' And I knew that he had fallen. I could tell from the sound he made after that. But I couldn't see down there, and I couldn't help him." Now Lyza was crying hard. Her words were little more than choking gasps.

Collins looked at her for a long time, studying her shaking shoulders, her lowered face. Saffron wanted him to look away, but he watched with an almost clinical interest. Finally, he gave cursory condolences and sent the girl on her way.

When Collins called Cyndi in, Byron strode in front of her.

"Just your wife, Mr. Carelli," Collins corrected. But Saffron could immediately see that Byron Carelli was a match for the overbearing MA.

"You interview us together or not at all."

Collins looked as if he might get ugly, but in the end, he merely gestured to the wicker loveseat and began his questions. It was apparent from the beginning that Bradley had made note of the conversation that Saffron had overheard between the man and his future son-in-law, and that Collins had read those notes with great interest.

"You didn't want Lieutenant Howard to marry your daughter, did you, Mr. and Mrs. Carelli?"

Cyndi looked around fearfully. Her hands fluttered in her lap like nervous birds. It reminded her of the way Lyza had twisted her hands. She must have picked it up from her mother. Byron eyed Collins coolly. Just as he was about to speak, a torrent of words poured out of Cyndi's mouth.

"I didn't want him to marry her. I didn't want her to be following him all over the globe and taking my grandbabies off to who-knows-where and being left alone while he was at sea. I admit it! It's my fault!"

"Your fault?" Collins leaned forward.

"Yes, I know. I cursed my own daughter's happiness on the eve of her wedding. I shouldn't have done it!"

"Done what?" Collins needed more specifics. Saffron had seen the look Collins was wearing now. She'd seen it on the strange predator that came after her chickens last week on the farm. He'd been hungry, and they'd been mostly defenseless.

"Stop talking." Byron's voice was stern, almost panicked. "Cyndi. Stop talking."

"I can't. I'll come clean. It's my fault. I killed Davis."

Marks scribbled furiously, glancing from the couple to his boss and back at his clipboard in a rapid loop. Collins remained cool. "How did you do that, Mrs. Carelli?"

"I took him away from the others, just before we went in, to talk him out of marrying Lyza. He had a flashlight, which he handed to me so I could see where I was going. When he refused to agree not to marry her, I said he was selfish and cruel, and I left him out in the black night with no light while I took it, and I went in with the others. He must have stumbled and fallen in the dark. I should have stayed with him and made sure he got back in!"

The woman was tortured, her face a mask of all the pain her daughter had endured the last few days. That was what scared Saffron about parenthood: the extent to which a parent's happiness was entwined with their child's.

Saffron stared as Collins, unbelievably, stifled a yawn. "Borrowing someone's flashlight is not a crime, Mrs. Carelli."

A nearly undetectable movement caught Saffron's eye. Byron patted his wife's leg. It shouldn't have seemed out of the ordinary. After all, a man should try to comfort his wife if she were in distress. But this was not a gesture of comfort. It was a gesture of pride. Saffron looked closer at Byron. His mouth was drawn tight in a lopsided smirk as if he were trying very hard not to smile. Collins didn't seem to notice. He was mentally marking the couple off his list, Saffron could see.

But why would Byron be smiling? Why, when his wife was so upset, would he be pleased?

Part of the answer was easy: Byron had gotten exactly what he wanted. Davis wouldn't be marrying his daughter. But the pride he seemed to feel in Cyndi's revelation seemed out of place to Saffron. She started to speak up, to urge Collins to press for more information about the timing of Byron's search for Davis, but Collins reprimanded her sharply.

"You're only here as an observer," he said. Marks shot her an apologetic look, and she could see that he understood being put in his place by Collins. She closed her mouth and tried to think why Byron would be, at this moment, so proud of his wife. It just seemed an odd emotion for him to have.

Until Collins asked the next question.

"Mr. Carelli, can you account for your whereabouts during the time your wife and Davis Howard were talking?"

Byron nodded. "I met her at the bottom of the stairs and escorted her inside. She was worried about Davis, so I went back to check on him. By then I suppose he had already fallen. I don't know. I didn't see the boy." Cyndi was crying harder now, and Saffron saw why Byron was pleased. He could weasel out of here using Cyndi's emotions as a shield. "I need to take my wife upstairs to lie down, Mr. Collins," he said, "if you'll please excuse us."

His wife was not only his alibi, she was also getting him out of more rigorous questioning by virtue of her distress. Insisting that they be interviewed together was a stroke of genius if Byron didn't want the MA digging too deep.

Collins dismissed them, and he put an arm around her and led her from the room. From where Saffron sat, she could see the smile that broke through Byron's facade of concern for his wife as soon as he turned his back on the Navy men. Byron had just dodged his own interrogation.

Chapter Eight

Next, Marks escorted Natalie into the tree room. "Shipmate," Collins greeted Natalie, but there was no warmth in his voice.

"Sir," she replied. No one acknowledged Marks, who sat scribbling on his clipboard next to Collins.

"Looks like we've lost a sailor."

"Yes, sir." She said. From where she sat, Saffron could see both participants in the discussion, and she felt a definite tension between them. Natalie's narrowed eyes, and the flush of red under the tan on her cheeks—something that only Saffron was likely to notice—belied her dislike for the MA.

"Tell me how you knew the victim," Collins asked. Natalie flinched at the last word.

"We were friends."

"How long have you known each other?"

"Two years." She said, "Since he was stationed on the Havasu." Saffron recognized the name of their ship.

"And what kind of relationship did you have, exactly?" The MA's voice was too hard for such a delicate question.

Natalie looked him in the eye. Her chin was raised.

"We were shipmates, Sir."

"Is that all? I seem to remember some disciplinary measures for fraternization."

Natalie was quiet, but her smoldering eyes showed how she felt about Collins.

"I myself found you two talking in the ladder well after darken ship more than once, didn't I?"

Natalie's steel jaw remained clamped shut.

"And we had to stop assigning you to roving watch at the same time because we kept finding you together on the fantail." Collins had dropped his pretense of friendliness. There was a hard edge in his voice.

"And you came up to Captain's Mast a time or two, didn't you?"

"We were never penalized. There was no proof we were fraternizing unduly." Natalie said, matching his tone.

Collins switched subjects. "And now you seem pretty close with another of our sailors." Collins jerked his head toward the closed door. "You and Prentice seem to be getting along well during your leave."

"No rules against that," Natalie said.

Collins sat and peered at her. A current of disgust rippled across his face. There was more to this than a simple breach of protocol or policy. He was taking this personally. And then Saffron saw it. Collins had romantic interest in Natalie.

"May I go?"

"We have one more thing to talk about," Collins said. "I did some interviewing on the ship before I came, and apparently you and Howard were involved in a pretty loud disagreement before he left the ship last week."

Natalie's eyes narrowed.

"You didn't think he should be marrying this girl, did you?"

Natalie clenched her jaw, "And if I didn't?"

"Well, it seems you had the motive to want to get back at

him. He'd rejected you. He was getting married the next day. Rejection can bring out the worst in a person."

"Know that from personal experience, do you?" Natalie spat the words back at him.

Collins glanced at his assistant, quickly, almost imperceptibly. His features hardened. Natalie had some power over him. It seemed likely that she'd rejected the MA's advances at some point.

"Don't risk your career for a relationship with a shipmate," he growled. Saffron could hear the echo of someone else's words in the phrase. Probably, she thought, Natalie had told him at some point that she wouldn't take such a risk.

Saffron was hardly breathing. Just like the long moment when she'd found the creature in the egg house, she sensed the danger Collins posed to the vulnerable Natalie. She wanted to cry out but seemed paralyzed by the scene playing out in front of her.

Collins reached out. He laid a hand over the scribbling pencil in Marks' hand. Marks froze and looked up.

"Next time you're called to court you won't be so lucky," Collins said. "I intend to make a full account of your relationship with Prentice, and you should know that I'll be waiting in every dark corner and every supply room on the ship. When you mess up, I'll be there, and I'm gonna get you discharged this time."

Natalie's military training showed in her direct gaze, her square shoulders. But her inner anger was manifest in the tight fists resting in her lap and the way she leaned forward as if in a challenge to her superior officer. The scarlet undertone had spread across her nose and up her forehead. She didn't speak, but the fire in her eyes made Saffron wonder, for the first time, what exactly the sailor was capable of.

Collins turned a cold gaze on Saffron, and she realized that she'd made a noise. He seemed utterly unconcerned that she was there, but she wondered if that were merely a facade.

"Dismissed, Crofts," he said summarily.

Logan's interview was more of the same: pointed questions about his relationship with Natalie, mostly. Saffron began to wonder what exactly Collins was actually investigating. He asked precious few questions about Logan's whereabouts during the party, but those he answered seemed to further incriminate him in Collins' real accusation: fraternization with Natalie.

"Where were you when the victim fell?"

"I was with Crofts in the media room," Logan said, looking the MA in the eye. "She can vouch for that."

"How long had you been there?"

"Since the old man showed up. I went up to turn off the lights and the music."

"And what were you doing with Crofts in the media room after you turned off the lights?" Collins' sneer made Saffron feel queasy.

"We were talking," Logan said, "arranging our plans to ride back down to Honolulu together." Logan glanced over at Saffron with a pleading look in his eyes, and she remembered, in a flash, seeing him and Natalie embracing. She tried to offer him a reassuring smile. She wasn't about to give Collins any more ammunition against the young couple who had so recently lost their friend.

Watching the two men was not unlike watching the sharks swim. Though there was no sign of bared teeth or outward aggression toward each other, the potential for violent conflict between them lay just beneath the surface. Saffron could feel it all the way over in the corner where she sat. They didn't move, but they circled each other with their words.

"Tell me about you and Davis Howard. Did you guys get along?"

"Sure. We were bunkmates, hung out on shore leave together," Logan looked down. "He was a good guy."

"You okay with the fact that Crofts had a thing for him?"

"I'm not sure that's a necessary topic."

Collins' voice was intense, "I get to decide what's necessary for us to discuss. And we're discussing this."

"Sure. Natalie dated him. But I think it's pretty obvious that he had moved on. It happens."

"Jealous?"

Saffron was impressed with Logan. He didn't seem to squirm under the pressure of Collins' questioning. "Nope. He was getting married. Wasn't really much of a threat."

Saffron noticed how Logan talked around the relationship. He never said outright that he was dating Natalie or anything that could be attributed to their fraternization. It was all general observations about Davis.

Collins noticed, too, and pushed harder. "But you are dating Crofts?"

Logan sidestepped the question neatly, "Are we being ordered back to the ship, or is our leave still approved for our full stay?"

This seemed to disgruntle Collins. Mostly, Saffron guessed, because they had gone over him to get the leave in the first place.

"You can stay," he said, "for now." He waved a hand toward Maika'i, out the windows, "the local law wants everyone here at least until they've made some arrests."

"Oh?" now Logan was questioning Collins, and the MA didn't seem to realize how the situation had shifted, "They're making arrests?"

Collins sneered, "of course they are. You really think this was just bad luck? An accident? I've read the reports, and Davis had plenty of people who wanted him gone."

Logan's face was clouded, "Like who?"

"The father-in-law, for one thing."

Logan was quick to jump to Byron's defense, "Well, sure, he didn't want Lyza to marry him, but he wouldn't kill someone. He doesn't have it in him."

"Listen, I've been in my rate long enough to know that *anyone* would kill someone, given the right motivation."

"That's a pretty dark view of humanity."

"Humanity is a pretty dark species."

WHEN LOGAN LEFT, Saffron found herself sitting through interviews with Lyza's friends: Rachel and Sylvia. The girls gave little information, having been with the group the entire time. Saffron remembered seeing them inside after Akoni's visit, and she told Collins as much when he asked.

The interview that surprised her was the one with Myra, Lyza's sister. The girl was young—maybe twenty—and quiet. She had big eyes, round as saucers, and a small mouth that she kept tightly shut. She'd been with the group, too, but when Collins asked her what she thought of her sister's wedding, Myra was vehement.

"I warned Davis," she said. "I told him to stay away from my sister."

Saffron wondered if she'd picked up on her parents' antagonism, but the girl's next phrase made it clear that it wasn't Davis she was against.

"For his own good. I warned him about Lyza."

Warned him about Lyza? The quiet, gentle bride?

"And what, exactly, did you warn him about?"

"That he shouldn't trust her. That she was deceitful and tricky and that if she didn't like what he was doing, she'd drop him like a stone." Myra laughed bitterly, and there was an edge of hysteria in the sound. "I guess she did. Literally."

Saffron squinted at the girl. Who took joy in someone falling off a cliff?

Collins must have found it an odd reaction, too, "How do you know she's deceitful? You got personal experience?"

"A lifetime's worth. And I've watched her throw away perfectly good relationships that anybody else would die for, just to upgrade to something more exotic, without any warning. She would have done it to Davis, too."

"Someone, in particular, you're talking about?"

"Logan. They dated in high school, but she just wouldn't commit to him."

"Why?"

"Because she's an idiot. She apparently couldn't see how hot he is, and how close he is with the rest of us, and how nice he is to everyone. She's totally blind to that, and to the fact that he has the brownest eyes and the best sense of humor ever."

So Myra was infatuated with Logan. Collins realized it, too.

"So you and your sister don't get along well?"

"I suppose we get along fine. I just don't trust her, is all."

Collins was direct, "Do you think she could have caused her fiancé intentional harm?"

"I don't see why not. She's caused lots of harm already."

Myra had evidently been carrying this opinion of her sister for some time. Saffron had seen, at the farm, how chickens would sometimes get obsessed with something about certain feathers, and they would pick at those feathers until their bare and bumpy skin was completely exposed. It was called feather picking. Myra reminded her of those chickens right now, baring her obsession to everyone in the room.

Collins nodded at Marks, who scribbled something down. Was Collins buying into Myra's theory? Had Lyza changed her mind? Could the bride have caused this tragedy?

Saffron thought about that all through the next interview with Lyza's cousin Tiff.

Tiff was casual and somber, but she tried to answer all of Collins' questions in a reasonably direct way, and as she was with the group the entire time, she didn't have anything new to add.

Collins looked at Marks' clipboard, left behind on the table while the assistant went out to get the next interviewee. "One more," Collins said to Saffron, "and then we'll go out to the cliffhouse and you can show me around there."

Marks came back in, holding his hands up.

"What?" Collins asked.

"We'll have to interview her later. She's gone off on a tour of the local flora and fauna."

Collins consulted the clipboard, "Evelyn Harris?" he said.

Marks nodded and Saffron's stomach twisted at his next words. "Owner said she was out with that local guy we interviewed this morning—Keahi something?"

Chapter Nine

From the back seat of the big black car, Saffron kept an
eye out as they drove to the cliffhouse. It was a perfect
Hawaiian day: the aqua water played against the
honey-colored sand. The vibrant green palms ran their leaves
across the breeze like emerald fingers playing an exotic instru-
ment. But Saffron couldn't stop peering at the parking lots of
the restaurants and the stretches of sunny beach as they drove,
looking for any sign of Keahi. She didn't see him anywhere,

but knowing that he was out there somewhere with Evelyn made her furious.

What were they doing? Why hadn't he mentioned it? Saffron pushed the thoughts from her mind as she hopped out of the car to key the code into the gate so that they could drive up the long driveway to the house.

Once there, they went inside, with Collins mentioning various details to Marks, which the assistant scribbled onto his clipboard.

It was cool and quiet in the cliffhouse. Saffron found herself walking more calmly.

Collins prowled the entire house, top to bottom, though Saffron insisted that there the party had been contained to the main floor. He questioned her in detail about the party and any place she remembered seeing Davis.

They ended up back in the dining room, where the gift table was still laden, and the anchor and ship details still hung. Saffron supposed she would need to come and take all the decorations down sometime, but both Bradley and Collins had insisted nothing be touched at the crime scene. She was secretly relieved because she didn't yet have the heart to undo the preparations she'd made for the happy event.

She snapped back at the sound of tearing paper. Collins was opening the wedding gifts.

"Stop!" Saffron said as he held up a "Best of Maika'i" cookbook and then tossed it into a growing pile of bare gifts on one end of the table. "You can't open their gifts!"

He barely glanced at her as his meaty hands ripped the silver paper off a box containing a set of glass tumblers. "These aren't gifts." He said gruffly, "they're evidence." Then, to Marks, he said, "tumblers from Ben Edwards." Marks scribbled each item and its giver on a list, and the question of whether or not Lyza would still have to send thank-you notes streaked through Saffron's head.

"That's absolutely ridiculous!" Saffron cried. "These are presents picked out by people who loved this couple, things they wanted them to use in their lives together!"

He held up a koa wood cutting board with the couple's names carved into it, reported that it was from Mano, and reached for the next gift: a small gold bag. "Not anymore." He said, pulling out an envelope.

"Whoo," he said, removing two long cards from the envelope. "Ticket vouchers for a trip to Kauai." He checked the bag, "doesn't say who they're from, though." He tossed the vouchers in the pile as Marks scribbled.

Collins' voice was lighter when he pulled the top off a rectangular box. "Cousin Evelyn's got the right idea for decent gifts," he said, holding up a pale pink silk robe, "though it's a little tame for my—"

Before she knew what she was doing, Saffron was across the room, snatching the delicate fabric out of Collins' hands and shouldering her way between him and the table.

"Enough." She said, and she felt her earlier fury returning, "Enough. I understand that you need to go through these, but you can do it in a respectful way."

Collins looked surprised. No, Collins looked astonished. His mouth was open, but he didn't speak as Saffron pulled the next gift from the pile and turned it over carefully, running a gentle finger under the strips of tape that held it closed, easing the heavy paper, covered with bells and hearts, open to reveal a box containing a crystal bowl.

"A crystal bowl, from Davis' mother," she said brusquely. When Marks continued to stare at her, she waved a hand. "Go ahead. Write it down." Marks blinked behind his big glasses and did as he was told. Saffron smoothed the paper back into place and put the present aside, taking pride that it only looked slightly rumpled.

She did the same for the rest of the presents: a set of

embroidered pillowcases, a cooler filled with beach towels and sunscreen, a book about intimacy. Every gift she carefully re-wrapped, arranging them neatly beside the mess Collins had made of the first several gifts.

The last gift was a small gold box tied with a deep red ribbon. Saffron slid the ribbon off and snapped the box open. Inside lay a key. It was a new key, shining silver nickel-plated, but unlike the generic keys, she'd gotten from the lawyer to her bungalow on the egg farm. This one had an ornate top, cut through to make the delicate outline of a butterfly for the handle. At the center of the butterfly was a five-petaled flower.

Saffron reported it to Marks, "A key," she said, then searched the box for a gift tag. When she found it, she read it aloud, "For Lyza." There was no giver's name, though. Saffron looked through the box again. The key was the only thing inside. There was no indication of who had given the gift. "Another gift with no name," she said, shrugging. Marks put a blocky question mark in the "Giver" column on his paper.

Collins was sulking in a chair in the corner.

"Is there anything else you need?" Saffron asked, "Or can I go home?"

Collins pretended like he hadn't heard her. "Wait," he said, standing and going over to the table. He picked up the box and turned its tag over in his hands. "For Lyza?" he asked as if he had never heard the name before.

"The bride," Saffron offered.

"I know who she is," Collins snapped. "But look at all of these," he jabbed a finger at the other gifts, "they say "to the bride and groom," or "For Davis and Lyza," or they don't have any names at all, but this one just says her name. Isn't that odd?"

He snatched the clipboard from Marks and dug through the papers at the bottom of the pile. He extracted one and put it on the table. Saffron could see that it was the guest list Marks had written down as Collins interviewed the people who had been at the party.

Saffron saw that he was crosschecking the list with the gift list. She tried to pay attention but found herself distracted by the tiny sketches that Marks had put next to each guest's name. All unique, they were doodles, really, and probably insignificant, but Saffron was intrigued by them.

Done in ink, they had a certain graphic quality to them that Saffron had seen, but couldn't quite place. Several names had snatches of rope and knots next to them, the Empress and Cyndi's names both had old-fashioned sailing ships. There was a star next to Logan's name, a rooster next to Natalie's, a harpoon next to Byron's, and next to her own name Saffron saw an intricately knotted rope. Evelyn had a delicately-drawn rose beside her name, and Keahi had an anchor. Davis' was the most detailed, though. Beside his name was a swallow, wings and head arched high, with a dagger plunged down through its breast. Drops showered out and down from it. They could have been blood or tears.

Collins didn't seem to care about the doodles. He checked each name off with efficiency before declaring: "Everyone here's given her a gift. I can't tell who might have given her a key." He pulled the ribbon off the box and opened it again, snatching the key out and studying it as if it might tell him the answers to the mystery of its origin.

Suddenly, he spun and looked directly at Saffron. "What do you think?" he asked calmly.

"About what?"

"About this key? About this case? I saw the notes Bradley made about what you overheard between Davis and his future father-in-law. You were here all night. What else did you see? If this was a murder, who do you think might be responsible?"

They were direct questions, and Saffron thought fast. If she'd been talking to Keahi or Mano, she might have poured out all the suspicions she'd had. But Collins was different. He was decisive, hard. He could very well take what she said and use it as a reason to attack someone.

And the truth was that she still wasn't sure it wasn't an accident. That cliff was steep, and the edge was treacherous. Everyone had been having such fun, and there hadn't been the air of caution that Saffron should have insisted on.

"In my experience," Saffron said carefully, "It's really a matter of deciding who might have been likely to do it."

Collins looked at her for a long time, his mouth a straight line and the muscles of his face puckered. Saffron was sure that he knew she wasn't giving him all the information she had.

Finally, he spoke, and he didn't address the issue. Instead, he said, "Show me this media room where the girls were having their party."

Saffron walked with him into the room down the hall.

It was a big, comfy room with couches and recliners, side tables, and a huge screen covering the wall that had the kitchen on its other side. There was a panel that slid open to reveal the stereo equipment, another for the television controls. Collins walked around carefully, peering at everything and Marks followed him.

Saffron noticed that the microphones were still out, laid hurriedly on one of the couches. She moved to put them away.

As she lifted them, horrible screeching feedback echoed through the room. They were still on. She apologized and switched them off before stowing them back in the stereo cabinet. There she saw that the stereo system was still on, too. As she reached to switch it off, she saw a red light blinking.

Peering closer, she read "REC" underneath the light.

One of Saffron's strengths was that she had always been curious. When she and her mother attended a neighbor's wedding when Saffron was just nine, Saffron wondered who had been in charge of the lavish party. Finding out had led her to her career as an event planner.

Now, she couldn't stand it. She had to explore this. Saffron pushed the "STOP" button and then the "REW" button to skip back through the digital files created by the system. When she began, the number of recordings glowed 14.

Number 14 was long—dozens of hours long—and it seemed to be all silence. She rewound for a while, then checked it. Nothing. Rewound again. Still nothing but a soft static indicative of the microphones being on in the empty house.

Saffron took it back to the very beginning of the recording. The sound of snapping fingers and a sweet cheery harmony filled the room as the Empress' voice belted out "Happiness in the Chapel."

The Empress had been glowing with happiness that evening, and she had been shattered the next. Saffron closed her eyes and tried not to see the two Empresses juxtaposed in her mind.

"Turn that noise off," Collins barked, and Saffron jumped as she opened her eyes. "We're trying to discuss evidence here."

Saffron cranked down the volume as the song went on.

"These are the songs the bridesmaids were singing," she told him, "they must have recorded themselves."

"How nice for them," his words were cutting, "the bride will have a wonderful memory of the night her fiancé died."

Collins turned back to commiserating closely with Marks as they peered at the outside wall of the room.

Saffron flipped back through a couple more of the songs. As she heard Davis singing, she thought maybe the recording actually would bring some comfort to Lyza. After all, Davis had sung to Lyza that night. The recording held the sound of Davis' voice as she had last heard it, and Saffron knew from losing her mother how much you missed the little things. She switched off the stereo with a plan to return and make a copy of this recording to give to Lyza.

For now, Saffron was growing interested in the conversation between the two Navy men. Collins was having Marks walk toe-to-heel down the length of the wall, speculating about an anomaly they were noticing: the square woodwork in the corner, which Saffron knew held the hinges for the transformable wall.

She could have stepped up and told them right away, but she was still miffed at Collins' overall demeanor in this investigation, so she let them waste some time on fruitless speculation.

"Maybe it's a pipe coming down from upstairs?" Marks suggested.

"There's no plumbing up there. More likely it holds wiring for all this media equipment." Collins said. Saffron liked that he was so confident in his assessment. She liked it because she knew he was wrong.

"What about over here?" Marks asked, striding to the other end of the wall and peering at the strange, ornate panel that sat about hip-height there.

Collins waved a dismissive hand, "Obviously a safe. Since everyone here was a guest, no need to explore that." He turned from the wall with an air of indifference.

Saffron stood and slid the cabinet closed in front of the now-dark stereo system. She walked to the ornate panel in the wall, which Mano had carved with palm trees. The cabinet had been carefully designed. There was a trick to opening it so that Doctor Evans' youngest grandkids couldn't open it accidentally when they were visiting, and Saffron happened to know the secret latch on the upper edge. She snapped the latch open and slid the panel back to reveal the controls for the wall.

"Wow!" Marks said, running a pencil-gripping hand across the controls appreciatively.

Collins said nothing, but he did turn to watch as Saffron

operated the controls and opened the wall up to reveal the balmy Hawaiian afternoon.

"Well that's interesting," Collins said, and though his words were dry and distant, Saffron heard a note of fascination in them. He strode past her, out onto the lanai, and looked down over the yard where the men had played football.

Saffron didn't follow him. Instead, she sank into one of the big recliners. She was remembering Keahi singing that night, his great voice, his smile. But the memory was bittersweet not only because of Davis' accident but also because that had been the night that everything changed between her and Keahi, the night that Evelyn had shown up and dumped ice water on their budding relationship.

She missed Keahi. During this most disastrous event she'd ever planned, she missed his stability and gentle humor. He was like an anchor, keeping her from being broken against the rocky shore of her emotions.

Collins had disappeared down off the lanai, but he returned momentarily and held up a glow stick.

"You want to tell me what all these are about?"

Saffron squinted. "They were for the scoreboard."

"Why aren't they all with the scoreboard, then? They're all over out there in random places."

Saffron peered outside, but couldn't make out any glowsticks in the lush grass below her. "I suppose the wind could have done it?" she said hesitantly.

"Not likely." Collins shook his head. "Write this down," he told Marks. "We're going to be thorough."

WHEN THE BIG black car finally pulled out of the driveway of Hau'oli Ka Moa Egg Farm, Saffron was very glad to see its tail lights. She went in and ate a malasada, then pulled a pork bun, called a manapua, out of the fridge and downed that. Collins had invited her to eat with them at the Oceanside Cafe, and though she got free meals there because of her Uncle Beau's lifelong generosity, she was tired of being with Collins and Marks. She needed some time to herself, time to think what to do about Keahi and Evelyn, time to watch the calming routines of her chickens.

She went outside and found her way to a beautifully carved bench she'd bought from Mano to sit on and watch her chickens. To her surprise, she discovered its creator there, too, sitting comfortably and sipping tea from one of her chicken-themed teacups. Mano often made himself a cup when he visited the egg farm. He was lazily tossing grains from a covered bin she kept there into the pens to draw the chickens out.

The late afternoon light was golden, and it painted highlights on the intricate web of wrinkles above Mano's close-cropped white beard.

Seeing him wasn't a total shock. Mano often showed up out here, fixing things up, feeding the hens, gathering eggs. She suspected he sometimes needed their calming influence, too. He looked Saffron straight in the eye as she approached.

"What is this girl I see my grandson riding through town with?"

Saffron closed her eyes as she sank onto the bench. She did not want to talk to Mano about Evelyn. She wasn't sure she could remain civil.

"His old girlfriend," Saffron said simply, opening her eyes and meeting Mano's gaze, "his beautiful, successful, elegant old girlfriend."

"He doesn't need his elegant old girlfriend. He needs you."

Saffron was surprised to feel the sting of tears in the corners of her eyes. "Apparently not, Tutu." She had taken to calling Mano by the Hawaiian word for grandfather since that was what Keahi called him.

Mano moved over and laid a heavy hand over hers on the bench. "Don't give up."

"I'm not giving up. I just don't like the person I am when I see them together. She's a nice person. I shouldn't dislike her so much. Envy's a flaw, and I don't know how to get rid of it."

Mano breathed a deep sigh. She thought he'd push harder, tell her to go and fight for Keahi, but he didn't. Instead, he let go of her hand and bent to scoop some more grains for the chickens, which he tossed in a wide arc through the wire sides of the closest pens. The chickens ran to snatch up the tasty treats just as Mano started to talk again.

"My mother once told me a story about a big shark who lived near a pleasant village. My mother was always telling me stories about sharks because she'd given me their name." Mano smiled, seeming to remember, "The shark was a gentle spirit and loved to watch the little children as they played in the surf. When the families of the village came to swim, the shark spoke to the waves so they would be gentle. Other sharks stayed away because he was so large and so powerful and they knew that this was his village."

Mano tossed another handful of grain and settled back against the bench as he went on. "The shark was lonely, though, and wanted badly to be a part of the village he loved so much. He began to swim closer and closer to the swimmers near the shore, to be near them. But the villagers were afraid. They had been terrorized by a bad shark many generations ago, and they snatched their children from the water whenever they saw this gentle giant approaching. This made the shark sad. He tried to call out to them, but the sight of his rows of teeth made them panic and run screaming away from the water.

"The shark began to hate his teeth. 'If I didn't have these teeth,' he thought, 'then the villagers would not be afraid of me. I could swim with them and play with them.' And so he began to pray to Kamohoali'li, the brother of Pele and the god of all the sharks, to take away his teeth from him. At first, his wish was refused, but the shark kept worrying the god about it until, finally, Kamohoali'li gave him his desire. The shark's mouth was smooth and soft as a loli."

Saffron didn't want to interrupt, but she wanted to understand, and she still only knew a handful of Hawaiian words. "Loli?" she asked softly.

"The sea cucumber," Mano explained, and Saffron thought of the soft, squishy creature as Mano went on.

"His top gums and his bottom gums—as smooth and soft as a loli. He was ecstatic! He waited for the villagers, and when he saw them come into the water, he rose up and opened his mouth.

"The villagers saw that he was toothless. They saw how he dove back under the water and came to them, asking for their friendship, and they weren't afraid anymore. He had no teeth. They invited him in. They cared for him and gave him chopped fish and the tenderest kalo leaves. He was so happy. The children swam with him and held onto his dorsal fin and skimmed along the water with them. They called him Hoaloha, or 'friend.'

"So the shark had everything that he wanted." Mano shrugged and paused, as if that were the end of the story, the "happily ever after." But Saffron had heard enough of his stories to know that there was more to come. She waited.

"But this happiness was not natural, and it could not last. The other sharks saw Hoaloha playing with his friends. They saw his smooth pink gums, and they saw the delicious villagers. One day, when Hoaloha was swimming with the villagers, the bad sharks rushed in and tried to gobble up the little children. Hoaloha bashed at them with his nose and flailed at them with his tail, but their teeth were too powerful. He could not protect his friends. So he cried out to Kamohoali'li in anguish to restore his teeth to him. Like volcanoes, they erupted from his gums, and he destroyed the bad sharks.

"In the aftermath, the villagers thanked him and begged him to remain on watch over their village. He remained a loyal friend to them until the day he died."

Mano went quiet then, and Saffron thought about the story. "So, you're saying that sometimes the things we don't like about ourselves are valuable, too?"

Mano's face lit up with the smile he reserved for her when she did something particularly well, like saying a new word just right or cooking a delicious new dish, "I'm saying that sometimes our curses are actually gifts." He looked her in the eye. "Use your teeth. Fight for my grandson."

Chapter Ten

Saffron was dressed in her best black sheath the next morning when she drove to Sandwashed and picked up the six hangers of clothes to deliver to the bed and breakfast. She handed off the two sparkling crackerjack uniforms to Logan and Natalie's rooms, then delivered the rest. Most people had brought clothes appropriate for a wedding, not a funeral, and Saffron wondered if the bright colors and flowing fabrics would bother the Empress.

When she arrived at the harbor, though, she was surprised. Rex, Carlo, and the Empress were all waiting on the deck of the boat dressed in richly-hued aloha wear. Logan and Natalie had made better time arriving than Saffron had, and they stood on either side of the gangway, resplendent in their white uniforms, offering a hand to guests. Logan gave Saffron a solemn smile as she accepted his assistance off the ramp.

Behind him sat the Empress in her chair. Saffron was startled to see her lap empty: Princess was not with her. Saffron leaned down and bowed her head as the Empress graced her with a sweet lei.

She greeted the Empress and her attendants and looked around. It was a medium-sized boat, with an enclosed cabin, a wide deck lined with seats, and bench seats all around the edges of the deck, stretching up past the center cabin to the prow.

A gentle breeze was blowing, and soft ukulele music played through speakers mounted on the cabin. Saffron jumped when she heard an incongruous voice cut through the still morning air.

"What in the world? You think you can just throw on any old array of clothes?"

Saffron turned to see Collins nose-to-nose with Natalie, his eyes narrowed and his voice hard.

"Sir, no, sir." She stood at strict attention, and from what Saffron could tell, she didn't even blink in the face of the onslaught.

"Then why are you here without your uniform on?"

Saffron was confused. She could see Natalie's uniform from here.

Natalie didn't respond.

"You think you're in uniform?"

"No, sir."

"Why not?"

"My neckerchief's missing, sir."

"I see that. How is it that you don't realize that wearing your *full* uniform is a sign of the responsibilities and authority given to you by your country?"

"I do, sir," she started, but Collins cut her off again.

"You do *not*, Seaman."

Logan spoke up, his voice strained with the formality of addressing his superior officer, "Sir, the cleaners must have lost it."

Collins didn't turn, just tossed a comment over his shoulder, "Well I can't very well hold the cleaners in violation of uniform regs, can I, Petty Officer?" He leered at Natalie, "But I can take disciplinary action against you, Seaman. Now, get outta my sight." He waved a hand toward the gangway, and Saffron was horrified to see Natalie turn and stride down it off the boat as the MA moved to stand at the back corner of the deck. He watched the guests with a fixed gaze.

Saffron ran after Natalie and caught up with her on the pier.

"Wait, Natalie, wait. Do you have to go? Isn't there something you can do?"

The tough sailor had tears in her eyes. "No. I don't have my neckerchief. I can't get my uniform up to regs without it, and I won't have time to change to civvies before the boat takes off. It's okay, Saffron. I'll be fine."

"But I'm sure you want to be there for the Davis' memorial."

There was a deep sadness and a flare of pain in Natalie's eyes as she looked down the long pier toward the water.

"Davis would understand better than anybody," she said, "He was always great at understanding people." Saffron wasn't sure if she was talking to herself or not. Natalie reached out and squeezed Saffron's arm in a grateful gesture, then turned and walked off down the ramp.

When Saffron returned to the deck, Lyza and her parents had arrived. The bride stood, disconsolate, at the prow of the boat. Logan left the gangway and went up beside her, slipping one arm into hers. Lyza slumped against him. Saffron was glad that they had each other to lean on.

Byron's gaze was sullen, and Cyndi was sniffling through her greeting with the Empress. Saffron wondered if she still blamed herself.

Saffron found a seat off to one side of the cabin, where she could sit and watch the turquoise water lap the sides of the boat. Evelyn arrived, and Saffron avoided looking at the slim figure as she took a seat in the enclosed cabin next to her aunt and uncle.

Saffron was surprised not to see Keahi, Adam, Tyrone, Sione, or Carl. None of Davis' local friends were on the boat. Maybe they had to work?

The colors of the morning seemed too vibrant, too cheerful. Bubble-gum pink hibiscus trees draped their flowers down over the water next to the boat, and tiger-orange fish slipped through the clear water beside the ship.

The sky, though, seemed to understand the solemnity of the day. Where it was usually clear and brilliant azure, today it was a pearly cornflower, blue with hints of gray mixed in. It was reflected in the steely water. The boat's engines roared to life, and the vessel moved very slowly, churning the cornflower color into white wake behind them as they cleared the harbor and moved into open water.

It was then that she saw them. Keahi and Mano in a canoe, paddling out from the shore. They were joined by Adam and Tyrone, Carl and Sione, and nearly twenty more canoes with people from Maika'i. They flanked the boat, moving as a fleet.

They went out to a point from which Saffron could see distant islands in every direction: some large, some small. The captain cut the engines, and a profound silence overtook them. The boat rocked gently below them, and Kahu Williams, one of the local ministers, said a few words before the Empress set a small, leaf-wrapped package adrift on the water. It floated gently beside the boat as she laid a beautiful lei on the water around it. At that point, Rex and Carlo began to pull flowers from their own leis and scatter them into the water. Here the sea was deep blue, and the flower petals made ripples in it as they landed. Saffron looked at the flotilla of canoes surrounding them. All her friends from Maika'i were doing the same, pulling the flowers from their leis and scattering them.

Saffron reached for her own lei. She grasped the delicate purple blossoms and tugged. They came free, and she dropped her hand over the side of the boat and released them, watching as they fell with the others and showered the package in color. Yellow, red, orange, pink, white, and purple petals made a delicate rainbow atop the water. The waves pushed the little bundle out away from the boat, and Saffron noticed the careful maneuvering of each canoe out of its way as the waves carried it off toward the horizon.

SAFFRON HAD LEARNED one thing about Hawaiian customs: if at least two people were gathered together, there would be delicious food. Today, back at the Empress' vast estate, the Ionas had been called upon to create a meal for the funeral of the groom they'd helped celebrate just a few days earlier.

Saffron made a point to find Enoch Iona and tell him what a fantastic job his catering staff was doing. He seemed pleased, and Saffron turned to the long-serving table covered in bright cloths and food warming trays. She took a lid off one and was greeted with a cloud of warm steam and the succulent smell of laulau—meat wrapped in layers of taro and ti leaves.

Saffron had eaten laulau before, especially at big family events. Keahi's mother, Iolani, made it. Saffron loved every incarnation of the meal, but the little leaf-wrapped bundles that greeted her this time were particularly fragrant and beautiful.

They sat as if having grown there, in straight rows, awaiting someone to pluck them. Saffron gathered up some and was just lifting her laden plate when she noticed Marks sitting all alone at a table.

Saffron saw Keahi and Evelyn chatting away at a crowded center table. Keahi and some of the others were telling stories about Davis, some of them laughing and some of them crying. Saffron left them to their reminiscences and went to sit beside Marks.

He glanced up, the laulau on his plate untouched. Saffron saw that instead of eating, he was sketching. What she could see from here was a half-finished bull.

"Where's your boss?" Saffron asked, setting down her plate and taking the accompanying seat.

"Not here. He told me he was going to interview the pastor, or, uh, the Kahu. My blood sugar was getting low, so I told him I'd better eat before I did anything else." He looked doubtfully at the leaves on his plate. "I'm not making much progress, though."

Oh, here," Saffron offered. She took his plate and split the deep green leaves to reveal a rich combination of chicken and butterfish. She cut into her own and took a bite.

Rich, sweet flavors flooded her mouth. Saffron gestured to Marks to try his, and he looked up in surprise as he began to devour it.

There were chicken and pork laulau, along with something the locals called POG: passion fruit juice, orange juice, and guava juice all mixed together and served cold. It was the perfect complement to the meal, sweet and slightly tart where the food was savory and salty.

"So you like to draw?" She asked Marks, trying to drum up a conversation.

"Always have," he responded. He was pleasant but preoccupied.

"A bull?"

"Right. This one's actually a commission. Blue's Tattoos in Waikiki buys a few of my designs when we come into port so they can have new stuff for their customers to check out. I sell them to other shops in other ports, too."

"Wow," Saffron said. "Do you have any?"

"Tattoos?" Marks shuddered. "No. None for me, thanks."

Saffron understood. She'd sooner be run over by a studded steamroller than have someone jab her and pump ink underneath her skin. She changed direction. "So what brought you to the Navy?" she asked.

Marks laughed through his nose. "My father." He said, tossing her a bitter expression, "Quite literally. He put me in his truck, drove me to the recruiting station, and said, 'Get out. You're joining the Navy. Maybe that'll toughen you up." Saffron's heart twisted to think of the young man being treated like that, but he was factual as he went on. "Serves him right," Marks sniffed, "that I became a Yeoman. I think he really expected me to come back a burly sailor with war stories and a girl in every port, but I work with mail and forms and office supplies mostly."

Saffron peered at him. "Do you like it?"

He looked up, his glasses framing his enormous eyes. He reminded her of the owls she had seen yesterday. "You know, I actually do."

That eased Saffron's mind.

Marks went on, "I like the order on a Navy ship. Everything has its place to be, and everyone has their job to do. There's no searching or stumbling for what to do with your life. It's already decided for you. A lot of people have trouble with that, but not me. I like it. I like knowing where I'll wake up every day and where I'll go to sleep, where my comb and razor will be, what I'll be wearing. I never had that growing up."

"No?" Saffron bit into her second laulau. This one was pork, and the sweet chunk of fish accompanying it had lent its unique flavor to the sweet potatoes and meat inside. She savored every bite as she listened, nodding to encourage Marks to keep talking.

"No," he confirmed. "My dad was an alcoholic. We couldn't pay the rent on our trailers or keep the lights on. We were thrown out of so many apartments that I lost count. Lots of times we didn't have water so I couldn't bathe, and kids teased me. It was pretty bad."

Saffron could see, then, what the Navy held for Marks. "And you get to create art, too."

"Sure. The best thing about office work is there's always plenty of drawing supplies around, and usually a fair amount of downtime, too."

Saffron watched him shade in the horn of the bull. As he did, she remembered the sketches she'd seen yesterday on his list.

"You drew pictures next to all the names of the people at the hen party, didn't you?" she asked.

Saffron had never seen anyone flush so red so fast. "You saw those, huh?"

She rushed to reassure him, "I did, and I thought they were great!"

He smiled, but his cheeks and ears remained red.

"Just something I do to keep myself awake sometimes," he said, then, leaning closer to Saffron, "and, if I'm with Collins, to keep myself calm."

Saffron was surprised to hear that the serene yeoman had to work at his docile demeanor. "Why?" she asked as if she didn't know.

"Because Collins is a bully. You've seen him. He treats people like dirt, whether they're in or out of the military. He's awful to most of the people under him. He's power hungry," Marks took a deep breath, "I should probably stop there. He's notorious for making charges of insubordination." Marks clammed up.

Saffron had plenty she'd like to say about Collins, but instead, she brought the conversation back around to Marks' art. "The sketches were terrific. Do they mean anything?"

Marks blushed again, bringing color back to his paling face. "No. Well, sort of."

Saffron leaned in, "tell me what mine means. I saw that it was a knotted rope, almost a decorative design."

Marks shook his head, "no, it's just dumb stuff I think of when I'm sketching."

"Well, what about mine? What were you thinking of when you drew it?"

Marks grinned, a slow expression that split his face and lit his eyes. "Okay, but don't be mad."

"Of course not."

"Navy sailors have particular symbolism in their tattoos, and the rope means someone is a deckhand, you know, someone who takes care of all the details on a ship, making sure things are maintained and in good working order. You don't always notice them, and they don't get much recognition, but they're the ones keeping the whole thing afloat."

Saffron smiled, too. She found that she liked that assessment very much.

Marks hastened to add, "It seems like you put together a really great party that night."

Saffron didn't want to think about that night. She wanted to hear more about his sketches. The quiet young yeoman seemed to have some real insight into people's characters that most people didn't have. She supposed it came from growing up rough and having to read every person in every situation. Saffron hadn't had nearly the difficulties he had, but she knew something about watching people to be sure they weren't going over the edge.

Saffron lowered her voice, "Okay, how about Keahi? I saw

your list had an anchor next to him." Discreetly, she pointed over to where Keahi was sitting.

Marks' eyes sparkled. "Oh, I see," he said, "You two?"

At this moment, with Keahi sitting five tables away and Evelyn between them, Saffron wasn't sure how to answer that, "Sort of," she managed.

"Well, his is pretty straightforward. The anchor means a few things to sailors, but one is stability. Guys get it to remind them of what is stable and constant in their lives—that's why they sometimes put 'Mom' on it. I just thought he seemed like a solid guy, a stabilizer, so he got an anchor."

That was one of Saffron's favorite things about Keahi. Marks really was good at reading people.

"Now you've got to tell me about the others," she said excitedly. But Marks wasn't listening. He was sliding a form over the top of his bull drawing and slipping his pencil into the side of the clipboard. Saffron looked up to see Collins striding through the tables toward them.

"Let's go, Marks," he said, "I've got to call in a report tonight."

"Yes, Sir," Marks flashed Saffron an apologetic smile, and she gave him a wave to let him know she understood. He gathered his things and followed Collins like an obedient puppy.

Saffron ate two more laulau and then let the Ionas serve her an enormous block of haupia, the bouncy coconut milk dessert whose texture reminded her of gelatin and whose taste was sweet, undiluted coconut.

Saffron took an extra plate of the dessert and carried it over to the Empress, who sat with Mano and Akoni at the head table.

She turned her sad eyes to Saffron.

"Where's Princess?" Saffron asked, not knowing what to say about Davis, or whether to mention him at all.

"She's in her hutch," the Empress said, referring to the

ornately-carved cage complete with nesting box and removable cleaning tray which the Empress kept in a room beside her own on the second floor of the house. Saffron had seen the hutch but had never known the Empress to use it. Princess was either on her lap, at her feet, or on the "chicken pillow" to which half of the Empress' ample bed was dedicated. The Empress didn't like to have Princess out of reach.

"I hope she's not sick," Saffron said, half in question.

"She's not. It's just that I think maybe I have given her too much attention lately. Maybe the 'aumakua are angry that she has all my devotion. Maybe if I had not loved her so much . . ." The Empress' voice cracked, and before Saffron's eyes, the woman crumbled, her hands sliding up to catch her falling head, a sob escaping from between her fingers.

Mano put a hand on the Empress' shoulder. "That is not how the 'aumakua work, my old friend," he told the Empress. "Sometimes these things simply happen."

Akoni, always one with helpful commentary, said, "they can be angered, though."

Mano shot him a scowl, then looked up at Saffron. "Go get Princess for the Empress," he said. "She needs the comfort of her little friend right now."

Saffron, glad to have something to do, put down the plates and headed into the house.

It was quiet and dark inside, cool as it always was. Saffron couldn't help noticing new items as she walked through the house. In the drawing room, the pictures of the Empress' parents and husband had all been replaced with photographs of Davis. In the hall were hung his childhood drawings, his handmade Mother's Day cards, more photos. It pained Saffron to see him growing up as she made her way to the bedroom.

Inside the Empress' grand bedroom, Saffron again admired the beautiful gilded bed, the heavy draperies at the windows, the pristine carpet. She heard Princess clucking her displeasure at being left alone. When Saffron reached the hutch, the chicken was pacing by the hutch door. Saffron opened it and allowed the silkie to hop into her arms.

Saffron carried Princess back down and settled her into the Empress' lap. The poor woman was still sobbing, but as the chicken turned and nestled into her usual place, Saffron saw the shaking shoulders still. The Empress' hand began to move in its familiar rhythm, and the storm of grief, at least for now, was calmed.

Chapter Eleven

Y*ou left without saying goodbye.*

The message from Keahi was on Saffron's phone when she woke up the next morning. She slid it in her pocket and went down to gather the eggs.

Tikka eyed her as she entered and gave a long bawk. She was in her pen with the chicks she'd hatched in the kitchen when Saffron had first come here six months ago. They were nearly grown now, the only difference between them and the other hens was the fluffy underfeathers that the older girls had developed. The lack of them in the chicks made the young brood look thinner than the rest of the flock, but Saffron suspected that in another month or two, they would look just like everyone else.

"I know, I'm sorry." Saffron snapped the door to Tikka's pen open just long enough for her to dart out. The chicks were hard to round up, so Saffron kept them inside, but she routinely let Tikka out while she worked so that the hen could explore and cavort with the farm's only rooster, Curry, who lived on Saffron's lanai.

Tikka didn't give her the courtesy of a response. Instead, she headed directly for the egg house door and strutted out into the sunshine. Saffron put off the egg gathering for a moment as she walked along the pens and looked carefully at each hen. Many of them were in the outside parts of their enclosures right now, and couldn't be coaxed from their bug-hunting to come back in for inspection, but those still in the indoor pens looked good.

Saffron took great satisfaction in the improvements her hens had shown since she'd arrived, cleaned up the pens, and caught the chickens, who had been roaming at large throughout the farm. Many of them had been scrawny and ragged when she'd come, but they were a beautiful mixed flock of healthy birds now.

A year ago, if someone had said chicken farm, she'd have pictured rows of small cages and white birds. That was not Hau'oli ka Moa. Here, her Uncle Beau had built something very different. A chicken paradise, with indoor and outdoor runs, nesting rails, windows for sunshine and ventilation. And he had loved all the different breeds of chickens. He'd had day-old chicks shipped in from the mainland, and he'd bought every kind of bird the island hatcheries offered, too. There was even an old incubator she'd uncovered from his foray into hatching his own eggs.

She tried to remember all the breeds she'd determined were here on the farm. There were gold-laced Wyandottes like Tikka, whose pointed, black-edged feathers looked like a suit of armor. Similar but much more aggressive were the silver-laced Wyandottes, whose plumage was exactly the same except silver instead of gold. Saffron loved to watch the huge, fluffy Orpingtons: buff and black colored, and a few that were a pale gray bordering on purple. She also loved her Brahmas, with their warm gold skirts and striking black-pointed collar of feathers, they were the grandmothers of her flock. They had feathered feet and a low, warm chuckle. There were lots of jungle fowl, more or less unremarkable brown birds that were the least friendly and most flighty of the hens, but did lay very well and ate the least feed, as they were quite a bit smaller than the other chickens, and seemed to be better foragers, too.

There were many more breeds: speckled and striped hens, hens with fluffy tophats and hens with beards and fluffy cheeks, even hens with frizzled feathers that stuck out like errant curls. She threw them all some scratch grains and watched them come running. She loved seeing them going about their usual chicken business even though her own world seemed out of order.

Saffron's phone buzzed in her pocket. Pulling it out, she saw Keahi's name and another message:

Go with us to the pineapple plantation today? I'm missing you.

Saffron typed before she thought: *Us?*

A breathless second passed, during which she knew what he would say.

Evelyn's never seen it. Thought she'd like to while she was here on the island.

Saffron felt the words more than read them. Like a sharp ache in her stomach, she felt Keahi slipping away.

"He wasn't mine anyway," she told the hens in the nearest pen. They responded with a chorus of low reprimands. "We've only gone out a few months, it's not serious. We've never even talked about only seeing each other."

She went to get the eggs. Having her hands busy made it easier to ignore her jagged thoughts. She'd gathered, washed, and packaged the eggs from the left side of the egg house when her phone buzzed again.

Want to?

Saffron typed, *No*, but didn't send it. She couldn't. She wasn't in the habit of lying to Keahi and the truth, she realized, was that she did want to go. She wanted to go and be with him, see the plantation again, do something besides mourning Davis. She wanted to be close to the man she had fallen for. She missed his hand holding hers, his kisses. She missed the way his eyes lit up when she said something funny. She didn't want to walk away and let Evelyn have him back.

"Use your teeth," she said aloud and found herself making a shark-like grimace.

Saffron pushed the back button and deleted the *No*. Instead, she typed *Sure*.

⁓

THE RIDE to the Golden Pineapple Plantation was less than an hour, and Saffron tried not to be too upset by riding in the back or by watching Evelyn brush Keahi's muscled forearm with the tips of her fingers whenever he said something funny.

Saffron was keeping an eye on her. She'd switched tactics. Instead of avoidance, observation. In fact, she'd invited Evelyn, and the rest of the wedding guests who were still being detained, to lunch next Tuesday at the Egg Farm. Being stuck in town was bound to be growing tiresome, and Saffron still felt responsible for entertaining them, even though—

maybe even because—the wedding she'd planned had gone so wrong.

Evelyn had accepted the invitation to the beach barbeque on Tuesday, and Keahi had raised both eyebrows in thanks at Saffron's attempt to make things more bearable for the guests.

But today it was just the three of them on the outing to the Golden Pineapple. The plantation was, first, a beautiful garden with every exotic plant Saffron could imagine. Three big sections were dedicated to bromeliads, the spiky family of plants to which pineapple belonged, and there were mango, papaya, and banana orchards where signs urged visitors to pick and sample the fruit from certain trees. They watched for the "RIPE: PLEASE PICK ME" signs. Freestanding slicing stations were located throughout the orchards, and it was easy to hand over your harvest and receive it back, ready to eat, on a plate.

"Here," Keahi said, plucking a mango from one of the marked trees. He tried to hand it to Evelyn, who threw up her hands to decline.

"I really only eat apricots," she said, "they're wonderfully low in sugar."

Saffron had nothing against apricots, but a ripe mango could beat them any day. She saw, in Keahi's face, a little disappointment. Saffron felt a surge of confidence. There was no doubt that Evelyn was beautiful, but there was something very distancing about her rigidity. Keahi turned to Saffron, and she snatched the mango with enthusiasm. A broad smile spread across his face.

Keahi and Saffron sampled bananas and papaya, as well as guava. Saffron couldn't help but savor the sweet and juicy fruits. Keahi smiled at her.

After the orchards, it was time for their tour of the pineapple fields. They traveled in a trolley, painted bright yellow and green, with pineapple eyes all over it.

The pineapple plants rose from the ground at varying heights in each field, planted in blocks of similar ripeness. In the first few fields, the pineapples atop the spiky plants seemed like tiny replicas of the ones she was used to buying in the Paradise Market back in Maika'i. The next few fields had larger ones, and in the next, they were even more substantial. Finally, in the last areas, the full-sized pineapples were being harvested.

Saffron found the whole process fascinating, and she and Keahi chattered about it all the way back to the extensive bungalow where the Plantation Cafe promised lunch with fresh ingredients.

The menu held a whole range of tempting recipes: Pine-snap-le, which was red snapper marinated in pineapple juice, cooked and served on circles of grilled pineapple; The Spiky Top Burrito, which featured chicken, black beans, avocado, and pineapple salsa; and Pineapple on a Stick, which was a plate full of steak and pineapple skewers drizzled with a honey ginger sauce. Evelyn clucked her disapproval and pulled a protein bar from her purse while Saffron and Keahi dug into their meals.

The warm honey reduction on Saffron's Pine-snapple was sensational. She felt sorry for Evelyn, crunching on her tasteless bar. Her expression said even she didn't like it. "You want a bite?" Saffron offered.

Evelyn wrinkled her nose. "I just don't take unnecessary risks with my body," she said dryly. Saffron was beginning to wonder what Keahi had ever seen in her. Evelyn reached out and touched his arm again.

"I once knew a doctor who felt strongly about the connection between food and health."

"I still do," Keahi said, taking a bite of his rice bowl, "It's vital. If more people would focus more on eating good, real food, we'd be a lot healthier society. That's what I love about being home. Lots of good food, and it's all fresh. These avocados were grown ten feet from here. Lots of nutrition for the body."

Evelyn eyed him hungrily. "It seems to be working for you." She tapped the table. "You're looking good."

Keahi kept eating, not seeming to notice anything out of the ordinary as Evelyn went on. "Remember when we used to work the night shift together, and you used to always eat the bacon burger at two o'clock?"

Keahi looked dreamily into the distance. "I loved that cafeteria," he said, "you could get anything you wanted, round the clock."

"Remember that night that nobody was on duty?" Evelyn giggled.

"Yeah, they were at a staff meeting or something?"

"And we had to sneak in and raid the fridge!"

Keahi laughed, "We found some good stuff."

"It was like a picnic in the cafeteria."

Saffron saw the memory pass between them. She looked away. A group of women was leaving the cafe, tourists in flowing dresses and big hats. Saffron squinted. The one in the back was carrying a woven bag. On it was what Saffron thought was a familiar symbol.

"Excuse me," she said, standing up. Keahi looked up in surprise. Saffron followed the woman.

Outside, in the parking lot, she angled into a position where she could clearly see the woven bag. Saffron felt her heartbeat quicken. On the bag was the outline of a butterfly, with a flower in the center. Saffron pulled out her phone and snapped a picture of the bag, trying to be inconspicuous. Then she ran toward the woman, who was just putting the bag into her trunk.

The woman looked surprised as Saffron approached. Saffron tried to smile.

"Excuse me," she said, "Can I ask about your bag? It has a beautiful design."

The woman glanced down at it in puzzlement. "Thank you. It's nothing special. In fact, I got it for free."

"Do you mind if I ask you where?"

"Sure. They gave it to me when I bought my condo."

"June!" Another woman called from the car, "our tour of Pearl Harbor starts in less than two hours. We need to go!"

"Coming!" June waved apologetically as she walked to the passengers' side of the rental car.

Saffron called out desperately, "What condo?"

"The Mariposa Building," she called back.

"Where?" Saffron's voice came out in a desperate squeak. The woman paused and looked at her suspiciously. Only then did Saffron realize that accosting a perfect stranger and asking where they lived might make them a bit uncomfortable. The woman called back, "Honolulu," then quickly slammed the door.

Saffron backed away, allowing the car to back out and speed off. *The Mariposa Building.* Holding the name in her mind, she went back to join the others.

When she got there, she heard only a snatch of conversation. Evelyn was saying, "It would be amazing if you came back. You know they've got the door wide open for you."

Saffron's heart stopped. She froze, and Keahi looked up just in time to see her grasp the back of the chair. His eyes held uncertainty, and he switched the subject when he saw her.

"You left quickly," he said.

Saffron nodded. She wanted to tell him about the bag, about the key, about everything, but not with Evelyn there, and not if he was considering going back to Boston. She tried to think of something to say.

Saffron had never fought for things. She had learned early that there wasn't much she could do to change most people's minds, and if they'd walked out of her life she'd usually been a spectator rather than an impediment. Her most recent serious relationship had been nearly three years ago, with a man named Reggie, who left Washington DC for a promotion in Honolulu. She hadn't even contacted him since she'd been here.

But it was different with Keahi. She couldn't imagine the island without him. Not only was he important to her, he was also crucial to his grandfather, to the community. His strength and stability helped a lot of people and made Maika'i a better place. For the first time in her life, Saffron fought back.

"Are you thinking of leaving?" she said, the words sounding too harsh, too accusatory, as they filled the space between her and Keahi.

He looked guilty. "I—Evelyn has been trying to convince me of that. But I'm not sure I want to." He reached a hand toward Saffron, and she moved forward and took it, sliding a chair close to him and sitting down. Keahi put a strong arm around her, and she looked up at him.

"I'm sure I don't want you to," she said. In that moment it was as if Evelyn wasn't even there. Saffron felt no jealousy, no threat from the newcomer when she was wrapped in Keahi's embrace.

"Well, I'm glad to hear you say that," he smiled.

SAFFRON FOUND the Mariposa Condos in Honolulu on her computer when she got home. The picture showed a blocky, unremarkable building emblazoned with the butterfly and flower image. It was one of many such structures, and nothing on the website indicated who might have given the key to Lyza. It seemed likely that Davis had bought a condo for Lyza to live in while he was onboard the ship.

Early the next morning, she called the Mariposa building and asked for Davis Howard's apartment.

"I'm sorry," the woman said, "That name is not registered with any of our condos here."

"How about Lyza Carelli? Or Lyza Howard?"

There came the sounds of typing. "Nooo," said the woman, "I'm sorry. No one by those names."

Saffron thanked her and hung up.

Maybe this was just another dead end. She wasn't sure what she had hoped to find, anyway. Just some clue to the tragedy that took Davis' life. She didn't like the way Byron had spoken to his almost-son-in-law, and she didn't like that he was missing when Davis fell.

Outside, a raucous dispute erupted on the lanai. Saffron stood to look out her window. There she saw Curry standing between Tikka and the edge of the lanai. Both were making loud, alarmed sounds. Saffron left the office, walked down the hall and through the kitchen, and came out onto the lanai just in time to see a long, furry body advancing across the boards toward the birds. Before she could even speak, Curry attacked, flapping up and raking the air with his claws. But the creature was fast. It darted sideways past the rooster and angled for Tikka.

Saffron shouted, running toward the animal. It was big—longer than her arm—and gray-brown, with a tapered snout and a long, bushy tail that it held perfectly parallel to the ground. When it saw her coming it froze, then retreated, casting one last glance over its shoulder as it leaped from the lanai and cut a trail through the tall grass into the bushes. Its tail floated straight out behind it as if it were a separate entity.

Saffron stood between it and the still-squawking chickens and dialed Mano's number.

"Aloha," came his cheery voice through the phone.

"Mano! Something tried to attack Curry and Tikka on the lanai."

"Rats again?" he asked. When she'd first come, rats had plagued the egg house, but they'd finally gotten rid of those.

"No, something bigger. It's like a squirrel, with a long bushy tail—only the tail isn't *as* bushy, and the face is more pointy, and it's big!"

"Ahhhh," Mano said. "Mongoose."

"*Mongoose?*" Saffron repeated. "What do you mean, mongoose?"

"It's a sad story," Mano said, and Saffron could picture his closed eyes and the slight shake of his head that always accompanied a sad story. "A century and a half ago, plantation owners were losing their crops to all the rats. So, they had mongooses," Mano hesitated, "mongeese? Mongeeses? How do you say it?"

Saffron had no idea what the correct plural form was, "I don't know. I've never had to talk about them before."

"We'll find out," Mano said, "but anyway, the plantation owners brought them over to kill the rats. Only, they didn't kill the rats, they just killed the birds and ate the eggs of the honu."

"The sea turtles?" Saffron was appalled.

"Uh-huh. They are everywhere, and they're driving some Hawaiian birds to extinction."

This was a sad story. "So I should lock up the chickens?"

"Yes. The pens are mongoose-proof. We built them well. But it might get anybody who's out alone, and any eggs you leave out."

"Will they attack people?"

"No, not usually. They're just looking for an easy meal."

Saffron glanced at Tikka and Curry. "I'll lock them up, then."

"And I'll bring out a mongoose trap."

"Thanks, Tutu."

"Wait," Mano's voice was insistent. "Before you go, tell me, are you fighting?"

Saffron tried not to smile. While the pressure from Mano was sometimes an uncomfortable part of her relationship with Keahi, right now it felt more like a gift. "I'm fighting, Tutu," she said, "I'm fighting."

She could hear his smile, "That girl is like the mongoose. She's sneaky. I've heard her talking to him about going back. I hope he stays."

"I hope he does, too," Saffron admitted. They said goodbye and hung up.

Saffron grabbed a feed can and shook it, tempting Tikka to follow her off the lanai and down the path back into the egg house. Usually, Curry followed as far as the doorway, and then he flapped off to continue his life of freedom, but he must have been shaken by the mongoose, too. This time, as she entered, Saffron made a special point to throw a few grains for him just inside the doorway, and he stepped in, pecking at them. When she opened the door to Tikka's pen and threw a few more grains inside, both chickens scrambled inside to scratch with the other hens.

Saffron latched the door, locking them both safely inside. Then she checked every other pen's doors, inside and out. She was not about to lose any of her flock to a sneaky, invasive predator.

Chapter Twelve

It was Tuesday again, and Saffron stood at the top of the driveway with her egg cart and handed cartons through the windows of a very long line of cars.

There was no time to chat, and by the time the last car disappeared, Saffron was exhausted. The sun was beating down, and a muggy Hawaiian day had settled in. She hurried to get everything ready for the lunch she'd invited the wedding guests to.

Keahi had to work today so he wouldn't be out, but Mano came to help, and Saffron always enjoyed his company. By the time everyone arrived, the stretch of beach in front of the farm was decked out with umbrellas, chairs, towels, drinks, and all the old beach toys from the shed.

It was a perfect Hawaiian day. The sun shone warm, and the breeze blew Saffron's strawberry curls into her eyes. She sat watching Byron and Cyndi in their chairs. Byron wouldn't budge from the shade, and every time Cyndi stood to go toward the water, something he said made her sit back down.

Lyza sat at the water's edge, drawing in the sand and letting the waves cover her toes. Her friends and cousins boogie-boarded and snorkeled. Saffron noticed the cooler was empty and headed back to the house for more drinks.

She had filled the cooler and popped back into her bedroom for her sunglasses when she heard voices inside the front door.

"We have to stay away from each other." Saffron recognized Natalie's voice. She didn't mean to eavesdrop, but she was trapped in the hall, and the intensity in Natalie's voice told her that revealing herself would cause the girl embarrassment.

"Nat, listen, this will all blow over. We're going to be back aboard the Havasu soon." It was Logan she was talking to.

"Right, and we're even more likely to get caught there."

"Collins is just on hyper-alert now because we went over his head. It will be fine."

"That's what you said about going over his head!"

"Don't do this, Nat. Please," Logan's voice was small.

"It's better, really." She was quiet for a while, "anyway, after what happened to Davis."

Logan's voice was angry, "What was it about him?" he said.

"What do you mean?"

"Why is he so irresistible? All the girls went for him. What makes him so hard to get over?"

There was shock in Natalie's voice, "He's dead, Logan. Dead. How can you still be jealous of him?"

Logan sighed deeply, and Saffron heard the squeak of the futon as he sat down, "I'm sorry. He's just a hard guy to compete with. Especially now that all he is is a perfect memory."

"He was your friend, too."

There was a long silence, and Saffron wondered what they were doing. Finally, Logan spoke again. "He was. He was a good guy, huh, Nat?"

"We had a lot of fun onboard."

"With the three of us, we could usually avoid Collins."

"Remember when Davis threw himself under the bus for us?"

Logan laughed, and it was a warm sound, "We would have been caught for sure. He knocked that entire stack of boxes over just to get Collins' attention so he wouldn't find us."

Natalie sighed, "That was after Rota, wasn't it?"

"Yep," Logan said, "after I introduced him to Lyza so I could have you all to myself." There was another squeak as he pulled Natalie down onto the futon next to him. "It was a pretty good plan, huh?"

Natalie's voice was sad, "It worked. He fell for her hard."

"He sure did."

"I don't even know if we ever talked about breaking up. It was just, one day we were meeting on the fantail, the next he was spending all his time on the phone to Spain."

"I'm sorry, Nat. I know that was a hard time for you."

This time it was her voice that was warm, "you helped me through it."

"Well, I could see that you were hurting. And I wanted to fix it if I could. I'm sorry I couldn't." The conversation was trending back toward the melancholy.

"I tried to get over him," Natalie said. "I really did."

"I know."

"I still think we could work," Logan said, but there was resignation in his voice.

"I guess I'm just tired of taking risks," Natalie replied. "If Collins decides to push this, we could both get dishonorable discharges."

Logan made a noncommittal sound.

"That's serious, Logan. And Collins is serious."

"Okay," Logan said. "I know you're right."

"So, this is it?"

He made a sound of grudging agreement.

"Let's at least go back out and enjoy our last few days of leave."

Saffron heard the screen door slam, and she stood for another few minutes in the hall. She felt sorry for them: Logan losing two girls he'd loved, and Natalie losing Davis, first to Lyza, and then to the accident. They seemed star-crossed for sure.

When Saffron returned to the beach, there was a digging competition going on between a few of the guests. Three big holes had been dug out of the sand, and they were trying to see who could dig the deepest one. Lyza watched from her place near the waves, and a tentative smile played at the corners of her mouth. Saffron was glad to see it.

Saffron was so intent on watching the competition that she didn't hear the police cruiser until it was all the way up the drive behind them. She turned to see Bradley pulling in on the other side of the line of palm trees that separated the beach from the farm. Collins' black car nosed its way in behind the cruiser and Collins and Marks got out.

Bradley strode unevenly across the sand toward them. He unsnapped a strap on his belt and released his jingling handcuffs.

"Officer Bradley?" Saffron asked as he approached.

"I'm here to make an arrest," he said. Saffron followed him as he navigated around the big holes, past Lyza, and to the beach chairs where Byron and Cyndi sat.

"Mr. Carelli, I'm arresting you in connection with the death of Davis Howard."

Cyndi made a small, horrified sound. Byron leaped to his feet, knocking over his chair.

"Oh, no, you're not."

"Mr. Carelli, please come quietly."

"Why me? Why would you arrest me?" Saffron saw the man's face flushing. It was reddish-purple in the shadow of the umbrella over him. Saffron noted a slight difference in his complexion from the time he'd grown angry at Davis at the cliffhouse. With the violet from the umbrella interfering, Saffron couldn't identify what he was feeling, precisely, but she could see the difference in the color of his face, indicating there was some strong emotion there."

"That's not a conversation we're going to have here, sir," Bradley said, "You'll be apprised of all that later. For now, please put your hands behind your back." Bradley's jaw was clenched, and his voice was hard. Saffron had seen him like this on very few occasions, and she knew he meant business. She avoided Byron's outraged stare. She was sure that the conversation she overheard between Byron and his future son-in-law was part of the evidence they would use to tie him to Davis' murder. But they'd barely questioned him before. What, she wondered, had changed to make them sure enough to arrest him?

"I'm not going anywhere until you give me one shred of evidence that I was even near that cliff when Davis fell."

Bradley sighed deeply, then obliged. "Another rescue team went down this morning. They found a business card case with your name on it just a couple dozen feet down the side of the cliff. Did you have such a case, sir?"

Byron backed out from under the umbrella. Saffron could see now that he had blanched, the blood in his face draining until his skin was the color of driftwood. This, Saffron thought, was the face of a guilty man. It was apparent that he had not wanted them to find the case. Saffron thought back to that night. She remembered that case—she'd picked it up for him in the dining room, and now she saw that it had been the bright object she had seen Byron kick over the cliff later that night. Keahi had seen it, too.

Bradley moved behind the man. With the click and ratchet of the cuffs, they began to move toward the car. Cyndi tried to talk to her husband, but he stared fixedly ahead, retreating into the same sullen place in his mind that Saffron had seen him go the night of the party.

The digging competition had stopped. Everything had stopped. As Bradley reached the top of the beach, he turned, keeping a firm hand on Byron's elbow. "I've got my suspect," he said. "I'm lifting the travel ban, and you can all feel free to go home now."

There was an uneasy response from the group, and Bradley walked past the silent figures of Collins and Marks and put his prisoner into the backseat of the car. As soon as his engine roared to life, Collins and Marks climbed back into their black car and followed him. Neither of the Navy men had said a word.

THOUGH A FEW OF the guests scrambled to get out of Hawaii and back to their lives, others stayed. Cyndi, Myra, and Lyza stayed to see if there was hope of getting Byron out on bail. Logan and Natalie still had leave left, so Logan stayed to support Lyza, and Natalie stayed to visit Davis' mother. Saffron wasn't sure why Evelyn stayed, but she had her suspicions, and she didn't like them.

THE NEXT DAY WAS WEDNESDAY. Wednesdays were Saffron's egg delivery day, when she took eggs to the local businesses. She made her usual stops: Paradise Market, the Oceanside Café, and the jail. When they had prisoners, they took a couple dozen eggs. Usually, Saffron waited for them to call her, but this morning she knew they had a prisoner, and she wanted to talk to him.

Bradley waved her on past his desk. "He's back there."

Saffron had never seen past the front lobby of the Maika'i Police Station before. She'd never had any reason to go into the part with the cells.

It was a small place, more of a holding jail than a prison. Inside a heavy door propped open with a chunk of coral, she saw four cells, two on each side. She couldn't help but think that it looked a bit like her egg house, with the center aisle and the pens down each side. Byron was in the first cell on the right, scowling at a TV mounted above Saffron's head in the corridor. She braced herself for a barrage.

But Byron didn't unleash any fury on her. Instead, he asked her why she'd come. She explained about the eggs, and he actually thanked her for bringing them. "All they had to feed me this morning was cold cereal." He grumbled, and then, in a pleading voice, he said, "I didn't do anything, you know. I don't know how they could think this about me."

Saffron tried to find words. She wasn't sure she believed him. He had been nothing but furious since he came to the island. "I guess, you know, you didn't seem very happy about the wedding," she managed.

"I wasn't! That doesn't mean I'd kill him!"

Saffron leaned forward, trying to see in this scared prisoner any sign of the angry man who'd come to the cliffhouse that night. His face now was pale gray under the dark stubble of his unshaven beard. She saw none of the angry red tones that had washed over his cheeks when she'd seen him charging his future son-in-law as Davis arrived at the party.

"Listen, I'd like to believe you, but I heard you talking to Davis under the lanai that night. I heard you say you'd never let him go through with it."

Byron's cheek twitched. A slight flush of purple stained his ears. That was something Saffron had seen before. It seemed to be an indicator of guilt in people she'd talked to before. But was it guilt because he'd said those things to Davis? Or because he'd acted on what he'd said? Those were two different things. "I meant that. I wasn't going to let the wedding go through. But—but," he stumbled, "I was going to stand up and protest during the ceremony, that's all."

Saffron considered that. "Well, you're in here. The police must think they've got some reason to hold you."

"They're saying that because I told them I wasn't out on the cliff, but then they found my case, I've cast 'reasonable doubt' on my story."

Saffron kept her voice low. "So you were out there?"

Byron closed his eyes briefly. When he opened them, he sighed. "Okay. I was there. I was outside because I didn't want to be part of the party, but I didn't want to ruin it for Lyza, either." His sigh was explosive. "It was just an impossible situation. I was walking around the lawn. It was really dark. I heard Davis cry out and I ran over there. I figured out that he had fallen, and I knew that they would suspect me, so I ran back to the lanai. I was just climbing the stairs when I saw my wife coming with the flashlight. So I lied." He waved a hand, "alright? I admit it. I lied. I was out there. But I didn't *kill* anyone." His face and ears had gone gray again, and Saffron fought the thought that he wasn't looking guilty now, as he talked about the murder. Was it possible that he was telling the truth? That his guilt was tied to *wanting* Davis dead rather than trying to kill him?

Saffron narrowed her eyes. "Davis knew that cliff. He'd been up there a ton of times when he was a kid. I don't think he just fell." Byron grunted. He was hard to believe. Even penitent and scared, Byron held a brimming hostility that scared Saffron. "And if you did think he fell, why didn't you run for help? Why didn't you get someone to try to save him? You should have known that they would figure out you'd been there. Did you know you'd dropped your case before today?" It was a test question, to see if he would tell her the truth.

Byron's eyes flicked sideways, "No," he said, and Saffron could tell that he was lying.

"Keahi and I saw you kick it over, remember? As we came up?"

Byron closed his eyes for a long moment. "I remember. I didn't think they'd find it." The guilty purple tinge seeped back into his ears.

Saffron nodded. He was like every other criminal—spinning one lie after another—sure he somehow wouldn't get caught. She took some satisfaction in the bars between them.

"I've got to go."

"Wait, no! Please, you've got to talk to the police."

"What would I say, Mr. Carelli? Everything I know about you, everything I've seen, tells me that you hated Davis and would have gone to great lengths to keep him from marrying your daughter. Isn't that right?"

The man's face was a mask of misery. "I admit that's right," He said, but he dropped his gaze to his feet. Saffron saw it clearly, in his shoulders and his voice: Byron was still hiding something. It was one more reason that she couldn't trust him.

"I'm going to go. I'm sure they've contacted your lawyer. Maybe he'll be interested in helping you get out of this."

"Please, *you* have to help me."

"Help you? How? You already got what you wanted. Davis is dead, and your daughter won't be marrying him."

"I just wanted her to be happy." Byron rubbed his fists at his eyes, "If she had just married Logan in the first place, none of this would have happened."

Saffron heard the warmth in Byron's voice. Logan. That's what he had wanted for Lyza. "But I thought you didn't want her to marry a Navy man. If she'd married him, she still would have been far away."

"Logan would bring her home eventually. I know he would. Logan is practically my son. He did everything with our family when they were dating in high school. He helped out, he went with us on vacation. She went to every football game he played in. He was a great quarterback. Fastest, most targeted passes in the country, they said." Saffron remembered him quoting that the night of the party. He must take great pride in that statistic.

"We loved to watch those games. We made plans. I *invested* in their relationship." Byron's fists were clenched, and there was a hard edge to his voice. "But then Lyza went off to college and dumped him, he joined the Navy, and I lost both of them within six months. Then, because he was in the Navy and we let her go to Spain to visit her friend, she met this Davis clown, who I barely knew, and next thing we know, she's calling to tell us they're getting married and can we just pop across the country and across the ocean to come to the wedding?" The rage had returned to Byron's voice, and he raised his intense blue eyes to stare at Saffron. "All I wanted was for those two kids to get married and live happily ever after. And you know what? Davis is gone, so there's nothing in the way of that. Maybe they will get their fairy tale ending now. And even if I rot in here, if it makes Lyza see, then it's worth it."

Saffron felt sick. She couldn't believe she'd felt sorry for him just a moment ago. Byron's hatred had returned, and in the face of it, there was little doubt that he was glad Davis was dead.

Chapter Thirteen

Cleaning the chicken pens was dusty work, but it was satisfying. First, Saffron locked the chickens in their outdoor runs where they loved to pluck the tender new growth off the long grass and snatch up centipedes. Then she propped the door to the inside run open with the wheelbarrow, raked, shoveled the worst of the soiled sand into the wheelbarrow, and dumped it outside in the old garden area.

Tikka scolded Saffron every time she passed her pen. She wanted out. On the eighth trip, Saffron paused. She hadn't seen the mongoose again after the first time. She'd also put out some poisoned bait like Mano had advised her to do. Maybe it was gone.

"All right," she said, "you can come out. But don't get yourselves eaten." She swung the door wide and let Curry and Tikka out, along with their nearly-grown brood. They made a picturesque flock, the multicolored offspring contrasting nicely with the golds and reds and blacks of their parents.

Then she got a load full of clean sand from the huge pile that the stream out behind the egg house had deposited over the years and took it back to spread it inside their run.

When she'd done all the pens, the egg house was beautiful: cool, clean, and perfumed by the gardenia bushes flowering outside the screened windows. Saffron let the other chickens back in, and they immediately began to scratch the new sand and explore their runs. She didn't go round up Tikka's family just yet. They could use a little more time to explore.

Saffron tried not to think about her visit with Byron yesterday. She tried not to think about Davis or the Empress or Lyza, whose grief still bowed her shoulders and glazed her liquid-blue eyes.

They would go home in a few days, they'd said, and let Byron's trial play out here. Cyndi seemed strangely resigned to her husband's fate, and Myra was filled with the same anger as her father, only she'd decided to direct it at her sister for the time being. Myra took every opportunity to inform Lyza that if their father spent the rest of his life in prison, it would be all her fault.

Saffron breathed deeply, trying to calm her troubled mind. The sweetness of the gardenias was almost intoxicating. She left the egg house and went nearer the bushes. They were called kiele in Hawaiian, sweet white flowers that left a heavy scent on the breeze. Saffron fingered the six symmetrical petals, newly amazed at the variety of blooming plants here. In Washington DC, there had been a single rosebush planted outside her building. Here, bouquets grew everywhere, a dazzling array of colors and scents. The big gardenia bush was flanked by a plumeria tree and a yellow hibiscus bush.

The hibiscus had no detectable scent, but its wide, gentle petals and the prominent pistil that projected from the middle made it showy. It was the state flower of Hawaii, and Saffron could see why. Just looking at it brought a feeling of peace and joy that Saffron had uniquely found here in Hawaii. It was bright and flashy and fun, especially compared to the more stately gardenia.

It was in that moment, looking from one flower to another, that Saffron remembered the key. She tried to shake the thought. She didn't want to think anymore about the accident or anything surrounding it.

But something was out of place, and, as usual, Saffron couldn't leave it that way. She needed to quiet this new, nagging thought.

Saffron was conscious of her own grime as she entered the spotless house. She tried to touch as little as possible as she went through to the dining room and searched for the box she'd seen when she was here with Collins.

It was there, among the torn wrapping paper and scattered presents.

She needed to clear the place out soon. She'd have to ask Lyza for an address where she could ship the presents.

As the lid slid off the box, Saffron saw what she'd thought she would see. A five-petaled flower in the center of the butterfly. She laid the key down and tapped at her phone to bring up the photo she'd taken of the woman's bag.

Yes, there it was. As Saffron had suspected: the key and the bag sported the same butterfly, but two very different flowers at its center. Though the angle wasn't perfect, the blossom in the center of the butterfly had the prominent pistil and floppy leaves of the hibiscus.

Saffron studied the key. Its flower had five petals, tapered slightly at the ends, so the whole blossom looked something like a soft star. Was there something significant about the flower in the symbol?

She used her phone to search for "flowers with five petals." A rainbow filled her screen: purple, blue, red, and yellow flowers, white apple blossoms and pale pink wild roses. But none of them was an exact match. Their petals were too blunt or too pointed, the gaps between them too wide or too overlapping. She swiped through several pages.

Suddenly, in the bottom corner of her screen, she saw it: the same flower as was on the key. She tapped it and read, quickly:

Mayflower or trailing arbutus. Grows best in rocky soil. Likes to be near evergreens. Flowers in early spring. State flower of Massachusetts.

Massachusetts. Winchester, Massachusetts. Lyza's hometown. Saffron searched through her recent calls and dialed the Mariposa Condos. When the same pleasant-sounding woman answered, Saffron nearly tripped over the words in her urgency.

"Yes, could you tell me if you have other buildings?"

"We do. Right now we have Mariposa buildings in over 30 major cities, including Los Angeles, New York, and Miami."

"What about Massachusetts?"

"We do. We have buildings in Boston, Cambridge, and Winchester."

Saffron blinked hard. "Do you have a number for the Winchester building?" She tried to keep her voice steady.

The woman rattled it off for her, and Saffron hung up and dialed with shaking fingers.

A young man answered, "Mariposa Building."

"Hello, are you in Winchester, Massachusetts?" Saffron asked.

"Yes, we are. How can I help you?"

"Could you please connect me with Davis Howard's apartment?"

Again, Saffron heard the tapping of a keyboard on the other end of the line, "I'm sorry, ma'am, but there's no one by that name in our building."

"Could you check Lyza Howard?" Saffron tried what would have been Lyza's married name. Whoever had given her the key may have planned for that, since it was a wedding present.

"Noooo," the man said slowly, "I've got a Lyza Prentice listed here."

Lyza Prentice? That was Logan's last name. "Is there anyone else listed?" she asked.

"A Logan Prentice and the owner of the unit, Byron Carelli. Shall I connect you?"

"Yes, please." Saffron couldn't hide the shock in her voice. She half-listened as the phone rang and a generic machine answered. She hung up before the beep.

So this was what Byron had meant by "investing" in Logan and Lyza's relationship. He'd bought them a castle to spend their fairy-tale life in. But he'd given her the key for her wedding to Davis, so maybe he was resigned to the fact that the tale had a different Prince Charming.

Saffron sat down on one of the dining chairs. She was conflicted. Obviously, Byron had both emotional and financial motives to do away with Davis. The thought of it made Saffron's stomach turn. But now, with Davis gone, maybe it was good that Lyza had someplace close to home to go. And perhaps it was good that she had Logan.

Saffron's phone buzzed. It was Keahi.

Wanna have Smoothie Tuesday today instead?

It was a weekly tradition, usually done on Tuesdays so they could call it "Smoothie Tuesday," but they'd abandoned for the last two weeks in the furor of the wedding and its aftermath. Saffron tensed. She wanted to see Keahi, but the thought of Evelyn tagging along gave her a hollow feeling. She texted back.

Just you and me?

The answer came back, *Of course.*

Okay.

Saffron glanced at the time. She'd just have time to get home and clean up. She slipped the key back into its box and laid it on the table, leaving its secrets tied up with the red ribbon.

KEAHI ARRIVED, as always, on time. His greeting was light, and his kiss was quick. Though he was pushing his voice to be bright and straining to keep his expression cheerful, he only succeeded in convincing Saffron that something was making him uneasy. She and Keahi had always been able to be straightforward with each other.

"What's wrong?"

Keahi shook his head and raised his eyebrows. If he tried any harder to hide whatever he was worried about, Saffron thought, his face was going to split open. "Nothing. Everything's good."

Saffron didn't believe him, and she couldn't help but speculate about what bad news he was carrying. Was it Evelyn? Was Keahi really thinking about leaving? Or was it something else altogether? Maybe the Laki Luau, where he worked, was in turmoil, or maybe—this one made Saffron feel weak—perhaps something was wrong with Mano.

"Keahi," she pressed, "I can tell something's bothering you. Now I'm imagining what it is and it's starting to scare me."

He reached for her hand, "No, no, it's okay. Don't be worried."

Saffron was honest. "Are you leaving? Are you going back to Boston?"

Keahi looked surprised. "No," he said, then hastily added, "not now, anyway."

Saffron didn't like that answer, but she was glad that wasn't what was bothering him. "Keahi, if you're worried, then I'm worried."

Keahi looked at her for a long moment. "Pueo," he said finally.

"Owls?"

"Right. Tutu has been talking a lot about them, and I guess it's just getting to me."

"I saw them the other day. There were a lot."

"More every day. The ones that have been gathering are now roosting over near the diving rock. So now you've got the sharks in the water and the owls in the trees. Tutu is sure it means something."

"An omen?"

"Maybe. Of some kind."

Saffron felt a chill. The memory of feeding the 'aumakua was still strong in her mind, and she wondered what the addition of the owls could mean. Not a jellyfish bloom, probably, like the time the manō had gathered before.

"Even the researchers are starting to take notice. There are three of them tracking the event. I talked to them in the Oceanside Café today, and even they can't figure out what's going on."

"What does Mano think it is?" she asked.

"He doesn't know, but to see them all gathering, well, it's kind of like an army amassing. It's both reassuring and unnerving." He seemed to consider for a moment, then squeezed her hand and led her into the house. "Nothing we can do about it right now. Tutu says we just have to watch and wait. Meanwhile, he and Akoni are out in the water and all up and down the cliff attending to the 'aumakua. And I guess part of me worries about that."

"Up and down the cliff?"

"Right. There's a path up the cliff from the diving rock. It makes it easy to get to where the owls are roosting. But it's steep, and with Davis falling, you know," he shrugged without finishing the thought.

The ocean filled their silence with its steady roar. The sound was punctuated by the contented clucking of Tikka and Curry and their family. She thought of the old men on the path.

"They've been up and down it a lot, though," she said, trying to be reassuring. "I think they'll be okay."

Keahi shook his head, as if to free the dark thoughts, and fixed his eyes on hers. "You can't convince them not to do anything they've set their minds on. We might as well make our smoothies and try not to worry about them."

It was nice having him here, with the shades drawn against the strongest of the afternoon light and the sweet breeze blowing through the back screen door. Saffron soaked in his laughter, memorized his gestures. When he reached over and kissed her, she wanted that kiss to last forever.

Saffron had bought her smoothie maker from the local kitchen store, Kukku Kitchen Appliances. The owner, Fumi, had advised her to always put yogurt in her smoothies.

"That way you get creaminess, sweetness, and protein!" she'd exclaimed.

Now it was the secret ingredient that Keahi craved in his smoothies. Saffron put in two large dollops of thick, white, vanilla yogurt, then turned to the mangoes she was slicing.

Saffron always resented the mango seed. Not only because it was a lot of work to get out, but also because it clung so desperately to the flesh of the mango that much of the juicy fruit was utterly wasted by the time the seed was extracted.

Still, she got several handfuls of mango cubes to toss in just about the time that Keahi put in two bananas and a sprinkle of shredded coconut.

They blended it and poured their smoothies into tall, hand-blown glasses that were made by a local artisan from recycled sea glass. The swirling colors in the glasses set off the bright orange smoothies.

Out on the lanai, under the shade of the big monkeypod tree, they sat sipping. The thick, sweet concoction was refreshing after a long day of shoveling. The gardenias perfumed the air with their heavy scent, and a light breeze wound its way through the palms and across the yard to stir long strands of Saffron's strawberry hair across her shoulders. Keahi looked at her.

"You are beautiful." He said simply. Saffron blinked. Her wide green eyes and freckles had never gathered many compliments, But Keahi's eyes shone with sincerity.

She blurted out what she was thinking with characteristic sincerity. "It's hard to believe you think so, after spending so much time with Evelyn this week." The words sounded more bitter than she meant them, and the other girl's name left a bad taste in Saffron's mouth. As soon as she'd spoken, Saffron wished she could take it back. She wished she were better at being cool and aloof, like Evelyn. She glanced over to see if Keahi's expression had changed to defensive.

But he was smiling, an almost disbelieving smile. "Evelyn?" he asked. "Saffron, you're beautiful compared to *anyone*. And you know why? Because not only do you have eyes someone could get lost in, not only are you so soft I want my arms around you all the time, but you are also always thinking about other people. You're always worried about Tutu, about me, about the Empress, about Lyza, who's a perfect stranger to you. That kind of compassion is beautiful. And you're cheerful, and you love everything. Do you know how attractive that is?" He was smiling at her, and Saffron didn't want him to stop talking. When he scooted out of his chair and knelt beside hers to kiss her, though, she didn't mind that he'd gone quiet.

When he pulled back, he looked her in the eye. "Saffron," he said, "I don't want Evelyn. I tried being with her, and it didn't work out. She's too cold, too driven in her own ways, and she lives too much on the surface. I could never talk to her about the 'aumakua. She wouldn't even try to understand how important that is. I couldn't tell her about Tutu. I couldn't even tell her why I left Boston."

Saffron remembered the night Keahi had told her about the 6-year-old patient he had lost, about how he'd never been able to forget that little boy. "She doesn't know at all?"

Keahi shook his head. "That's why she keeps needling me to come back. She thinks I just got bored or something, or that I wanted to come hang out on the beach, so I came home." There was bitterness in his voice. "That's another reason we're not together. She doesn't know me at all, even after all that time we spent together." Keahi moved back into his chair, but he took Saffron's hand. "Although I suppose that's my own fault."

"What do you mean?"

"That if she knows only the surface of me, it's because that's all I let her see. Like I said, she's not a person I'd share anything deep with."

Saffron could understand that. She'd lived her whole life on the surface before coming to Hawaii.

"It's easier to get into the deep stuff here," she said, waving a hand at the swaying palms and the curls of white waves chasing each other to the shore.

"Maybe," he conceded. They sat in silence for a long time.

Their peace was shattered by an uproar from the back of the house. Tikka's brood suddenly erupted into a chorus of frantic squawking, crying out in voices that Saffron had never heard them use.

By the time she and Keahi made it around the house and down the path, the little family had scattered. Only one hen remained—a black-and-white speckled one that Saffron had named Pepper. She lay struggling in the sand beside the stone pathway. The flowing tail of the mongoose was disappearing into the bushes.

Saffron's breath stopped. She rushed over, but then she saw the blood on the sand, streaking the feathers. It was the color of hibiscus flowers, the deep red of lychee husks. When she saw the glistening gash in the hen's upper leg, she froze. The hen wobbled and flapped sideways, heaving in the sand as it tried to stand.

Keahi didn't freeze. With strong, sure hands, he reached down and gathered the wounded animal to him. Heedless of the blood soaking into his aloha shirt, Keahi headed for the kitchen. Saffron snapped into consciousness long enough to follow his directions to open the door and get old towels. As he wrapped the bird, he sent Saffron for the first-aid-kit from his car.

When she returned, he had the hen calmed. Laying on a towel on the table on her side, wrapped securely in another towel, only her head, the long gash, and her tailfeathers were exposed. He took the kit and popped it open to reveal a first-aid kit like Saffron had never seen before. Instead of a few band-aids and some calamine lotion shaking around in the bottom of an old pencil case like hers, Keahi's kit was a miniature doctor's office. Multiple tiers inside it folded out, each holding rows of carefully placed supplies and instruments. He extracted a black case with scissors, scalpels, and pre-threaded needles. She watched, fascinated, as he tidied the wound, knotted the thread, and stitched with a precision she'd never seen before.

It was like watching an artist paint, or a musician play. Saffron was completely lost in the skill with which he put right the gash that looked so wrong among the gleaming feathers.

Saffron didn't know if Pepper understood he was trying to help, but she lay very still until he was done. When he unwrapped her, she rolled onto her side and tucked the injured leg under her. She was still calm, and she closed her eyes.

A passage from *The Rewarding Art of Chicken Keeping*, an old book left at the farm by her uncle and used by many chicken keepers, if the varied notes in the margins were to be believed, came to her mind.

Injured chickens will often spend several days after an accident in a state of shock. Chickens should be provided with food, water, and a sufficiently warm, quiet place to rest. Do not place with other chickens, as picking may occur.

Saffron went for the shed, where there were several boxes made for chicken isolation. She scooted aside the brooder box, the large wooden box where Tikka had raised her chicks and extracted a smaller box made with one side of wire instead of all four sides of wood. It was called an isolation box and allowed a chicken to be in with its flockmates without their being able to reach it. She put it in the run and filled its feed and water dispensers. Then she put soft sand and straw in the bottom.

Keahi appeared in the egg house with his patient in his arms. Together, they arranged her, then gathered up the rest of the flock and locked them securely away.

Keahi sighed. "I think she'll be fine. It wasn't too deep, and just muscle."

Saffron leaned against him, her gaze falling down to the rusty stain on his shirt. "I'm sorry about that," she said.

He kissed the top of her head and waved a hand, "It's not the first time." His complete steadiness, his calmness, soothed her. He really was an anchor. Saffron straightened. *An anchor.*

The image of the sketched anchor next to Keahi's name on the guest list flashed in her mind. But this time, that wasn't all she saw.

"Keahi," she said, "you were amazing. Thank you."

He waved away the praise. "Keep an eye on her. I put some electrolyte solution into her water. It should help her recoup. I have to go, so I have time to change before I perform tonight, but I'll be back to check on her tomorrow. You should probably get someone to come out and trap that mongoose, too, before it has little baby mongooses." He shook his head, "mongeese?"

Saffron wanted him to stay, but she let him go. She had just realized something. She needed to talk to Marks.

Chapter Fourteen

Marks was packing, and Saffron was glad to find him alone. He said that Collins had gone off to the cliffhouse to wrap up the rest of his investigation. With a suspect in custody, they could leave.

"Listen, Marks, I just wanted to ask you about something."

Marks put a perfect crease in his last pair of pants and folded them into a small duffel. "Sure."

"Your notes—the sketches on them—what do the rest of them mean?"

The kid looked embarrassed. "Mean?"

"Yeah, like you told me about Keahi's stability, and me being the deckhand. They're really insightful."

He held up his palms in protest, "No, really, they're just sketches. I didn't mean anything by them."

Saffron could see that he was getting nervous. He had that kind of disposition anyway, and his art was obviously something he kept under wraps. She needed to think of a way to convince him to let her see the rest.

Saffron peered at him and switched the topic. "Did you finish your bull design?"

He nodded, glancing cautiously at her, "And two more."

"What were they?"

"Standard stuff. An eagle and a three-dimensional skull."

"Cool. Could I see them?" He looked doubtful, then she went on. "You know, I think of myself as a bit of an artist, too. Only instead of pen and ink, I use flowers and cake as my medium." It was true. She often thought of her celebrations in terms of a painting: where was the focal point? What colors blended best, and which made great accents? How could she incorporate textures? She told Marks all this, and soon he pulled out his clipboard and offered it to her shyly.

The new sketches were in the back, and they were magnificent. Saffron had seen countless depictions of eagles, but this one captured all the majesty of the bird while avoiding familiar tropes like the gaping beak and awkwardly arched wings. Instead, it had an almost field-manual feel, like a sketch you could use to identify the bird, and it was all done in this clean, bold style that Saffron was sure that Marks' clients—the tattoo artists in the ports he visited—could replicate. The skull was equally impressive.

"These are sensational," she said. "They almost make me want to get one."

Marks squirmed.

"Not you?" she asked.

"I told you, needles make me pass out," he said. Saffron thought about the irony of that.

Before she thought, she blurted, "We're alike, you know."

"How's that?" His voice held a note of hope, and she thought it was probably rare for him to be like anyone else he was around.

"Well, you make these beautiful tattoos, but you don't use them yourself. I make what I hope are beautiful parties, but they're all for someone else, too. Both of us make art meant to be consumed by other people."

There was a light of kinship in the kid's eyes when he nodded. "That's true."

"I think even your sketches were meant for someone else to see." She said it boldly, but the warmth between them smoothed the harshness of it. She went on, "you know a lot about people. I can see why—you had to watch out for your dad all those years, and now you're surrounded by people who demand things of you all day. You have to be able to read them and see who they are and what they're capable of in order to know how to prioritize all the things they want you to do."

He was smiling now. "It's nice to talk to someone who understands," he said.

"Marks," she said, then, "Actually, do you have a first name?"

"Seth."

"Seth," she started again, "I know that you're getting out of here, and you'll probably never think of any of this trip again, but I have to live here, and I need to know who really killed Davis. His mother is my friend. I know his childhood buddies. I think it was Byron, but I'd love to see your sketches and hear your insights."

Marks hesitated, shifting from one foot to the next and raising a hand as if to take back the clipboard. Then, he pressed his lips together and nodded. "Okay," he said. "You can look at it. It's somewhere near the end."

Saffron flipped through the pages, seeing several forms and notes before she got to the list of names.

There was her name, with the knotted rope beside it. There was Keahi's, with the anchor.

She found Byron's. It sported a harpoon. The tip gleamed menacingly. Saffron pointed to it. "Tell me about this one."

"Well, traditionally, the harpoon meant a sailor had served on a whaling vessel or a fishing vessel. But more recently guys get them as a sign of protection. I just thought that Byron had a strong protective vibe like he'd do anything to protect his daughter."

Saffron heard the longing in Marks' voice. He saw Byron as the kind of father he'd never had—one who worked to protect his children and shield them.

"Whether he was right or wrong," Marks went on, "he saw Davis as a monster who threatened Lyza's future and happiness." He said. "That's why I did the harpoon."

Saffron glanced at a few of the others.

"Ships for both Davis and Lyza's mothers?"

Marks nodded. "There's a passage on the sea, around Cape Horn in South America, that's extremely dangerous. It's stormy and hard to navigate. Sailors who've been through that get to wear a fully-rigged ship."

"So it's symbolic of what their mothers have been through?"

"I can't imagine what a mother would feel, having to see her child suffer," Marks said. There was an exquisite softness to his voice when he said the words *mother* and *child*.

Saffron left that alone. Prying into the grief and longing that Marks was so obviously still carrying would be unnecessarily cruel. She pointed to a palm tree. The same design was sketched next to several of the names.

"Hawaii. Sailors who have been to Hawaii often get tattoos of palm trees or hula girls."

Saffron saw now that the palm trees graced the names of Davis' local friends.

Davis himself had a beautiful sketch. Saffron remembered the poignant symbol: a swallow with wings and head arched high, and a dagger plunged down through its breast. She ran a finger over the drops of blood or tears raining below it.

Marks spoke, "symbol of a fallen shipmate," he said simply.

A detailed sketch of a sea monster caught Saffron's eye. It

was writhing and arched, twisted around on itself. It was sketched next to Lyza's sister's name: Myra.

"What is this one?" She asked.

"Easy. That one practically drew itself. She's so jealous of her sister that it's all she sees."

"The sea monster—"

"Represents any kind of danger at sea. In this case, jealousy."

Saffron had certainly seen Myra's animosity. The monster was a good representation of that.

"All she could talk about was how crushed Logan was going to be at this wedding, even though it seems pretty obvious he'd moved on. And you'd think she'd have been happy about the wedding," Marks' voice was high and emotion made his words flow faster, "because she's obviously stuck on him and with her sister marrying Davis, maybe she'd have a chance at him."

Saffron pointed to the next name on the list: Akoni. "Why crosses? He isn't overtly Christian."

"Crosses on the soles of a sailor's feet are supposed to ward off sharks. It's an old superstition, and he was obviously superstitious. When we interviewed him, all that old man could talk about was the sharks down by the big rock."

Superstitious seemed like too strong a word until Saffron remembered Akoni's insistence that Davis was bad luck.

What had he said? That Davis was a "bad luck boy," and that he had to go because he was upsetting the 'aumakua. And he had been out there. For some reason, Akoni had left his range rover just outside the gates. Where had he gone from there? Saffron needed to find out.

"Can I take a picture of this?" she asked. She didn't want Marks leaving with it forever.

"I don't know," he ran a hand across the back of his neck.

"Seth, please. I think you have real insight into this case."

He nodded. "Okay. Go ahead. But don't tell Collins. The present list is there, too."

She thought about Collins as she snapped pictures of both pages. "Seth, you said that Collins had come up here the day the accident happened. You don't think he would—" she couldn't bring herself to say it.

"Sure he would." Marks' voice was bold. "Collins hated Davis. Collins had fallen for Natalie Crofts, but she told him she wouldn't get involved with him. It was obvious that she just didn't like him, but she didn't tell him that, of course. She told him it was because of the Navy's fraternization policy. He found out that she had a thing for Davis and figured out that's why she wouldn't have anything to do with him. I've been afraid for months that he'd toss Davis overboard and not get caught."

"Do you think he still thinks he has a chance with Natalie?"

"At this point, it doesn't even matter. He's not after her anymore. He's after revenge. He wants them all out of the Navy."

Saffron was quiet. "Do you know if Collins has an alibi for that night?"

"Not that I know of. He didn't come to get me until the next day."

Saffron handed back the clipboard.

"Thank you," he said.

"For what?"

"For talking to me. I'm used to being the guy nobody sees."

Saffron nodded. "Well, I think you're pretty noticeable. Talent like this is not something that happens every day."

Marks smiled. "You let me know if you need anything else," he said. He scribbled on a card and handed it to her. "That's my cell number." He said. Saffron smiled and slipped it in her pocket.

"Keep drawing," she said.

"You keep throwing parties. Who knows, maybe you'll throw one for me someday." Marks smiled, and Saffron smiled back as she left the room.

"Thanks, Seth."

AKONI'S HOUSE looked the same as it had before. His old range rover sat out front. Saffron wondered briefly when he had gotten it back from up the cliff.

She tried to talk herself out of Akoni as a suspect as she walked toward the front door, but his vehemence and the certainty of his beliefs about Davis being bad luck were hard to discount. And Bradley had told her about his stealing all those pigs.

Raising her hand to knock, Saffron heard raised voices.

"Hello?" she called. The voices stilled. When the door opened, Akoni peered out at her from the dim interior. She was about to speak when Mano leaned around Akoni.

"Aloha!" He said, his voice genuinely bright. "Come in!" Mano ushered her into the dim, cramped living room where he and Akoni had apparently been having tea.

"Sit!" he said, "Stay for a cup with us."

Saffron was more of a soda girl, but the warm smell of chamomile was inviting. She allowed herself to be guided to a wicker chair with a cushion on it and she sat as the men fetched another teacup and poured. She took plenty of cream and sugar as they watched her expectantly.

"You're here about the pueo?" Akoni said.

"The owls?" Saffron blinked, "uh, no."

"Well, they're here," Akoni said.

"I saw some of them," Saffron was trying to be polite.

"Did you acknowledge them? Or offer them anything?"

Saffron tried to explain that she'd been a passenger in

Collins' car at the time, that she couldn't stop, but Akoni waved her off with a sputter.

"Aaak, that's no excuse," Akoni said. "That's the problem. Everyone thinks that reverence should be easy. They want protection, but they don't want to do what they need to show the 'aumakua their deference."

Mano had been quiet. Saffron took that he agreed somewhat with their host. When he did speak, it was to offer general support, "You're doing a lot for the 'aumakua. You've got families out to help that I haven't seen in years."

Akoni grunted.

"It's true," Mano went on. "And you go out night and day."

This was getting at Saffron's reason for being here. "Akoni," she said, "I need to talk to you about the night Davis died."

"Yes," Akoni said, shaking his head. He and Mano exchanged a look.

"They found your range rover by the road after we thought you'd left."

"That's right. I was done with you guys, but I still had work to do."

"What kind of work?"

This time Mano spoke up, "We were setting up some feeding stations for the villagers to use for their pueo."

Saffron had seen those as the villagers set them up near the road. "You were together?" If Mano vouched for Akoni, then Saffron would have no problem scratching him off the list of suspects. Mano knew people, and Akoni was only on the list because he hadn't seemed to like Davis.

"Right. I came up the path from down here, and he said he had an errand—I guess it was going to yell at you guys." Saffron found that Mano's cheerful outlook made even difficult conversations easier. "Then we met on the path and set them up."

"Isn't that dangerous? At night?" Saffron was thinking about what Keahi had said.

"No more dangerous than in the day, or in the rain. The cliff is always dangerous," Akoni said. "Nobody respects it anymore. Nobody respects anything."

Respect. The word resonated with Saffron, because that was what she saw in Akoni. It wasn't superstition. It was respect. Beneath his cranky exterior, there lay in him a deep respect—for the natural world, for things he found sacred, for living things. That's what truly vindicated Akoni—his deep respect for life. He would not, she now saw, be so callous as to take that from another being, even one he clearly didn't like.

"You have to Mālama Honua," Akoni said. "You must."

Saffron, without even realizing it, cast a glance at Mano, who translated smoothly for her. "Mālama Honua is to care for and protect our island—Earth, all living things, and the people around us. It's taking care," he said, "and we honor our 'aumakua and our ancestors by showing reverence and respect for Earth and everything on it."

"If you don't have respect," Akoni went on. "Then bad things can happen. That's what happened to that bad-luck boy."

Saffron didn't correct him. Davis' fall was seeming more and more like very bad luck.

SAFFRON HAD ENJOYED her visit with the two old men. She had even related her traumatic mongoose experience, and they'd promised to come set some traps and take it away.

On her way home, she stopped by the cliffhouse to be sure everything was in order after Collins' had been here this afternoon.

Saffron decided to come back tomorrow and take everything down. Perhaps she should start tonight with loading up the gifts and taking them over to the Empress'.

The house was quiet. Only the rush of the sea outside kept her tumbling thoughts at bay.

Saffron stacked the tumblers and the cookbook and carried them out to the car. She came back to fetch the cooler and the crystal bowl. She put in the key, the books, everything she could find, glancing at the photo of the gift list on her phone to make sure she didn't miss anything.

But as she checked it over, she realized that something *was* missing. Saffron checked again. The envelope with the flight vouchers. It wasn't where she'd left it. Saffron went through the stack of discarded wrapping paper. Nothing. She sorted through everything she'd taken to the car, emptying the cooler and riffling through the pages of the books. The voucher was completely gone. Someone had stolen the vouchers.

Collins. He'd been here just this afternoon. Saffron tried to remember the last time she'd seen the vouchers. She didn't remember seeing it when she came to look at the key, but she hadn't been thinking to look for it then, either.

But it wasn't only him who had access to the place. She knew that both Bradley and Collins had done walk-throughs with several of the guests as they had with her, gathering evidence. Even Lyza had been here. Maybe she had taken the vouchers. And if so, there was really no problem with that— they were hers, after all.

Saffron checked the time. It was nine o'clock, well past time to gather the evening eggs, So she headed back toward Maika'i. She needed to drop these gifts off at the Empress' and get back to the farm.

Keahi was working tonight-performing at the Laki Luau. Saffron shivered and sent a little prayer up that he'd be okay. He did a fire-knife dance that Saffron had found both thrilling and terrifying the more she'd come to care about him. He'd be exhausted after the show, and though he'd probably send her a couple texts, they wouldn't see each other again tonight.

Traffic was slow along the stretch of highway to Maika'i. Saffron watched the ocean as she rolled behind a brightly painted Volkswagon Bug. The waves were crystal blue, gentle here, and the sky made an unbroken line where it met the water.

The flutter of a sail on the beach caught Saffron's attention. Pulled up onto the shore was Oke Cooper's canoe. He was setting up to sell his catch, and Saffron pulled over in the nearest wide spot with a craving for the taste of fresh steamed kūmū fish.

Oke was hunched over a cooler with the top open when Saffron approached.

"Good catch?"

Oke grunted. He could speak, but most of his communication was non-verbal. Saffron found herself talking more to make up for the quiet.

"I'll take two," she said brightly, indicating the paper-wrapped packages he had ready.

He held up two hands, the pocked fingers spread, and Saffron extracted a ten-dollar bill, plus a few loose ones for a tip, and handed it to him. Oke grunted his thanks.

Saffron turned to leave, her mind already on the buttery flavor of the fish she'd have for dinner. But a color anomaly down the beach, near Oke's canoe, caught her attention. She looked at it. Brown canoe, blue water, white sail, golden sand. The picture was an island still life. Big and steady, the boat sat on the shore waiting for Oke to launch it out for more adventures on the sea. But Saffron knew color, and something wasn't right. Though Saffron couldn't explain why the color she'd seen was unusual for the canoe. Maybe a sea bird had landed on it? Or a pale crab had scuttled behind it? Both species loved the fish-filled vessel. But she squinted and didn't see any creatures near the canoe.

Saffron had never been able to leave anything alone if it seemed out of place to her. She supposed that came from the turmoil she and her mother had been thrown into after her father left. She learned that things had a place, and if they were out of place, chaos happened.

She crossed the sand, peering at the boat as another group of buyers vied for Oke's attention. The damp shore gave slightly under her feet, the ocean's gentle breath filled the air, and Saffron's gaze fell on a slight patch of warm brown contrasting with the golden sand in the shadow of the wooden canoe. Saffron stopped and stared. Sticking out from behind the canoe was a human foot.

Chapter Fifteen

S affron clutched the package of fish more tightly. She glanced back at Oke, who was busy with his next customers. Closing her eyes, Saffron took two more steps forward.

When she opened them, Saffron's heart stopped.

Davis Howard lay in the shade of the boat.

He wore only his white crackerjack pants, ripped off at the knees, and a navy neckerchief with faded white letters wrapped around a wound on his left bicep. On his head was a makeshift bandage made from what Saffron could now see were strips of the missing pant legs. The center of the dressing was stained with old blood. There were bruises and cuts all over his torso and lower legs. His eyes were closed.

Saffron stammered out his name, unsure whether or not he was alive.

Davis opened his eyes.

"Davis!" she cried, rushing toward him.

Davis, his eyes wide and frightened, scuttled backward on the sand, deeper into the shadow of the boat. His tensed body showed her he was ready to run. Saffron backed off just as Oke came flying around the boat, shouting at her.

"Get back! Get back! Leave him alone!" Oke put himself between the two of them, and Davis curled his knees up to his chest and dropped his head, making himself as small as possible.

Saffron did as she was told, but couldn't stay quiet.

"This is Davis Howard. We thought he was dead!"

Oke peered at her, his weathered face scrunched. "He from here?" he asked, waving a hand toward Maika'i. Saffron's gaze followed the gesture, and she saw the other customers beating a hasty retreat back to their car, startled by the shouting. She nodded.

"Where did you find him?" Saffron asked, trying to keep her trembling voice down.

Oke squinted at her, and Saffron felt as if she was being carefully evaluated. A long silence stretched between them, punctuated only by Davis' ragged breathing.

Finally, Oke spoke, and Saffron sensed a deep reverence in

his words. "The 'aumakua," Oke said. Saffron nodded to show she was familiar with the word. "They brought him to me."

Saffron tried to picture that. Her questions must have shown on her face.

"I was leaving this harbor. Out. Way," he waved a hand toward the horizon, "way out. In the moonlight, I see the 'aumakua coming. Their fins cutting the water."

"Were you afraid?" Saffron blurted.

"No. All the time, the 'aumakua visit me," he said, shaking his hand. "I give them fish. Only this time, they were swimming strangely."

Saffron stayed quiet, nodding.

"They didn't approach with their mouths open, like usual. They came pushing him," Oke jabbed a finger in Davis' direction, "ahead of them. One swam under, supporting him. They brought him to my boat, you see?" Oke laid a hand on the boat. "He was bleeding—his head, his arm, torn up."

"By the sharks?"

Oke stopped talking, pressing his lips together in a stern, disapproving glance. "I told you, they were helping him. These were not shark bites. These were wounds from falling—from lava rock, I think."

"He's been with you this whole time?"

Oke nodded.

"Why didn't you take him to a hospital?"

At this, the unflappable fisherman shrunk a little himself. He glanced quickly up and down the beach as if he were afraid of being heard. "I can't leave my canoe," he said, but Saffron sensed there was more.

"He needed medical help. And his family—his mother," Saffron felt a growing excitement in her chest as she thought of telling the Empress that her boy was alive, "his mother has been in mourning."

Oke looked, for the first time since Saffron had met him,

sorry. "I can't go into the towns," he said, trying to explain, "because I'm not a US citizen. If I get caught, they'll arrest me. I'll lose everything." His hand was clutching the boat now as if he could hold himself to it. Saffron looked at his *everything*. It was, as far as she could see, the boat, the cooler, and the dirty dungarees he was wearing. Still, she understood what it was like to cling to things. And Oke was a man of the sea. He would not survive in a cell.

"I thought he would get better and I could just send him home," Oke said. There was no deception in his voice. "Only he don't know who he is, or where he comes from." He waved toward Davis' curled form, and Oke's voice was pleading, "I took care of him," he said, "I took him on my route around the islands. I fed him, I let him help me on the nets. I fixed his wounds. I helped him feel safe when he had nightmares. I took care of him."

Saffron could see a great tenderness in Oke's eyes. For the first time, she considered how very lonely his life must be.

"I can see that," she said.

"But now, I see it's time for you to come in," Oke's voice was sad. "You are meant to take him home. Take him to his mother."

Saffron looked at the huddled figure of the groom. He was so different than the striding, confident man who had walked into the Empress' garden that morning. Oke followed her gaze and nodded. "It's okay. You go over by your car. I will talk to him."

Saffron backed away, keeping an eye on him. She got to her car and slipped into the driver's seat. Oke crouched next to Davis, taking the younger man's face in his scarred hands and speaking to him in a low, even voice. Saffron had no idea what he was saying, but he pointed Davis' face toward her, and the sound of his words was encouraging.

As they stood together, Davis gave Oke his hand like a child and allowed himself to be led to Saffron's car. The footprints of the two men followed them across the sand. Oke opened the passenger's side door and helped Davis in, and Saffron heard the injured groom murmuring. He was softly repeating a word that she recognized: *Mama.*

———

SAFFRON TRIED to be absolutely quiet on the ride to the Empress' house. She wanted to call ahead, but couldn't risk frightening Davis. She had wanted to take him to the hospital, but he was so fragile, and there was only one person he wanted to see. His health didn't seem under imminent threat, so she took him home.

She didn't know what Oke had told him, but he must somehow have convinced Davis that Saffron was a friend, because when she opened the door to the car, he offered her his hand in that same childlike way. She took it, and together they walked up the wide marble steps of the estate house.

Davis' bare feet made a soft shushing sound as they crossed the veranda and knocked.

Carlo opened the door, and for the first time, Saffron saw shock on the man's face. He began to speak, but Saffron felt Davis pulling back toward the stairs. She waved Carlo away.

"Get his mama," she said quickly.

Carlo disappeared, and Davis settled.

Rex pushed the Empress' chair through the doorway, then disappeared back into the house clutching Princess.

The Empress' face was drawn, pinched by days of weeping. Saffron had seen, since her time here in the islands, the magic of a Hawaiian rainbow chasing itself across the sky after a storm. She saw that magic now, as the Empress' gaze fell on the disheveled sailor, as her eyes widened, as her arms reached for him.

The Empress didn't speak. She simply spread her arms. Davis released his grip on Saffron's hand and fell into them.

He was a big man, and the Empress' arms didn't reach all the way around him, but the strength of her embrace made up for it.

"My boy, my boy," she kept repeating, "my son."

Davis knelt beside her chair, his bandaged head on her shoulder.

After a long time, the Empress looked up at Saffron over Davis' head. "You have always been special to me," she said, "but now, you are my ohana. My family."

Saffron did not trust herself to speak.

"You have brought my son home to me," the Empress forced formality into her voice, and Saffron could see that it was holding back a roiling torrent of emotion, "raised him from the dead."

Saffron opened her mouth to explain, but the Empress stopped her.

"I will hear about it later. Now is the time for homecoming."

The Empress raised a hand, and Rex and Carlo appeared from the shadows of the doorway behind her. She took her son by the shoulders and pushed him back so she could see his face. "We're going to your room now, Davey," she said, "and the doctor will come to see you."

Davis' powerful voice was small and thready when he spoke, "Mama, stay with me."

The Empress' brilliant white smile spread across her face. Her deep brown eyes shone, and the mahogany tones of her skin caught the evening light and set her face aglow. "I will not let you go, my boy. I will be with you every minute." She held his hand with both of hers as he stood and they went, together, into the house.

"Come in, Saffron," the Empress called, "and please tele-phone Doctor Weiss."

Saffron, glad to have something to do, made her way into the parlor. It was quiet and serene inside, and the photos all around the room stared at her. She saw that every one with Davis in it had been graced with a thin, colored ribbon, and she imagined the Empress holding each gilded frame in her lap beside Princess, looping the ribbon and tying it in a careful bow in memory of her lost sailor.

The phone call was quick and the Doctor's response even quicker. His orange jeep pulled up outside within a quarter of an hour.

Dr. Weiss was Maika'i's general practitioner. He was middle-aged and had come here from the west coast of the mainland. He practiced old-fashioned care, and though he did have an office downtown, more often visited patients in their homes, arguing that treating them properly required knowing not only what was in their charts but what was in their refrig-erators.

Saffron followed him upstairs past the chair lift that carried the Empress' chair up and down the staircase. She followed him down the hall to the door of Davis' room, which, Saffron noted, was right next to the Empress'. Rex and Carlo stood guard by the door, their calm deportment restored. They let the doctor in, and Saffron sat in a Louis XVI gilded armchair in the hallway awaiting news.

It was over an hour later that the doctor emerged. Saffron sat eating a sandwich that Rex had provided for her.

It was a delicious concoction that the Rex often served. Saffron called it Aloha Chicken Salad. It had chunks of honey-pineapple marinated chicken, chopped smoked macadamia nuts, and crisp lettuce on toasted poi rolls. Saffron hadn't real-ized how hungry she was until she started in on it.

Doctor Weiss smiled as he accepted one himself. He ate

standing up, talking around the bites of chicken salad.

"I guess this one will go down in the history books," he shook his head, obviously pleased at the outcome.

"Will he be alright?"

Doctor Weiss' eyes clouded, "that's too general for me to commit to. Brain injuries are tricky. He'll live. He'll learn. I just don't know what all he'll be able to recover from before."

Saffron had been wondering something, "Doc, Oke said that he hadn't been attacked by the sharks."

Dr. Weiss nodded, "That's right. Not a bite on him."

"So what happened to his head? His arm?"

Dr. Weiss shook his head. "He was struck. That's the wound on his head. And I think the lava rock tore up his arm on the way down. His shoulders, too, and one calf."

Saffron remembered the other wounds, but it was the doctor's first comment that stuck with her most, "Struck? You mean someone hit him?"

"Definitely."

Saffron sucked in her breath. "Did he say who?"

"Poor kid can't remember anything after he was about seven. In fact, he thinks he's still seven. Thinks he dove off the diving rock and almost drowned."

Saffron's eyes widened. "He did. *When* he was seven."

The doctor nodded. "That's what the Empress told me. Looks like the two traumas have merged in his mind and everything between them is folded up somewhere between them."

"And there's no way for him to tell us what happened the night he fell from the cliff?"

The doctor looked up and snapped his fingers. "That reminds me. I left something in there." He poked the last bite of sandwich into his mouth and went back to the door. Knocking lightly, he let himself in and then slipped back out holding two plastic evidence bags.

Through the clear bags, Saffron could see the strips of

bloodied pant legs and the neckerchief. He held it up, and Saffron could see the ragged edges of the pant legs and faded letters on the neckerchief. "There's no way he can tell us," Weiss said, "but these might."

SAFFRON STOPPED at the bed and breakfast on her way back. Most of the remaining guests were leaving in the morning, and she wanted to be sure they knew the news.

The warm Hawaiian night wrapped around her like a song as she stepped out of her car at the Felicity Inn. The place was lit up like a birthday cake, and Saffron found herself trembling with excitement about the news she had for Lyza. Though the news wasn't all good—Davis had no memory of Lyza—he was alive, and that was a start.

The doctor hypothesized that Byron had struck Davis with something blunt—maybe a rock—and he had fallen over the cliff. Most of the damage was sustained on the way down. Saffron was glad Byron was in custody.

The first guest she met was Natalie. Saffron was glad to see her. The girl had suffered so much with the loss of Davis, and Saffron was sure she would be overjoyed to hear of his return.

"Natalie!" she said, "Davis is alive!"

The girl's expression was puzzled. "What?"

"It's a strange story, but he was picked up by a fisherman and has been traveling around the island with him. He's—"

Natalie interrupted, "Where is he?"

"He's home," Saffron smiled.

Natalie seemed less overjoyed than stunned. She turned for the door, muttering, "I've got to get over there."

"Wait," Saffron caught her arm, "you should know that he's got some memory problems."

Natalie tipped her head in a question.

"He doesn't remember anything after he was about seven."

Natalie nodded, wrenched her arm free, and strode out of the Felicity Inn.

Saffron watched her go. She couldn't tell if Natalie was happy, angry, worried—Saffron was finding the girl's military training to be an impediment to reading her reactions. She was in such control that her face never changed color in the characteristic ways that other people's did.

Saffron went to find Lyza. What she found, instead, was Myra and Cyndi in their room, staring vacantly at flickering reruns on their TV set. Their blinds were drawn, and the only other light was from the half-open door of the bathroom. When she asked about Lyza, she found that the two of them had no idea where the bride had gone.

"Haven't seen her for a couple of hours," Myra said. The girl was characteristically sullen.

"Does she have a phone?"

"Yes," Cyndi said, then pointed. Saffron saw a pink phone with the word *Lyza* bejeweled across the case lying on the side table. That wasn't going to be of any help.

"What did she say when she left?" Saffron pressed.

Slowly, Myra raised her hand. In it was the remote. With an air of great annoyance, she pressed the mute button. "She didn't say anything."

Saffron imagined being in this room with the two of them moping for hours at a time. She suddenly felt guilty for not doing more to distract Lyza these last few days. She supposed that she wouldn't bother to tell them where she was going, either. She wondered if she should tell them, but something about Cyndi's mournful expression and Myra's overt anger made her hesitant. She wanted Lyza to know first.

"You said it's been a couple of hours?"

"Mmmmm," Myra snapped the sound back on, and the TV blared to life.

Saffron let herself out. She went to Logan's room. No one answered her knock. She felt a bit better thinking that maybe they were together somewhere.

Letting herself out onto the veranda, Saffron tried to think what to do. The evening was getting late—her watch said 9:00 —and she'd had a long day. But she really wanted to find Lyza, and Logan, too, if he was with her, and tell them both about Davis. She pulled out her phone and searched her contacts.

She had known she didn't have Logan in there, but she thought she'd check anyway,, as much out of pure hopefulness as anything else. There was no number there, though. Just Lyza's.

But Lyza would have Logan's number in her contacts, and though Saffron didn't have Lyza, she had the next best thing: Lyza's phone. She went back to Myra and Cyndi's room.

Cyndi answered the knock, and Saffron could see in her the pure exhaustion of a traveler at the end of a very grueling trip. Cyndi tried to smile, but the gesture was more of a grimace.

"I'm sorry to bother you again," Saffron said, "but it's important that I talk to Lyza. I thought maybe I could get Logan's number from her phone. Do you mind if I look at it?"

Cyndi shrugged and paced to the side table. She picked it up and brought it back to the door.

"Here," she said, and Saffron said thank you to the room door closing in her face.

Flipping the phone over and locating the button, Saffron saw the screen glow to life with a picture of Lyza and Davis. They were standing at a railing, a beautiful city in the background. It had white adobe buildings and red tile roofs—Rota, Spain. It must have been a picture from their first date. Even then, they already had a glow about them that Saffron could only attribute to love.

The screen was locked. In front of the smiling couple, nine

dots dared Saffron to decipher them. She tried a couple of sweeping strokes.

Incorrect pattern. 3 more tries before lockout the phone read.

Saffron got serious. A square? An X? She tried the second one. *2 more tries.* Saffron realized that this was mostly hopeless. She tried a Z. *1 more attempt.*

Of course. Saffron started at the top left, went down three dots, and across two, tracing a perfect L. The phone unlocked. *L for Lyza.* Saffron wondered how many other things she made unnecessarily difficult for herself.

As she tapped the screen, looking through the contacts, a missed call popped up. The number was local, with an 808 area code and a Maika'i prefix. It had come in a couple of hours ago, likely just after Lyza had left her phone. Maybe it would give Saffron some idea of where the bride had gone.

Saffron pulled out her own phone, and, holding the two next to each other, dialed the number.

The line rang three times. Five. Just as Saffron was about to hang up, a machine answered.

"Thanks for calling Tropical Adventures! We're out making someone's dreams come true right now, and we're sorry we missed your call. Please leave your name and your number and a brief message, and we'll call you back to make your own Hawaiian travel plans!" The message was followed by a jarring buzz. Saffron hung up.

Tropical Adventures. She'd heard that before. Of course, she'd visited the travel agency in the old post office building on one of the side streets in Maika'i, but she'd heard the name more recently. Saffron tapped the photo gallery app on her phone and a grid of the recent pictures she'd taken sprung up.

She tapped the present list. There it was, in Marks' neat handwriting: *Tropical Adventures Flight Vouchers—No Name.*

Saffron ran a finger over the screen. She had solved the mystery of the missing tickets.

Chapter Sixteen

Saffron tried all night to reach Logan on his phone, but there was no answer. She checked with Cyndi several times, but Lyza never reappeared. But it was no use. Logan wasn't picking up. No matter how badly she wanted answers, Saffron had no choice but to wait until Tropical Adventures opened late the next morning.

Saffron even tried to call Logan while she was gathering the eggs and inspecting the mongoose trap that Akoni and Mano had installed last night.

She stooped down and peered into the long, rectangular wire cage, then jerked back with a cry of surprise as a snarling ball of fur threw itself at her, stopped only by the trap. With shaking hands, Saffron called Mano.

It wasn't just Mano who came to take the animal away. Akoni came, too, and Keahi drove them there. Saffron was glad to see them all.

The anticipation of telling them about Davis made Saffron bounce on her toes as they climbed out of Keahi's SUV.

They had barely reached the lanai when she called out, "He's alive! Davis is alive!"

Keahi quickened his step. "What?"

"Davis is alive. He's been with Oke Cooper. In his canoe. I found him on the beach yesterday."

Mano and Akoni stood speechless.

"Where is he now?" Keahi said. Saffron saw in him a desire to see his friend.

"At home. With his mother."

Akoni and Mano approached slowly. A murmured conversation had begun between them.

"Mo'opuna," Mano said, calling Saffron 'grandchild,' "how is this possible?"

This was the best part. Saffron reached out and took Mano's hands.

"The 'aumakua saved him. They took him to Oke's boat!"

Mano's face broke into a grin. Akoni, on the other hand, closed his eyes. Saffron's giddiness was tempered by the sight of him standing very still. His lips were moving, but no words were coming out.

Keahi leaned close to her. His voice was quiet, but his eyes were sparkling from the news she'd shared. "It's okay. He's praying—it's called pule. He's giving thanks."

When Akoni opened his eyes, he spoke softly. "I was wrong," he said to Mano. "Davis is not a bad luck boy. The 'aumakua have saved him. He is a blessed boy."

There was humility in the words, and in how Akoni spoke them. His reverence for the 'aumakua had helped him change his mind about Davis. Saffron admired that—the ability to let go of past judgments.

Keahi checked on Pepper and said he thought she'd make a full recovery. The men took the snarling mongoose trap and put it in the SUV. Saffron did not know what they would do with it, and she didn't want to know. So she didn't ask.

They were too busy to stay for tea, though Saffron invited

them. Mano and Akoni had work to do for the 'aumakua, and Keahi wanted to go see Davis.

She thanked them profusely for getting rid of the menacing mongoose and waved from the lanai as they drove away with it. Glancing at her phone, Saffron realized that Tropical Adventures would open in fifteen minutes. When they did, she would be waiting for them.

THE TRAVEL AGENCY was owned by a couple who, Saffron thought, always looked like they were having a tropical adventure themselves. They had five or six kids—Saffron couldn't ever count them properly, because they were always moving around—who were, much of the time, scattered around the travel agency building getting into various kinds of mischief. The father, Val Tucker, was generally a smiling, easygoing type, and his wife, Belle, was the opposite. She was tense and nervous, always snapping at the children and whipping out a pen from behind her ear to jot down notes or scribble a check to someone. Saffron suspected that Val dreamed up the adventures and Belle made them actually happen.

Belle always seemed very happy to see Saffron, maybe because if Saffron got within arm's reach, Belle handed her a baby to hold.

This time was no exception, and Belle handed off the youngest Tucker as she unlocked the doors to the agency. The baby was a little girl, with chestnut curls and colossal violet eyes. Her chubby cheeks bunched in a gummy grin, and Saffron couldn't help but smile back. She offered the baby her finger, and the tyke grabbed on and held fast.

"She likes you," Val called from the side of their minivan, where he was changing a diaper on another Tucker.

"I like her," Saffron said, smiling at the baby. "Hey, I

brought you all some eggs. They're on the floor by the back seat of my car if you want to grab them."

Val grinned, and Saffron saw where the baby got her smile. "Thanks!" There was genuine appreciation in his voice—the Tuckers had a lot of mouths to feed.

The door swung open in front of Mrs. Tucker, and Saffron followed her into the stuffy office.

The old post office was a fascinating building. In the early days of Maika'i, it was both a general store and mail outlet. Large shelves lined the walls up to the ten-foot ceilings, where the merchandise had been displayed. There were still a few odd cans and boxes and bottles with unknown contents up on the highest shelves. The little Tuckers had cleared anything within their reach, so all the lower shelves were barren.

The building had a room where the postal workers used to do their part of the business. It had a heavy door and a classic service counter, with a high arch above it and bars separating the customer from the worker. The Tuckers never used it for business, but the older kids often played outlaws and locked each other inside.

"So, you're ready for a vacation already?" Belle said, her terse tone revealing a hint of bitterness.

"No, no. I just need to ask you a few questions about some travel vouchers you sold."

"Sure." Belle sat heavily in her chair as a toddler climbed onto her lap. Saffron sat, still holding the baby, in one of the mismatched chairs across the desk from Belle.

"The ones that Lyza How—I mean Lyza Carelli got for her wedding."

"Oh," Belle nodded. "Right."

"Lyza's missing, Saffron said, and the tickets are, too. I wondered," Saffron didn't get to finish.

"She flew out last night," Belle said.

The sound of the words was jarring, and not only because the toddler on Belle's lap had begun to howl.

"Flew out?" Saffron asked.

"Yeah. She redeemed the vouchers right before we closed last night. We barely got them on a flight out of Honolulu."

"Them?"

"Right. She and someone named . . ." Belle pulled a paper out from under a stack on her desk and scanned it. Saffron knew what Belle would say before she spoke. "She and somebody named Logan Prentice."

Saffron shifted the baby and gripped the edge of the desk. "Did they have to pay a fee to change the names on the vouchers?"

Belle looked startled. "They should have," she said, and Saffron could see she was concerned they'd made a mistake. Belle shuffled, one-handed, through several papers, then held one up. "Nope. That's what I thought. The vouchers were already in their names. No change charge needed." Belle looked relieved for only half a second before her face tensed up again as she looked across the room. "Don't climb those shelves, Andy!"

Saffron sat in stunned silence, the baby entangling its fingers in her hair. The vouchers, which had been purchased before the party, were in Logan and Lyza's names. Whoever had bought them had planned for her to use them without Davis.

Saffron's mouth was dry, though her lap was a bit damp.

"I think the baby needs—" she waved a hand.

Val was approaching, carrying the four-year-old. He set the boy down and took the baby. Saffron turned back to Belle.

"Belle, this is important. Who bought those tickets?"

This was a moment that Saffron was glad Belle was never one to worry much about privacy. The haggard woman looked at the paper again.

"They were bought," she said, "over the phone."

Saffron leaned toward her, trying to communicate a sense of urgency.

"And," Belle said in a leisurely way, "on a credit card. The name's Bison? Carel? Carelli? I can't read my own handwriting."

Byron Carelli.

SAFFRON SAT IN THE CAR, slightly damp and fuming. This whole tragedy was seeming to be less senseless tragedy and more orchestrated crime. Byron Carelli. The father who couldn't let go of his vision for his daughter's life. It was hard for Saffron to understand. Her own father had left when she was a toddler to take care of his brother, her Uncle Beau, back here on the island, and he had never come back. She had never expected to have him at her wedding or living nearby to go get a soda with. She had never had him chase off a suitor or pressure her about who to marry or where to live. The thought of paternal love so strong that it would move Byron to murder was foreign to her.

And now she had no idea how to contact Lyza and let her know that Davis was alive. Logan wasn't answering, and Saffron was desperate to tell him what was happening, too. He was an unwitting pawn in Byron's devious scheme, and the deeper Logan fell back in love with Lyza, the harder the revelation that Davis was alive was going to be.

But there was no forcing them to answer. She was sure Logan was trying to get Lyza's mind off the tragedy. And though she tried to be angry at Lyza for running off so quickly with Logan, thinking of the ruined wedding, the girl's father in jail and the bleak scene in the bed and breakfast with her mother and sister made it hard to judge her too harshly.

The drive to the farmhouse was short, and the morning sun had set the beach afire when Saffron pulled into the driveway. She didn't go into the house. Instead, she went to the egg house and let Curry, Tikka, and their brood out. The farm was safe now, and she wanted their company.

Together, they wandered toward the water, then walked down the long stretch of sand, the chickens stopping to scratch here and there, and Saffron stopping to watch them.

The waves had polished the edge of the sand clean and smooth. Saffron kicked off her shoes and dug her toes into it, feeling the satin press of it against her soles. Her beach was shielded by a coral reef, so the waves were relatively gentle here. Still, the power of the ocean was evident. Its constant tumbling, its flashing crests, its steady rumble, all its details attested to the might of the water teasing around her toes and filling in the depressions she'd made in the sand. And, like obedient soldiers, the grains of sand rearranged themselves in the wake of the waves, wiping clean the sand and erasing all trace that she'd been there.

Erasing. Saffron played with the word on the edge of her mind. For more than a week, since Davis' fall, she'd been trying to erase the thought of it from her mind. And Davis' memories had been erased by that fall. And Byron had tried to erase Davis from Lyza's life.

A little bit of seafoam caught on Saffron's foot. The bursting bubbles looked like cursive letters written in an old-fashioned style.

Curry squawked as a particularly sneaky wave splashed him. He turned with his neck arched and his wings bowed to face the ocean. A low, warning sound: *tuk, tuk, tuk,* came from his chest. Saffron tried not to giggle as he flapped and clawed at the next wave.

Curry had become defensive since the mongoose had

visited. He regularly spooked at anything out of the ordinary, and he rushed at anything he thought might be dangerous.

As Curry continued to battle the advancing waves, Saffron sensed a shadow passing. She looked up to see an owl gliding silently overhead.

Tikka let out an alarmed bawk, and Curry turned from the waves toward his brood just as the shadow crossed them.

In an instant, he was bounding back across the sand to them, raising an alarm and spreading his wings to increase both his speed and his size. The flock bunched together and scurried in front of him, allowing Curry to herd them under a bush near the top of the sandy beach. Tikka and her nearly-grown chicks huddled under it, and Curry followed, sticking his head out and swiveling it so that one eye searched the sky.

The owl seemed oblivious to the chaos it was causing. Amid Curry's warning calls to Saffron, who he felt was also in danger, the owl winged its silent way up the coastline. Just as it grew too small to see comfortably, another shadow passed, setting Curry into new fits of warning.

This was another owl, much bigger. Saffron watched as it traveled behind the other up the coast and out of sight, in the direction of the diving rock.

Before this week, Saffron had seen only one pueo in the entire time she'd lived on the island. The gathering of the birds near the diving rock was undeniable. She thought about Mano and Akoni, about all the other people she'd seen attending to the birds and to the sharks over the last few days. She even thought about the researchers who had come to determine why the animals were gathering. Though Saffron didn't know what, it was obvious that something significant was happening.

Curry must have thought the coast was clear because he squawked an order to his family and they all emerged in a beautiful burst of color from under the bush. To Saffron, they were a kaleidoscope: golds and silvers and reds and blacks, shining pointed feathers that caught the Hawaiian sunlight and flashed back a pattern unique to Saffron's mixed flock.

Curry and his family were headed back to the egg house. Saffron followed them. She watched how Curry darted around them, keeping them bunched together and trying to watch every side of the group for danger. She thought again of Byron.

The picture was becoming more clear now. Byron, who had apparently always wanted a son, had gotten his wish when Lyza began dating Logan. He had planned their whole future, even buying them a condo. He must have still believed there was a chance for them to get back together because he had held onto it. When Lyza had called to say she was getting married, Byron must have panicked. He had planned Davis' death and arranged for Lyza to have somewhere to go with Logan.

But Saffron's perfect memory for color nagged at her. Byron's face, its gray undertones when he denied killing Davis, cast a doubt. She had seen him when he felt guilty about the argument when he felt guilty about trying to get rid of the evidence of his being on the cliff, and she had seen that distinct purple flush that seemed to be a revelation of guilt. He had not had it when he talked about killing Davis.

But even thinking through it seemed ridiculous. Saffron had no idea how she would tell something like that to Bradley. Most people didn't understand the true subtleties of color anyway, and she'd given up trying to explain the different hues and shades she seemed to see. Maybe she was a tetrachromat like Keahi had suggested, but knowing the name probably wouldn't make her hunch any more persuasive. The fact was that there was no solid evidence that Byron had not tried to kill Davis and a lot of solid evidence that he had. Why couldn't she let it go?

Maybe she should explore some ideas for other suspects,

just to further reassure herself that they had the right guy in the cell.

Saffron opened the door to the chickens' pen and let them back in. She closed it tight and saw Curry visibly relax. He must have known the enclosure was secure and his family would be safe there. Saffron thought of Byron, locked in the cell in Maika'i. Did he feel safe there? Did he feel that the sacrifice was worth it? She wondered how he would react when he learned that Davis was still alive.

It would certainly change the charges against Byron. He wouldn't be wanted for murder anymore. But there was still the fall and the intent he would need to answer for.

Saffron shook her head. She would let Bradley deal with that. She walked down the row of pens, checking each one. Her attention was drawn back to Curry and Tikka as they noisily disagreed over something evident only to them. Saffron looked up just in time to see Tikka deliver a firm peck to Curry's floppy comb. He squawked and ran to the other side of the pen.

It was impossible to know precisely what he was thinking, but seeing his mate attack made Saffron suddenly think of Lyza.

Lyza. Saffron had never considered her as a suspect, but what had Myra said when Collins was interviewing her? That she didn't have trouble suspecting Lyza. That her sister had "caused lots of harm already."

At the time, it had seemed like a ridiculous theory. But now that Lyza had, within a week of her fiancé's death, flown off to Kauai with Logan, and had left behind her phone, it seemed more plausible. What if Lyza had fallen back in love with Logan? What if the second thoughts she was having had driven her to try to get rid of Davis before the wedding? And what if she'd run off to Kauai not to escape her grief but her guilt?

Saffron considered this a long moment. Lyza had no alibi and was on the cliff at the time Davis fell. After the accident, Lyza had rushed right into Logan's arms, and he had wasted no time breaking up with Natalie.

And what about Natalie? What if she couldn't stand the thought of Davis with anyone else? The last two weeks, with Evelyn here, had given Saffron a glimpse into the power of jealousy. Natalie could be a suspect, too. The whole thing made Saffron's head hurt.

Chapter Seventeen

The next morning, Saffron drove to the Empress'
house and was ushered in by Rex. He and Carlo
started to unload the presents from Saffron's car while
she went upstairs. Rex had assured her she would find Davis
and his mother there. Natalie was out, they said but should be
back anytime to take a shift watching over Davis.

"He'll let her stay with him?"

"He remembers her," Rex said. "He's said her name a few times. Probably because they were childhood friends."

"How about Lyza?"

Rex shook his head. "Nothing yet. But he does a lot of sleeping. The doctor says he'll probably come to sometime and then we'll see if the amnesia is permanent or temporary."

Saffron left them to their task.

"Don't knock," Rex called after her. "You may wake them."

Saffron nodded. She climbed the stairs and walked down the long, ornate hallway.

It was quiet and dark up here, and the heavy curtains at the end of the hall were drawn. Portraits of past owners of the house seemed to glare down at Saffron as she walked between them. The hallway was quiet except for a soft, insistent trill coming from the Empress' bedroom. Saffron whispered a promise to stop in to visit Princess in her hutch on the way out.

The door to Davis' room was nine feet tall, with white lacquered cherubs carved into it, flying with gilded banners streaming behind them. Saffron pushed it open and slipped into the room.

The room was dim, brightened only by ribbons of light around the edges of the windows. The ornate furniture contrasted strangely with Davis' memorabilia: a pennant from his high school, a poster of his favorite band, an oversized stuffed dog won at a long-ago carnival. There was a glass plaque proclaiming him the 2nd place winner of something and a trophy with a runner atop it. Stuck to the walls without the frivolity of frames were snapshots of camping, surfing, and cookouts with his friends.

In the center of the room was an enormous gilded bed. Saffron wondered if he had slept in it as a small child, and if so, if his mother had ever lost him in its vast hills of pillows.

Even the Empress, with her impressive size, was dwarfed by it. This was the only time Saffron had ever seen her out of her wheelchair, and without it, the powerful woman seemed vulnerable and human. She sat on the bed, her back propped against the headboard and her legs stretched out in front of her. Davis' head rested on her lap, his eyes closed.

The Empress held Davis with all the tenderness of Michaelangelo's Pieta. Her eyelids drooped, and her hand brushed his forehead as she dozed. Saffron wondered if she'd gotten any sleep at all.

The Empress opened her eyes and focused on Saffron. She smiled gently and waved Saffron over to her.

"He's still so fragile," she said in a whisper. Saffron could see the delicacy with which the Empress ran her fingers across his cheeks. It reminded her of the way Tikka had preened her chicks when they were small.

"How are you holding up?" Saffron asked.

"My boy is alive," the Empress said. "I could fly." She reached for Saffron with her free hand, and Saffron stepped closer.

"Tell me about finding him," the Empress said. "Tell me about Oke."

Saffron had been wanting to tell the Empress the story. She related it as best she could. "From what Oke says, it was the 'aumakua that saved him."

The Empress' eyes shone a rich shell-brown in the dim light. "I knew they would protect him. I knew, when he went into the Navy, when he wrote home about crossing the ocean, that even though I could not be with him, he wasn't alone. Our ancestors would watch over him, and the 'aumakua would be there to help him."

Saffron nodded. "It's nothing short of a miracle."

"He is special. Akoni says he is bad luck, but I know better. I know this boy is good luck. I could have lost my legs and my husband and spent my life alone, but instead, I gained this boy. He got me through so many tough times. And when he should have died before, Mano saved him. And now, the manōs have saved him. He is lucky, and I am lucky to have him."

Saffron nodded. She couldn't argue with that, and she admired the Empress' view of it. Quietly, she told the Empress about Akoni's visit yesterday, about how he thought he'd been wrong, how he thought Davis was blessed.

The Empress' grip on her arm tightened, "Saffron! Where is Lyza? She's Davis' sweetheart. She must come to see him. I think that will be what brings him back completely."

Saffron's voice died in her throat. She couldn't tell the Empress that Lyza had gone to Kauai with another man. For all the Empress' optimism, she had endured a harrowing two weeks, and Saffron didn't want to burden her with that news just yet. "I'll—" she stuttered, "I'll try to find her."

The Empress looked at Saffron skeptically. "Find her?"

"Tell her," Saffron corrected. "I'll try to tell her. I just didn't know if you wanted everyone to know."

"Natalie is here," the Empress said. Her voice was flat and devoid of enthusiasm. "She has been since yesterday."

"Do you not want her here?"

The Empress closed her eyes and heaved a deep sigh. "Oh, Child, things are complicated. I do want her here. She's been a big help, bringing me things and sitting with him for a few minutes here and there. But Davis—I have never seen him like he was with Lyza. She is his true love, and it's she who should be here now. The longer Natalie stays, the less sure I am that Davis will come fully back." She shook her head, "He may get stuck at seven, with nothing to remind him of the rest of the life he has lived. What if he never remembers Lyza? What if he never gets to have that look of love and joy in his eyes again?"

Saffron took a deep breath. The air in the room was sweet

and heavy, a product of the lowering skies outside. She didn't know what to say to the Empress.

The door opened, and Natalie came in, her steps measured and her jaw set. She didn't even acknowledge Saffron. Instead, she stepped close to the bed and looked directly at the Empress.

"Rex and Carlo are ready to take you in for some rest," she said softly. "I'll stay with him."

The Empress looked as if she might protest, but instead, she made a sound of agreement. Saffron stepped back and watched as Natalie went to the other side of the bed and climbed on. Rex and Carlo entered, ready to help. They leaned over, sliding Davis off his mother and onto the center of the bed, where Natalie sat beside him and took his hand. Then the Empress' helpers expertly maneuvered her into her chair.

Natalie brushed her fingers across Davis' chest, smoothing the fabric of his pajamas.

"He looks different out of uniform," she said. "More like the old days."

The Empress' gaze lingered on her son. "He does look so young." Rex turned her chair and wheeled her out the gilded door.

Natalie gazed down at Davis.

Saffron didn't know exactly what to say to Natalie. It was obvious that the girl was still in love with Davis, and with Lyza coming back in a few days, there was no telling what fresh pain lay in wait for Natalie.

"I notice she hasn't shown up," Natalie said, and Saffron heard a knife's edge in the word "she."

"Lyza?"

"Somewhere with Logan, no doubt?" This time the sharpness was in the word "Logan."

Saffron didn't speak. There was no hiding the truth from Natalie. And having this conversation across the inert body of the wounded sailor made it impossible to tell her where Lyza was, anyway. There was no way to share that information without Lyza coming off as harsh and cold.

"You think you're close with the Empress?" Natalie said, her short hair flipping as she looked up to find Saffron's eyes in the dim light.

Saffron stuttered, "I'm not sure we're close. But we're friends."

"Trust me. You're close. She had the lawyer in here this morning. You're in the will now."

The news shook Saffron. She didn't want to be in anybody's will. That seemed like it would complicate what was so far a delightfully casual friendship.

"You and the chicken," Natalie sneered.

Saffron understood that Natalie had undergone a terrible two weeks, as well. She realized that loving Davis and losing him in so many ways was unbearable. She knew that Collins' unwanted attention and the power he had over Natalie on the ship was uncomfortable. She even understood that Natalie was hurting from her recent breakup with Logan. But she didn't understand the bitterness in Natalie's voice right now.

"I'm sorry for what you've been through," Saffron said.

"What I've been through? You don't know anything about that." Natalie said. She looked down at Davis, beside her, resting on a mountain of pillows.

"Davis is really the only one who knows about that," she said. "And this morning he said my name. *My name.* Not *Lyza*, not *shipmate*, like he usually calls me now. He said my name." The girl's voice trailed off.

Saffron fought the urge to throw open the drapes and flood the room with light. Natalie's melancholy had filled the place in the same way that the Empress' optimism had, only that had been invigorating and this was suffocating.

"I have to go back to the ship in two days," Natalie said,

tracing a finger through Davis' short black hair. "And Davis is being discharged. There's a good chance that once Lyza comes back, I'll never even see him again."

Saffron saw in Natalie's face the same look she'd seen that night on the cliff—an empty resignation.

Saffron's phone chimed, and she tore her eyes away from the grieving girl to glance at it. It was a message from Logan: "Saffron, what's up? I see that you sent me some messages, but they're not downloading, so I don't know what they say."

Saffron laid the phone against her leg to cut the brightness of the screen. "I'm sorry," she managed, "I have to make a call."

The words hung weakly in the air as she slipped out, and she wished she'd had something better to say, but there was no help for Natalie's situation, and anything Saffron could think to say just made that more obvious.

She stepped into the hall and tried to call Logan, but he didn't answer, and there was no more room in his voicemail. She tried messaging him: *Come back. Davis is alive.*

But the "sending" wheel started spinning and didn't stop as it usually did. A warning popped up: *Message Failed.* She wondered if the heavy plaster of the hallway was interfering. She'd go outside and see if it would send there.

But on her way, she heard the insistent sound of Princess' trills and the Empress calling softly from her room.

"Princess wants you to say hello before you leave!"

Saffron stuck her head into the big bedroom and saw the empress propped on her pillows.

"You're supposed to be resting," she chided.

"I would be, except that I need Princess beside me so I can go to sleep. Would you bring her to me?" The Empress made a scooping motion with her hand toward the hutch.

Saffron crossed the room and peered at the silkie. The white bird stuck her beak through the bars of her hutch. Her call was unlike the calls of Saffron's hens. Princess' voice was a constant buzzing hum that barely ceased for the hen to take a breath.

"I think she wants you to know she's laid an egg!" the Empress said, with obvious pride. "Look in her nest box."

Saffron raised the hinged lid to check Princess' nest. Every few days Princess laid a perfect, oval-shaped mini-egg. This was one of the lucky days. On the deep blue satin pillow was a gleaming cream egg. Seeing it, Saffron's perfect memory for color made other things flash through her mind: the bubbles from the sea foam yesterday were the same color as this egg. It was also the same color as the icing on the cake she'd ordered for Davis and Lyza's wedding. It was the same color as the ginger flowers in the leis. And it was exactly the color of the faded letters on the neckerchief in the bag Doctor Weiss was holding yesterday. Saffron remembered how the waves had licked up and erased the seafoam bubbles from her toes. Saffron stared at the egg and thought of erasing. The faded letters on the neckerchief. They'd been nearly erased by blood and salt water. But she strained to remember every detail she'd glimpsed through the clear evidence bag. She remembered a few numbers and an 'N' and an 'L.'

That was what was off. There was no 'N' and no 'L' in Davis' Howard's name. Why would those letters be on his neckerchief? Maybe Dr. Weiss had been right. Maybe the items Davis had with him could tell them something about what had happened on that cliff.

Saffron held the thought close in her mind as she deposited Princess on the chicken pillow next to the Empress.

"I need to go," she said, "and you need to rest."

"All right," the Empress conceded, "but please open my curtains before you go. I want to watch the rain."

"Rain?" Saffron raised her eyebrows. It had been a clear morning. But when she opened the drapes, she saw that the

Empress was right. A soft pattering sounded on the window-panes as dozens of small drops showered down.

Saffron smiled and slipped out into the hall, down the stairs, and into the rain. As she climbed into her car, her phone chimed again.

It was a surprise to see that the screen was lit up with a yellow box instead of a message. The box read: "Severe Storm Warning this area beginning 6 am tomorrow. Check local media. Stay indoors. Avoid low areas."

Saffron scanned the sky. The raindrops falling seemed fairly unremarkable. The pearl gray cloud cover looked light and calm. She tried to send her message to Logan again, but again, the message failed. Saffron slid the phone into the car's console. She'd seen several storms since she came to live on the island, and so far this one didn't seem too worrisome.

The police station looked lonesome when she pulled up in front of it. Only Bradley's police cruiser sat in the parking lot. Saffron parked next to it. Turning off the car, she sat for a moment, thinking. She glanced down at the front passenger's seat and saw that the Empress' helpers had missed one gift: the box with the key inside. She'd have to get it to Davis or Lyza at her first opportunity. She slid it into a compartment in the center console with her phone and went inside.

Bradley was scratching his signature on a form. A stack of papers as high as his coffee cup sat next to him. He looked up as Saffron walked in.

"That looks like a lot of paperwork," Saffron said lightly.

"Always. You know, when I first wanted to be a cop, I thought it would be all car chases and shootouts." He snorted and waved a hand at the stack of forms. "It's not."

"You have caught a few bad guys, too, though," Saffron reminded him.

"Well, that's true. Although some of them," Bradley jerked

a thumb at the door that led back to the cells, "are kind of slippery."

"Is he still here?" Saffron asked.

"For now. Davis being alive really puts a crimp in this murder investigation." Saffron was sure Bradley didn't know how cynical that sounded. She sat in a chair across from him.

"Listen," she said, "I might have some ideas that make the investigation easier."

"Really?"

"Maybe. Could I see the evidence bag?"

Bradley looked at her for a long moment, and she tried to think of a good reason he should show her restricted access evidence. But Bradley's distinguishing characteristic was his lack of protocol and cavalier attitude about his job. For once, that worked in Saffron's favor. He stood and went through a door to the left of his desk. Saffron made a mental note that it must be the evidence room.

Bradley emerged with a plastic bag which he dumped on a table under the front window before sitting back down to his paperwork with a heavy sigh. "Got that back from the lab pretty fast. Nothing interesting about it. But take a look. Maybe you'll see something they missed. Let me know if you have any ideas," he said, handing her a pair of thin plastic gloves.

Saffron put the gloves on and unsealed the bag. In it were Davis' jumper, one black shoe, the football, and the neckerchief. Only this neckerchief was still crisp, bloodstained, but not faded. Carefully, she unrolled it and looked at the name printed across the middle: Howard, D., followed by a string of numbers.

She looked in the bag again. "Where are the strips that were on Davis' head?"

"From the doc? I sent those in way later. They haven't come back yet."

Saffron looked at the neckerchief again. This was part of Davis' uniform. She read the thick black lettering on the bag: *Recovered at the scene*. This neckerchief had come from the cliff, where Davis had fallen. But there was another neckerchief—the one that had been wrapped around his head wound. And two of the creamy letters marked on it were an n and an l. Saffron was willing to bet that the name on it was Natalie's.

"When will that evidence be back?" she asked Bradley.

"Probably tomorrow. Doesn't take too long."

"There's nothing here, but will you let me know when that comes back? I'd like to take a look at it."

"Sure thing." Bradley didn't look up. The rain was falling harder now, and the sky outside was the color of an old bruise. Saffron needed to get home and check on her chickens. She thanked the officer and ducked out into the storm.

***

SAFFRON WAS SURPRISED to see a rental car in her driveway. She was even more surprised to see Evelyn sitting in it. The lithe woman didn't wait for an invitation, just watched Saffron go up to unlock the door and then dashed through the rain and pushed inside the house with her as Saffron opened the door.

They both burst into the living room at the same time, and Saffron was annoyed to see that Evelyn was barely even wet, while she, by contrast, was dripping onto the rug.

"Sorry to barge in," Evelyn said. There was no apology in her voice.

Saffron had lived on the island long enough to know a thing or two about hospitality. She forced a smile. "No worries. How can I help you?"

Evelyn looked pointedly at the futon in the living room. "Can we talk?" she asked.

Saffron resigned herself. This wouldn't be a short visit. She was also intrigued, though.

"Can I get you a soda?" she asked, "Or some tea?"

"Coffee?" Evelyn demanded.

"Sorry," Saffron shrugged. "The smell of it gives me a headache."

"And you don't have a beer in here," It was a statement.

"Soda?" Saffron offered, making her voice cheery, "tea?"

"Bottled water is fine," Evelyn made no mention of the fact that Saffron hadn't offered bottled water.

She played a good hostess and fetched it anyway.

As much as she hated to admit it, Saffron could see why Evelyn was a good nurse. The woman was decisive, efficient. She didn't make excuses and didn't seem to accept them. They were good qualities . . . in moderation. Being able to see some of Evelyn's strengths seemed like progress to Saffron.

Evelyn cut right to the chase when Saffron handed her the bottle of water and sat awkwardly trying to face her on the other end of the futon.

"I'm here because you're holding Keahi back and I don't think you know what that's going to cost him."

Saffron opened her mouth as the words sank in. Of course, it was about Keahi. Why else would Evelyn be here? "Holding him back?" Saffron managed.

"Right," Evelyn's words were clipped, as if giving orders to a patient, "you need to let him go back to Boston, where he belongs. He has a promising career in front of him. The administrators at the hospital are prepared to offer him a lot of money to come back."

Saffron absorbed those words. "I think you're giving me too much credit here. Keahi and I are barely dating. He hasn't made any commitments to me."

Evelyn lost her cool momentarily. She stood up and paced around the room, throwing an arm wide as she did so, "It's not just you! It's this whole place, this whole island culture! He thinks he's so free and easy here, but he's just wasting his potential." She spat the last few words toward Saffron, and they sounded like she'd said them before.

"What does Keahi say?"

"He says he's happy, but I know him. I know what he can do, and it's just not possible that he's really happy with this lifestyle."

Saffron was honest, "I can't speak to that," she said, "I'm still getting to know him. But I do know that he's incredibly sincere, and if he wasn't happy, I don't think he would say he was."

"He can't stay here," Evelyn growled, plunking her water bottle down so hard on the side table that a small eruption shot out the top and splashed on the tabletop. "It's ridiculous." She took two steps toward Saffron. Saffron stood up to meet the nurse's gaze. Evelyn went on. "You know you have a part in keeping him here. He's told me so, and if he's as sincere as you say he is, then he's told you so, too."

Saffron thought back to the discussion she and Keahi had a few days ago, to the things he'd said about her. She did have some part in keeping Keahi here. She let her eyes flick away from Evelyn's just for a minute.

Evelyn pounced. "See? See? You do know."

"What do you want me to do?" Her eyes settled on Evelyn's manicured nails, poised in the air, pointing at Saffron. They were painted a deep red with a purple undertone. Saffron's color memory dredged up plums she'd eaten and a pair of sneakers she'd worn when she was eight.

"Talk to him about his potential. About his opportunities on the mainland. Talk to him about going back to the operating room. If you really care about him, you won't be so selfish as to let him ignore all that."

Saffron's heart was pounding. The color of Evelyn's nails

was also the color of Saffron's father's shirt in her single memory of him. Deep red, his smile above the crisp collar. She wished she had a good answer to give the nurse, wished she could refute what she was saying. But the memory of her father stopped her. There was a part of her that remembered how her father had walked away from his life to come back here, and she wished someone had told him that what he was leaving behind was too good to ignore. She didn't say anything.

Evelyn seemed to sense that she had made her point. "I didn't come out here to cause problems. I just think you could make a difference. Keahi is at a critical point, and what he decides now could affect the rest of his life." Evelyn thanked her for the water, and her voice rang hollow in Saffron's ears.

Saffron stumbled through a goodbye, and Evelyn showed herself out into the rain.

Sinking onto the couch, Saffron felt adrift, as if she were losing her anchor already.

Chapter Eighteen

The rain was falling harder the next day. Saffron slogged through rivulets down to the egg house.

She noticed with dismay that only a few grains rattled down the pipes when she turned the crank on the big feed hopper that supplied the pens with feed. She pulled her raincoat over her head and spent the next hour making trips to the storage shed to get bags of grain. She piled them all in the work area, then went back to close up the shed.

Filling the hopper took another half hour. Saffron had to open each bag, set it on the lift, then crank the lift up until the bag poured into the hopper.

Her arms were aching when she finished. She leaned against the counter as she cranked the conveyor belt that carried all the eggs to her from the nest boxes. The eggs were muddy from the hens' foraging into the outdoor pens. She thought with envy of Princess and the pristine eggs she left on her satin pillow.

The egg washer ran on water power, and at the end of it was a buffing track that dried the eggs as they came out. Saffron spent a long time feeding the muddy eggs in the machine and placing the clean, dried eggs in cartons as they came out of the buffing track. She took some pride in their gleaming browns, greens, and blues.

Saffron's sensitivity to color meant that she could see more variation in the eggs than most people. Not that the knowledge had ever made much difference. All the eggs tasted the same, after all.

Just as she placed the last egg in the carton and switched off the egg washer, the door to the egg house burst open.

"Saffron!" Keahi called, and the fear in his voice made her spin to face him. She walked forward with a question in her eyes.

"What are you doing here?" she asked.

"Where's your phone? I've been trying to call you!" Keahi pulled her into his arms and hugged her tight. His jacket was slick with rain. There was panic in his embrace.

She felt her pockets. Her phone was gone. "It must have slipped out while I was hauling the feed up," she said. "Keahi, what's wrong?"

"There's a storm coming. There have been all kinds of cell phone alerts." He took her hand. Saffron had never seen him this worried.

"I know there's a storm coming," Saffron pulled him along out the back door of the egg house. Her phone must have fallen along the path somewhere as she went to the shed. The wind lashed them as they pushed through the bushes along the path. Saffron spotted her phone ahead, lying near the shed. The screen was alight with messages—probably from him. Snatching it, she waved a hand toward the lowering clouds, the whipping palms. "I got the alert yesterday, but I didn't think it would be this bad," her voice strained to rise above the sound of the thrashing palms and the howling wind.

"But the weather service updated it. They say it's going to

be bad," Keahi said. "They're predicting awful flooding and winds over a hundred miles an hour."

Saffron turned back toward her chickens. "I have to close up the egg house," she said, starting back up the path. Keahi took her hand.

"They said to get to high ground. We're going to the cliff-house. I came to get you. I don't think your car will make it. There's already flooding along the highway."

Saffron glanced past the egg house and saw his big SUV. She was comforted by its bulk and height. She tried not to be annoyed that Evelyn was sitting in the front seat.

"Okay, but I have to close them up first."

Keahi nodded, though his shoulders were tense as a ukulele string. "I'll help you."

Together, they made their way through the wind back into the egg house. The gusts snatched the big door from Saffron's hands and slammed it back against the wall. Keahi ushered her inside, then wrenched the door closed behind them. The airy henhouse was now a wailing wind tunnel. The chickens huddled next to their feeders, as far from the doors that led to the outside runs as they could get. The tall grass in the runs waved and arched in the wind. Saffron went down the rows, counting birds and peering out into the runs to make sure no chickens were stuck outside before she closed each door. Keahi worked on the other side.

Coming back down the aisle, Saffron reached for a lever she had never used before. High up on the outside of the pen, it controlled the shutters on the outside of the pens' windows. She pulled it down, and the shutters snapped closed. Their heavy clasps made a sharp click as they engaged. Saffron felt the wind shut off immediately.

Moving quickly, she pulled the lever on each pen, barricading every window.

The chickens settled more and more as each window

closed. When all were snapped shut, the howling wind outside had been reduced to a high whine through the cracks in the shutters.

Instead of huddling, the chickens moved onto their roosts, looking like rows of fluffy cupcakes. They must have known there was danger because it was rare for them to roost this early in the morning. She was relieved that the roosts were graduated from low on the ground to up above head-height. If there was flooding, the hens could get to high perches for safety.

Keahi was pulling the lever that filled their feeders from the big hopper at the front of the egg house, and feed rushed down the pipes into each feeder. Saffron was glad she'd spent the time filling it.

He called her name, and she looked up to see him holding her phone aloft. "Found it again," he said. Saffron sighed. It must have fallen out again. This time, Keahi slipped it into his own pocket as Saffron double-checked the automatic watering system.

By the time she met Keahi at the front of the egg house, she was relatively sure the chickens would ride out the storm safely in their cozy coop. She tried not to think what would happen if the roof came off or the farm flooded higher than their highest roosts.

"Will they be okay?" she asked.

"I think so," he said, but she saw anxiety in his gaze. He couldn't promise her that they would be, and she wouldn't ask him for that promise.

They pushed back out into the storm. In addition to the wind, sheets of rain had begun to fall. Hawaiian rain was, so often, like a light mist, but this was different. It was torrential, soaking. It hurt when it hit Saffron's cheeks and arms.

They ran through it to the house, which they locked down as well as they could. The shutters on it were much more unwieldy, and it took them several minutes to circumnavigate the house and close all the shutters against the coming storm. She grabbed a bag from inside and stuffed a few changes of clothes, her toothbrush, and her makeup bag into it. She had no idea how long they'd be staying at the cliffhouse, and the thought scared her.

She dashed to her car and locked it. Seeing the gold box, she snatched it in hopes that she could return it to Lyza when she finally saw the bride. Keahi said lots of people were heading to the cliff house.

When they finally scrambled into the SUV, they were both drenched and breathing hard. Saffron couldn't help but resent Evelyn's still-perfect updo and pristine makeup slightly. She looked as if she were on the cover of some adventure magazine, with the bending palms and the slick sheen of rain behind her out the window. Saffron pushed a wet strand of hair out of her own face and buckled her seatbelt as the SUV lurched into a u-turn and headed for the highway.

SAFFRON WAS STILL wet when she walked into the cliffhouse. The scene was eerily similar to the night of the hen party nearly two weeks before. Saffron supposed it was good that she hadn't taken down the chairs, because half the town was there.

Mano was coordinating the influx of people. He waved Saffron, Keahi, and Evelyn in and directed them to the great-room. Rex and Carlo followed, bringing the Empress through the big front door in her wheelchair. Saffron stood transfixed as Davis and Natalie came in after them. Davis was steady on his feet, his eyes were bright, and his arm was around Natalie. She looked blissful.

"You'll take one of the first-floor bedrooms," Mano said to

the Empress with his trademark good humor, "unless you've brought your chair lift."

The Empress waved off his joke, and Rex disappeared with her bag into one of the bedrooms. Behind her, Fumi from the kitchen appliance store and Bernadette from the Oceanside cafe made their way in. They were laden with boxes and bags of food.

"We brought supplies," Bernadette announced. She was not small, and neither was her voice, "there's more in the truck!"

Behind her, the new owners of the Paradise Market were hauling in supplies, too. Bags of produce and meat and bread. At least they'd have enough groceries to weather the storm, Saffron thought.

Behind them, a pack of children began to pour into the cliffhouse. The Tuckers had arrived. Belle stepped through the door and handed Saffron a baby on her way past. The little girl tucked her head under Saffron's chin.

Evelyn sniffed. Saffron glanced at her.

"You know her?" Evelyn asked.

"Sure," Saffron responded. She found she was having a hard time looking Evelyn in the eye after their discussion last night. "Everyone knows everyone in Maika'i."

"Hmmm," the sound was derisive, and Saffron suddenly felt defensive about the Tucker family.

"They're good people," she said, "and their kids like me." She patted the baby's hair.

"What's not to like?" Keahi asked, squeezing Saffron's arm.

Evelyn didn't hide her disgust. "Doc, I'm going to stake a claim on a decent bedroom."

"No bedrooms," Mano said lightly. He'd obviously been listening. "Those are for the old folks and the babies and the sick folks. Everyone else bunks together," he held up a warning finger, "Girls in the media room, boys in the game room."

The group of researchers who had been in Maika'i studying the gathering sharks and owls stumbled through the front door, laden with bags of equipment.

"I'm glad you found your way here," Mano said. "Let's put your instruments in the garage. Have to have all the room in the house for the people."

They nodded. Saffron saw how they, like everyone else, looked shocked and drenched. The storm had come up so fast.

A palm frond smacked through the open front door, slapping against the legs of the volunteers carrying in groceries. It was driven by the wind and left a wet mess on the floor. Saffron peered out into the driving rain. The baby, startled, began to cry.

Val Tucker appeared at Saffron's shoulder and took the little girl. As he turned to walk away, Saffron stopped him.

"Val," she said, "Any word from the bride that went to Kauai? Lyza? Or Logan? He went with her," she explained.

Val nodded. "Scary, but they're out in this. Their flight was due back a while ago. As fast as this storm came up, they were probably in the air before the planes were grounded. They've probably been flying right through it," he shook his head, "Not a trip I'd like to take."

Saffron wondered if they'd know where to come. She still had Lyza's phone, and she couldn't get a message through to Logan. She glanced toward the greatroom, where Davis stood with his arm still around Natalie, and wished Lyza back safe and soon.

"You okay?" Keahi's voice was low. He had leaned down and put his mouth close to her ear. She looked up at him.

Was she okay? She didn't know. Everything was in chaos, and Saffron didn't like chaos. Nobody was where they were supposed to be, the balmy island weather had turned into a howling nightmare, and she couldn't seem to remove the wedge that Evelyn had been driving between her and Keahi since the nurse arrived.

"Keahi," she blurted, "have you really thought about going back to Boston? Really considered it?"

His amber eyes widened in surprise, then narrowed as his brows drew together. "No, I haven't. Not really. I told you, I'm happy here. I'm not interested in Evelyn."

Saffron tried to explain. "I know. But this isn't really about her. It's about you. She says that the hospital would have you back, that you could be a surgeon again. Do you not want that?"

Saffron waited for him to confirm that, for him to say he didn't want it and for the future to be certain again. She waited, but he didn't speak. There was turmoil in his eyes.

"You do want that," it was, she could see, as much a revelation to him as it was to her. As always, when Keahi didn't know what to say, he stayed quiet.

The big wooden door slammed behind them, sending a reverberation throughout the whole house. The wind had picked up.

Saffron looked at Keahi, her words failing.

"It's not about Evelyn," Keahi said, and Saffron heard the truth of it. She also heard what he was not saying: *It's not about her, but I do want to go.*

Saffron searched his face. She couldn't tell him not to go, couldn't deny him the chance to do what he had trained for. She didn't want to be the reason he gave it up. But she had always been honest with him. "I don't want you to leave," she said.

A heavy thud rang through the house, making Saffron jump. She and Keahi rushed to the front window. A big palm had fallen at the edge of the lawn. Its broad leaves tossed in the wind, which stripped them off one by one and sent them tumbling over the edge of the cliff.

Keahi slipped an arm around her. "I'm not going anywhere right now," he said, and Saffron took comfort in his strength.

EVEN THOUGH ONLY girls were bunking in the media room, everyone gathered in there as reports from across the island flashed on the big TV that took up one whole wall.

The storm was worsening. According to the news, it was the fastest-moving storm in the island's history. Within hours of Saffron's arrival at the cliffhouse, it had been upgraded to a hurricane, and it was headed directly for Maika'i.

Saffron's instinct was to flee. But there was nowhere to go. Airports were closed. Highways were flooded. Saffron wondered briefly where Lyza and Logan were and if they were safe.

The cliffhouse was full of people, and though they were subdued—even the children seemed quieter and more still than usual—there was a palpable tension throughout the house.

Saffron left Keahi watching the news and slipped out of the media room for some air. Waiting for the storm to arrive was exhausting.

The door burst open. Inside came a soaking pair—Bradley and his prisoner, Byron. Bradley struggled with a big duffel bag in one hand and Byron's arm in the other. Byron's hands were handcuffed together in front of him. Saffron rushed to help them close the door.

"Whew," Bradley breathed. "This is some storm."

"It's a hurricane," Saffron said, "we just heard that they upgraded it."

Bradley grunted. He reached for his keys and took the handcuffs off Byron. "You might as well go see your wife," he said, "I don't worry about you making a break for it with that storm outside." Saffron pointed Byron into the media room.

"You got a place I could change?" Bradley asked, hefting the duffel aloft.

"Sure. Any bathroom. Just lock it. There are a lot of people here."

As he went down the hall, Bradley called back, "Hey, I got that evidence back from the lab just now. It's in the car."

Saffron's pulse quickened, "What did the report say?"

"Didn't read it yet. I came straight here. You can check it out, though, car's unlocked. I didn't have an extra hand to lock it, and nobody's going to be bothering it right now, anyway."

Saffron turned to the door. Just as she put her hand on the knob, though, a terrible racket started up. She peered out the window beside the door and saw the heavy wooden furniture from the lanai lifted and slammed against the house, the lanai, and across the lawn. A bench skidded along the lanai in the wind as if it weighed no more than a palm frond.

This was not the time to venture outside.

Several people poured out of the media room to catch a glimpse of the fleeing furniture.

Bernadette called from the kitchen. "Everybody come eat!"

She had brought a veritable picnic of plate lunches, and she scooped them deftly onto plates: two scoops of rice, a fan of breaded chicken with a splash of sweet-savory sauce, and a scoop of the Oceanside Cafe's famous mac salad lent a distinctive flair with shredded carrots and diced scallops.

Everyone crowded into the kitchen, taking plates in a more-or-less organized way. Saffron, distracted by the blaring news from the media room, slipped in to turn it off while people ate. They could see the storm. They could hear the wind howling outside the door. They didn't need to listen to the news droning on about it the entire day.

No one but Saffron was left in the media room. She switched off the TV. The room quieted but did not fall silent.

She could hear a soft buzzing over the speakers. They must, she thought, still be on.

Saffron stepped over the sleeping bags, duffels, and backpacks to get to the audio cabinet. Peering inside, she saw that it wasn't just the sound system she was hearing. It was the recording of the karaoke session from the night of the party.

Saffron was about to switch it off when she heard the soft murmur of voices. Leaning toward the nearest speaker, she reached over and cranked the volume. Even still, she had to strain to hear. Someone was speaking.

"What did you do?" it was a man's voice.

"Just what I said I would."

"No, Nat. You can't."

"I already did," Saffron felt cold. She knew what this was. Natalie and Logan had been in this room the night of the accident. She'd seen them embracing and assumed they'd been in there a while. But what if Natalie had not been in with him the whole time? The microphone had apparently been left on, and they'd had no idea that their conversation was being preserved.

"Oh, no, Natalie. No." Logan's voice was heavy.

"I had to do something. I couldn't just let him marry her. I still love him, Logan."

"Then how could you do this?"

"Because I won't lose him to her." There was a sob in Natalie's voice, barely audible in the soft recording.

The next sound was a far-away screaming. Saffron recognized it as the Lyza's voice the moment she came in to say that her fiancé had fallen.

Saffron switched off the recording.

Natalie. She had confessed to doing something horrible. Saffron guessed that was pushing him over the cliff. And Natalie was with Davis right now. Would she still try to hurt him? Saffron made her way back through the media room and down the hall. As she neared the wide staircase in the entryway, the big door burst open. The howling wind screamed through the room, and cold rain splashed across Saffron's arms and face.

Lyza and Logan were blown in with the rain.

Saffron stood and stared at them. Logan wrestled the door closed behind him, then pulled Lyza close to him.

"You okay?"

She nodded. There was still a vacant, aching expression etched across Lyza's face.

"We're safe now," he said.

Just then, Davis and Natalie strode into the entry, having finished their plate lunches in the greatroom. They stopped short, and Natalie gasped as she saw Logan and Lyza. She stepped protectively in front of Davis.

But it was no use. They had seen each other.

Lyza let out a cry of surprise, and Davis took two hesitant steps toward her. His brows were knit together, his lips parted. There was a cautious light in his eyes.

He made a soft sound: "Llll?" It was almost a question.

The shell of grief fell away from Lyza, and she broke free of Logan and ran across the hall to Davis, pulling him into her arms.

"Ly-" he began again, "Lyza?"

It was as if the word were magic, or maybe, Saffron thought, the magic was in Lyza's touch. Either way, Saffron saw Davis awaken. Whatever had stolen his memories of his bride disappeared. He said her name twice more, burying his bandaged head in Lyza's shoulder.

Saffron looked at Natalie. Her shoulders were rigid, her eyes wide. Was it fear or sorrow Saffron was seeing? As always, it was hard to tell with Natalie. But Saffron saw, for the first time, the depth of emotion in the girl. The recording flashed in her mind, and she stepped forward to protect the reunited couple from whatever Natalie was capable of.

But there was no time. Natalie cried out, her uncrackable facade falling away.

"No!"

Davis looked at her in alarm, a hint of the fog he'd been living in returned.

"Do you even know where she's been?" Natalie cried. "Do you even care?"

Davis held out a hand to her as if to offer some comfort, even in his confusion.

Natalie scoffed, "She's been off on *your* honeymoon with *your best friend*," Natalie waved an erratic hand at Logan.

Davis turned his gaze to Lyza, "What?" he asked for clarification.

Lyza, still enraptured by discovering him alive, held him tighter. "Logan and I went to Kauai," she said, "just as friends. Just to get away. I needed a distraction. Davis, I thought I'd lost you."

Saffron stole a look at Logan. His usually smiling face was stony. He seemed embarrassed, but Saffron couldn't tell whether it was because of Natalie's behavior or because of where he'd been. He made no attempt to explain.

"You can't seriously expect Davis to fall right back into your arms," Natalie cried, moving forward. Saffron registered a threat just as the girl struck out at Lyza.

Logan must have seen it sooner. He moved like lightning to intercept Natalie, pulling her back with a firm grip and wrapping his arms around her.

"Come on," he said, guiding her down the hall, "Come with me a minute and cool down."

Saffron was grateful for his quick action.

"What happened out there?" Lyza asked. "Are you all right?"

Davis held her close. "I am now." He stepped back, and Lyza raised tentative fingertips to his forehead.

"What happened that night?" Lyza asked.

"I don't remember," he said. "Just that I was out gathering things up. I heard Natalie calling me. I tried to find her, but it was really dark."

"Didn't you realize you might fall?"

Davis seemed to think for a long moment. "It didn't occur to me, no. I used the glowsticks I was carrying to mark where I'd been. I dropped them as I looked different places for her. So I'd know where I'd been." That explained why they'd been scattered, Saffron thought. "I remember being worried about her—that she'd fall. I was looking for her." Davis put a hand to his head. "It gets fuzzy after that."

"You don't remember the fall?" Lyza asked.

He shook his head. "Nothing."

Chapter Nineteen

So many intertwined relationships: Davis loved Lyza and Natalie loved Davis and Logan loved Lyza. And that didn't even take into account the situation Saffron found herself in with Keahi and Evelyn. Saffron wished there was a better way to navigate the stormy seas of human relationships—a love compass that would point each person in the right direction. Of course, it would need a lot of needles. The thought brought an image to Saffron's mind: a compass with many needles. Where had Saffron seen that before?

She knew. It was one of the sketches that Marks had made. Wanting to see it again, Saffron left Lyza and Davis in the entry and slipped into the greatroom. She went over by the big wall of windows as she pulled up the photo of the sketches on her phone.

Saffron scanned the sketches: Byron's harpoon-a symbol of his protection for his daughter. Myra's sea monster—a symbol of her jealousy for her sister. Keahi's anchor-a symbol of his steadiness and dependability.

Next, to Davis' name, there was a swallow with arched wings and a dagger through it—symbolic, Marks had said, of a fallen shipmate. She wondered briefly if there was a symbol for someone who'd come back from the dead.

Halfway down the page, Saffron found what she was looking for—the compass. It was next to Logan's name. Saffron wondered about that. What could the symbolism be?

Saffron tapped into her phone's contacts and called Marks.

"Hello?" The yeoman sounded strained.

"Seth? This is Saffron."

"Hi," he said, and Saffron heard a clatter behind him, "what's up? We're in the middle of a hurricane here."

"Us too," Saffron said, though she realized she was much more steady in the cliffhouse than he probably was on his ship.

"How can I help?" Marks was polite but impatient.

"One more question about your sketches. Logan Prentice's name has a compass next to it. What does that mean?"

Marks laughed, "Man, you're obsessed with those drawings. Nothing. It's just an old superstition that getting a compass tattoo will ensure you can always find your way home. I just thought of that one since Prentice is on his way home."

"Wait, what? Logan is leaving the Navy?"

"His term of service is up. He's not re-enlisting, so he's being discharged." There was a brief pause. "Technically, I probably shouldn't tell you that. I just processed the paperwork, so I know, but probably not too many other people do."

"Does Logan know?"

"Sure. He had to sign the papers." There was a screech. "Look, I gotta go. Call again when the world's not being torn apart."

"Thanks, Seth." Saffron hung up.

Logan was leaving the Navy. This was news. Byron's dreams for Lyza's future—settling down in Winchester with Logan—didn't seem so far-fetched now. Could the father of the bride have known? Is that why he decided to try for one last attempt at salvaging the relationship?

The wind had reached a fever pitch. Its whine set Saffron's teeth on edge. Behind her, the drone of a weather announcer on the news told her that someone had turned the television back on.

". . . Set to make landfall over the town of Maika'i," the announcer was saying. Saffron looked out at the sea, stretching away from the cliffs. Like a living thing, the waves rose and fell, heaving in crests that tumbled chaotically over each other. Whitecaps delineated each breaker, and the size of the swells and power of the ocean made Saffron afraid.

She thought of the houses along the beach, hers included. She thought of the Oceanside Cafe and the bookstore, the park and the Paradise Market. Once those waves hit, there would be no Maika'i left.

She thought the cliffhouse was high enough to be safe, but not everyone from town was here. Some of the residents had stayed in Maika'i to sandbag and board up their houses. Saffron shivered as she thought of the deluge heading toward them.

A dark shape cut across the bank of windows. It was one of the pueo, laboring hard against the howling wind. Instead of the silent, steady flight Saffron had seen when the owls had passed over her on the beach, this time the bird was buffeted, tossed up and then down on the fierce hurricane winds.

Saffron wished she could help. She wanted to reach through the glass and bring the bird inside.

Another pueo struggled up beside the first. It was followed by another. Suspended in the air outside the window, more owls began to gather, fighting past the line of palm trees that were bent like tightly strung bows in the wind. Saffron watched, fascinated, as twenty or more of the owls gathered and made a rippling knot outside the bank of windows.

A soft voice beside her said, "it's happening."

Saffron turned to see Mano, his lined face serious, his bright eyes filled with wonder. "What?" she asked.

Mano handed her a pair of binoculars she saw that they were emblazoned with the logo of the research institute. The researchers must be sharing their equipment. As she looked around, she saw them at the window, too, along with Akoni, who was murmuring a pule—a prayer—as he watched.

"Look," Mano urged. "Down there. At the 'aumakua."

Saffron looked down. Through the driving rain, she could see the bay below. In it, the sharks. Their distinctive rocket shapes and cresting dorsal fins were shaping into a rough line.

"What are they doing?"

One of the researchers, the wiry girl with the cloud of jet hair, said, "We think it may be some kind of feeding stance. Fish can detect the drop in barometric pressure that comes with a storm, and they head for deeper water in droves. Bigger fish usually eat a lot more as the pressure begins to drop, to sustain them through the storm. We think the sharks are lining up to gorge on an easy meal as the smaller fish rush past them out to sea."

Mano didn't correct her, but he didn't agree, either. Instead, he spoke to Saffron. "They are protecting their families," he said, his voice solemn. "It was like this when they protected Maika'i from the jellyfish bloom, too, years ago."

Saffron watched, fascinated, as the sharks assembled. She had seen their weaving and shifting patterns before. Now, though, they moved with determination and purpose. It was as if each had a place, and each knew that place. They lined up parallel with the cliffs, tails to the coming waves, and swam suspended in the turbulent water.

As the sharks aligned and the owls continued to tumble together in the wind, the people of Maika'i gathered in front of the big windows.

"What about the owls?" Cyndi asked the researcher. The bride's weary mother was sitting in one of the chairs, watching the tumbling birds outside the window.

"Many birds fly ahead of a storm," the researcher said. "And because they're all trying to leave at once, it may look like they are gathering together."

"But they're not leaving," Cyndi said.

The researchers were fascinated by this, as well, and they didn't have a ready answer. "We do know," the bearded one said, "that Hawaiian Owl males do amazing aerial acrobatics to attract their mates. It could be a variation on that behavior. They're a bit disoriented from the storm."

"It's called sky dancing," the curly-haired researcher said.

Whatever was happening outside the windows, Saffron thought, sky-dancing was the perfect name for it.

After that, the storm grew in fury, and the spectators grew quiet. The turmoil outside was contrasted by the complete silence in the room.

The wind screamed around the doors and windows. The house groaned. The pueos flapped, and the manōs swam.

There was a haunting symmetry to the owls and the sharks.

Both seemed to hold their position against the incredible forces of air and water that were accosting them.

They fought the elements, small against the vast sky and sea. Saffron found herself barely breathing. The beats of the pueo's wings became more aggressive, the waving tails of the manō became more forceful. The owls beat against the wind as the sharks thrashed against the water.

Keahi arrived at Saffron's side. Mano caught their eyes and gestured. "They are fighting for us," he murmured. His tone held the same reverence as Akoni's prayer.

Saffron listened. Was the howling wind easing? She shook the idea out of her mind. That wasn't possible. The hurricane was almost upon them. There was no changing its course now. The animals were, like everything else, being acted upon by the weather, not acting upon it.

But there were signs. Undeniable signs that something was happening outside. The arch of the palms was distinctly less. The screaming of the wind in the cracks was now an ebbing whistle. The pueo were no longer tumbling. They were now holding steady with powerful, controlled strokes instead of flapping wildly. Saffron raised the binoculars again and looked at the sharks below. Their flashing tails moved rhythmically, and they, too, seemed under less strain.

The weather announcer's voice wound into the room, "Storm seems to be turning . . ." Saffron shook her head, unsure she could be seeing what she was seeing.

She glanced at Mano. He was grinning, his eyes pressed closed. It was an expression of pure gratitude.

Akoni was suddenly beside him, his eyes shining. Mano put a hand on his friend's shoulder.

"Do you see it?" Akoni said with awe in his voice.

"I see it."

"The 'aumakua are turning the winds and the tides."

THE WIND HAD EASED. The weather announcer could barely contain his amazement as he recounted, again and again, the dramatic turn in the storm. The national meteorological agency had a dozen theories about what had happened, none of them involving sharks or owls.

The researchers in the cliff house had theories, too, but they were less sure of them. They had watched the 'aumakua, had seen the undeniable shift in the storm, and they were conflicted as they sat in a circle and tried to reconcile what they thought they knew with what they had seen.

Saffron looked outside at the flagging palms. It was no worse than a breezy day out there now, with a sprinkling of rain. There was no sun yet, but Saffron knew it would return.

The knot of pueo began to loosen. One by one, then a few at a time, the beautiful speckled birds winged their way off over the cliffhouse and out of sight. A few rested in the trees outside, and a few of the people of Maika'i whose 'aumakua were still nearby went outside with gifts of thanks.

The sharks, too, dispersed, leaving only a few dark shapes slicing through the water at the base of the cliffs. The researchers said they'd eaten their fill. The kahuna said their work was done.

Saffron glanced around and found Keahi in deep conversation with Mano. She left them to talk and walked out onto the wide lanai.

A gust blew by, sprinkling Saffron with a burst of fresh rain in the heavy, damp air. The pressure had lightened a bit, and the breeze was refreshing. Saffron stepped over and righted one of the remaining chairs on the lanai. She was glad to see that there wasn't much damage to the outside of the house. As she lifted the chair, she saw, huddled under it, a bright butterfly. Its wings were a rich red—the exact color, Saffron recognized, of the ribbon on the gift box that held the key. The butterfly was damp and bedraggled, but alive. Saffron set down the chair, then slid a hand in front of the creature.

The butterfly climbed onto her hand, and she carried it to a sheltered windowsill and set it there to rest and dry.

Along with the color of the ribbon, the curve of the insect's double wings and the gently tapering body brought the image of the key to Saffron's mind. She skipped down off the steps of the lanai and made her way around mud puddles and palm fronds to Keahi's SUV.

The box was still on the backseat. Saffron fetched it. She might as well give it to the couple now. On her way back, she passed Bradley's car.

She'd almost forgotten about the evidence bag. Saffron didn't really need to check it. She knew the neckerchief would be Natalie's. She knew that Natalie had been outside when Davis fell. She knew the anger she had seen in the girl's eyes. And now, because of the recording, she knew that Natalie had done something terrible out there.

What she didn't know was whether Natalie or Byron had been the one to actually push Davis over the cliff. Both had been there, both had valid motives.

Both evidence bags were there. She got the one that Dr. Weiss had filled, with the black silk neckerchief and the shreds of stained white fabric. As she pulled the plastic bag from the front seat, she knew that the neckerchief would have Natalie's name on it.

Saffron pulled it from the bag and unfurled it. The letters were faded to that sea-foam color, just as she remembered. And there was an N and an L. Diagonally across the middle of the tattered square of black silk, were the indiscernible strokes of a name and number. A faint line, then a gap, a fairly clear 'N,' then another sizeable blank space broken only by a few stray lines and the odd curve, then a bold 'L' followed by a period and a string of sporadic numbers.

Though Saffron was unsure what the faint line before the 'N' could be, the 'N' and the 'L' seemed to be in the right places, more or less, to make up Natalie's name.

Saffron grasped both bags and the box, slammed the door to the police cruiser, and strode back into the cliffhouse.

The still-tossing sea glistened in the late-afternoon light outside the big bank of windows. People had left the windows to go outside, or to gather in the media room. Only a few people remained in the greatroom, and they were the bedraggled members of the wedding party. The chairs had been moved around into various configurations, and they sat in a large half-circle facing the windows.

Lyza and Davis sat leaning on each other, talking softly. Logan sat on the other side of Lyza, and next to him was a smoldering Natalie. Also in the group were Myra, Lyza's parents, the Empress, and Evelyn.

Saffron felt protective. Someone in that circle had deliberately tried to hurt Davis, and they might try again. Or they might hurt someone else.

She thought of the deep respect that Akoni and Mano had for life. She didn't sense that in some of the people in this circle. They valued other things: their ideas of life, their own desires. It was no way to live.

Saffron carried the box to Lyza. "This is yours," Saffron said. "One of your gifts. It was left in my car."

Lyza laid it on her lap, exchanging a look with Davis. Saffron stood in the center of the half circle and set the evidence bags on the floor. She crossed to Natalie, holding the neckerchief.

"You'd better take this," Saffron said, trying to keep the anger out of her voice, "If you're going back to your ship." She held up the neckerchief and watched for the guilty tinge to spread across Natalie's skin.

But it didn't. Natalie's sullen expression only turned quizzical. "What?"

"Your neckerchief," Saffron said.

"How did you get that?" Natalie demanded. Saffron saw the girl's head turn, just slightly, to glance at Logan.

No one else would have seen it, and Saffron herself nearly missed it: the slight reddening of Logan's cheeks, and the blue tinge to his forehead and chin—*he* was surprised to see the neckerchief.

For the first time, Saffron saw Logan—really saw him, not just as the ubiquitous supporter of all the women in his life, but also as the boy who'd been in love with Lyza.

"Why did you look at Logan just now?" Saffron asked, a suspicion forming in her mind.

Natalie glanced over her shoulder as if checking for anyone who might overhear, "Because I gave that to him."

"You gave your neckerchief to him?"

"Yes," Natalie said, "Just before the memorial service. I knew that Collins was gunning for him, and he couldn't afford another uniform violation. I knew Collins would go easier on me because he was still hoping I'd give in to him."

The seafoam-colored letters flashed through Saffron's mind. She dug in the other bag for the neckerchief they'd found over the cliff the morning after the accident. Unfurling it, she saw, clearly stamped diagonally across it the name of the sailor it was issued to:

HOWARD, D.

The last name first.

She dropped it and grasped both sides of the silk square that had been found wrapped around Davis's wounds. She held it in front of her, studying it.

That was where she'd gone wrong. She had seen —N——

L. and her mind had read "Natalie." But uniforms were marked with the sailor's surname and initial. What she was seeing was the remainder of PRENTICE, L.

Logan.

This wasn't Natalie's. That was, apparently, with Logan's uniform in his suitcase in the game room.

When Saffron raised her gaze to Logan, she saw the red shade in his cheeks had faded. A slight, very pale blue had replaced it and spread from his forehead down between his eyebrows. Saffron knew that hue—it was fear. She spoke slowly, using her peripheral vision to locate Officer Bradley talking to Bernadette in the doorway at the back of the room.

"Why did you need to borrow Natalie's neckerchief, for the memorial service, Logan?"

There wasn't the slightest tremor in Logan's voice when he answered. "Mine was lost at the dry cleaners." A story he'd practiced, Saffron could tell.

"It's remarkable, then, that Davis was found gripping it. That Oke Cooper used it to wrap the wound on his arm when he found him days before I took those uniforms to the cleaners."

Logan didn't speak.

"I don't think it got lost at the dry cleaners," Saffron said. "I think it got lost the night Davis fell. Then you borrowed Natalie's to stay out of trouble with Collins, and just stood there while she got in trouble for not having it." The pieces were falling together.

Saffron spoke evenly. She knew, now, where the mystery gift had come from. Without taking her eyes off Logan, she spoke. "Lyza, open that present."

A flash of red, bright as a butterfly wing, fluttered as Lyza untied the ribbon around the box in her lap. She removed the lid and lifted the key. It hung, twisting gently, from her hand.

"Logan?" Lyza breathed.

The sailor didn't look at her. His shoulders had squared, and he had shifted his gaze. He sat at rigid military attention, eyes forward, staring past Saffron, out the wide windows.

"Logan?" the bride said again.

Saffron spoke to Byron. "What was your gift to your daughter for her wedding, Mr. Carelli?"

Byron, stirring out of his sullen stupor, had less growl in his voice than when Saffron had first met him. "I didn't bring a gift. I figured all the expense to get here was enough."

Saffron nodded, remembering his eruption about the cost when he'd arrived for the party.

"So you two didn't give her anything?" Saffron had wrongly assumed he'd given her the key.

"No," Byron said, but his wife shifted in her seat uncomfortably. Saffron pinned her with a direct gaze.

"Cyndi? You seem to disagree with your husband."

The woman ran her fingertips across her disheveled hair. She looked at Byron pleadingly, "I had to give her something. I didn't get to plan the wedding. I wanted at least to contribute to the honeymoon."

He scowled his question and his disapproval at the same time. "What?"

"Just a short trip. I told Logan, not too extravagant."

"Logan?" Byron asked, "What does he have to do with anything?"

A fine beading of sweat had appeared on Logan's forehead. Saffron explained. It was all so clear to her now.

"Cyndi asked Logan for help, didn't you?" Saffron registered a slight, miserable nod from Cyndi. "You gave him your husband's credit card number and asked him to get the newly-weds something nice from you and her father. You knew you could explain the charge to him later when you were all back home." She swung to face Logan. "And you did buy something. A honeymoon—not too far away, just over on Kauai. But you never intended for Davis to use it. You made the reservations in your own name. You were planning to kill Davis and take Lyza there yourself."

At this, Logan's gaze snapped to Saffron. His voice was shaking, but not loud. "That's not true."

"Which part?"

"I was never going to kill Davis. I just talked to him. Natalie and I both talked to him, right, Nat?" Logan turned a pleading face to his shipmate, but she had recoiled from him. Her hand was over her mouth, and she choked a little on her breath.

Logan went on, his words rolling over each other, "I really thought he'd be reasonable if we talked to him. Everything was lining up wrong: him and Lyza together left me and Natalie out in the cold. Natalie was in love with him. If he broke it off with Lyza, he wouldn't be alone. And I'm always going to be in love with you, Lyza," here, he swung his head back toward the bride. She shrunk back against Davis.

"No, no," he said, "don't be afraid. I know this seems bad."

"Bad?" her voice was high and strained, "Logan, you said the trip to Kauai was to give me space, to let me grieve. But you knew beforehand that I would be grieving?"

"No, no, I swear, I didn't mean for anything bad to happen to Davis. I just thought I could talk him out of it and he wouldn't go through with the wedding. Natalie knew it was wrong, your dad did." He waved a hand at Byron. Saffron heard the older man grunt. "We all knew you shouldn't marry him. You've only known him for a few months!" He grasped Lyza's hand, "we've had a lifetime to love each other."

Lyza pulled her hand back, standing as she did so. The key clattered to the floor and lay between them.

"Where did this come from?" Lyza asked slowly. She looked at Saffron as she stooped and retrieved the key, "my dad gave us these for graduation. When we broke up, I gave mine back, but Logan," she looked at him, "did you keep yours?"

Logan's jaw tightened, and Saffron answered for him. "Until now. He's given it away. That's Logan's present to you. Right, Logan?"

He turned his fierce gaze on Saffron, "What do you know?"

"I know you planned to pick up where your dream got side-tracked after high school. I know you planned to wreck the wedding, then make up for it by whisking Lyza away to Kauai and surprising her with the key to the condo at the Mariposa building in Winchester. After her devastating loss, you could offer a new dream, a place to run home to."

"No, this can't be right," Lyza said. "He wouldn't plan that, because he's going back to his ship," there was a bitter edge of denial in her voice, and a tremor of fear behind it.

"No, he's not. Are you, Logan?" Marks' sketched compass spun in Saffron's mind—the symbol of a sailor finding his way home. "Your term of service is up, and you're not re-enlisting."

Logan's face was a mask of surprise, and his voice was low, "How do you know that?"

Saffron didn't have time to answer before Lyza spoke again. "So you thought you'd just wreck my wedding and then give me this key so I'd come back to Winchester and live our happily ever after with you?"

Logan opened his mouth. His voice was hoarse when he spoke, "Lyze—"

She held up a hand. "Lies is right. You've been lying to me for a long time. Logan," her voice held exquisite pain, and she locked her eyes on Logan's, "did you hurt Davis?"

For the first time, Davis spoke up, "He grabbed me," he said, almost to himself. "I remember that." He looked at Natalie. "It was right after I found you."

"I'm sorry, Davis," she said, "I shouldn't have done what I did."

Now Saffron stepped forward. The recording sprung to her

mind. Natalie wasn't entirely innocent. She had admitted that she'd done *something* out on the cliff. Had she been Logan's accomplice?

Davis looked at Lyza, and there was shame in his face. "I remember now. She kissed me," he said, "and told me she still loved me." That's what Natalie had confessed to in the recording—kissing Davis on the night before his wedding. Saffron was relieved that she hadn't tried to kill him.

Lyza didn't respond. Saffron could see the flood of revelations washing over her.

Davis went on. "But I told her I loved you, Lyza. I told her I was sorry. She left crying." Davis was staring up at Lyza, who stood in front of him and to his right. Logan stood to his left. He looked between them as remembrance spread across his face like dawn breaking. "And then Logan was there. He told me I couldn't marry you. I tried to explain to him that I had to, that I love you. He knocked the rest of the glowsticks out of my hand and pushed me. He said he'd stop the wedding. And we fought. "

Davis's voice was stronger now. His hands clenched into fists. "You tried to push me over, but you couldn't do it. You weren't strong enough."

Logan's jaw tensed. He was clearly bothered by Davis' recollection.

"I tried to talk you out of it, but you kept coming after me. I remember. It was so dark. I could tell we'd moved close to the edge of the cliff, because we kicked a couple of glowsticks while we were fighting, and I saw them go over. He said he would kill me and you'd come running back into his arms." Davis' I grabbed his neckerchief. It was tied wrong, like always, and when he pulled away and ran, it came off in my hand."

"And then you fell?" Lyza's voice rang with concern.

Davis shook his head, "No. I was fine. I was standing there, trying to catch my breath. I knew you were nothing more than a coward, Logan. You tried to push me over, but you couldn't do it."

Logan jumped in. "See? See? When I left him, he was fine. Even if I wanted him dead by then, I didn't push him off the cliff. Have we considered that maybe he was just clumsy and fell over himself?"

"No," Davis said, "I didn't fall, and I wasn't pushed. I was hit. Something slammed into my head." His hand went to the stitched wound on his forehead. "That's when I remember falling. And darkness."

Saffron looked at the evidence bags at her feet. She reached down, slowly, and extracted from the first the vibrant orange football. She knew how Logan had done it. And Davis was right. He hadn't even had the decency to end it hand-to-hand. He had done it from afar.

Byron had figured it out, too. His voice rang through the room, "Fastest, most targeted passes in the country, they said."

Chapter Twenty

I t turned out that in spite of all his anger, Byron was innocent. He had arrived at the cliff's edge after Davis had fallen, just as he'd said. He and his daughter had a long talk, and he recognized, finally, that he had misjudged Logan and tried too hard to push her into a life she didn't want. Byron promised to be more supportive of her choices from now on.

He was taking the first steps in that direction by walking her down the aisle the next morning.

The delicate strains of the wedding march trailed along the petal-strewn floor to meet the bride and her father, advancing in perfect synchrony toward the big windows that overlooked the sea.

Davis stood alone at the front of the aisle, his eyes alight with the love Saffron had seen the day she met him, watching Lyza's approach.

The light scent of ginger leis and the rich smell of plumeria brightened the room. Saffron took in the scene from the back row of chairs. The room was full of family and neighbors and sailors, many of whom had weathered the storm together here in the cliffhouse yesterday. They were all there to celebrate the couple that had weathered such a tumultuous storm of their own to reach this moment. The lineup looked slightly different, with Lyza's friends already back on the mainland, the best woman back in service on the *Havasu*, and the man of honor locked up in the brig back on his ship, but it was beautiful nonetheless.

The sky outside the big wall of windows was a perfect, creamy blue. It met the azure ocean far off at the horizon. A triangular sail accented the water, tiny from this perspective, and Saffron knew that Oke was attending the wedding, too, in his way.

The decor had been freshened, the caterers re-booked, and Saffron reveled in the moment that Lyza and Davis said: "I do." It was the culmination of all her work and the happy ending that they deserved.

Afterward, over light refreshments in the dining room, Mano slid an arm around Saffron's shoulders.

"A beautiful event," he said, sweeping his hand wide, "and the food—so ono."

Saffron smiled at the praise.

"I couldn't have done it alone. Thank you for your help cleaning everything up outside." Mano had headed an effort to gather the palm fronds, saw up the fallen trees, and generally shine up the outside of the cliffhouse for the event.

"We got to Mālama Honua, eh?" he said.

To care for our Island Earth. Saffron remembered. And to care for those around us and the animals and oceans. Saffron nodded, "I've learned something about that these last few weeks." She lowered her voice. "Have the 'aumakua gone?"

"Mmm-hmmm," Mano closed his eyes in a moment of reverence. "But they were here when we needed them."

"They sure were. I'm still in awe."

"Awe is a good word," he said, then repeated it, "Awe. The

'aumakua turned the tides and the winds, and in the end, the storm was no worse than a bad rain on a stormy day." Saffron thought of how scared she'd been for her chickens. But the egg house had kept them warm and dry, and she'd come home to find them all safe. Even Pepper was back on her feet.

Mano went on, "The 'aumakua sent that storm turning, right out into the open ocean where it couldn't hurt their families." He leaned in close and said it again, in case Saffron hadn't gotten it. "The 'aumakua protected their families. We look after them, they look after us. It's what ohana does."

Ohana. Family. Saffron glanced at Byron. He was free, all charges against him dropped. And in the wake of the revelation that Logan was not what he seemed to be, Byron was also free of the limiting vision of his daughter's future. Though Davis was medically discharged from the Navy, he and his new bride were staying in Hawaii. Byron had proven his new resolve to support them by exchanging the condo in the Mariposa building in Winchester for one in the Honolulu building. Byron and Cyndi had made plans with the Tuckers at Tropical Adventures to come back for a visit in a few months, once the newlyweds were settled.

"Hey, planner," Keahi said, approaching with a clear plastic cup of ginger ale for Saffron, "great party."

Saffron forced a smile as she took the cup. She felt her eyes stinging. Keahi's eyes softened. "Hey," he said gently.

Mano patted her shoulder awkwardly, then turned and went to congratulate the Empress. Saffron knew he was giving them space to talk.

Keahi moved close, standing in front of Saffron and putting his hands on her arms. "It's okay," he said, "I'm not going to work all the time. I'll come back as often as I can."

Saffron nodded, not trusting herself to speak. Keahi had contacted the hospital. They had begged him to come back, and when he'd asked Saffron what she thought, she'd swallowed her own sadness and said what she knew she had to say —that he should go. And it was the right choice. He was a gifted surgeon. She'd seen it when he worked on Pepper, and she didn't want him to waste that gift. But she was still sad and scared. It was five thousand miles to Boston from here.

"We're still going to keep this going," Keahi said. "I'm not ready for this relationship to end."

Saffron looked up at him and blurted, "I'm just going to be so alone here, with you gone."

Keahi's usually warm eyes were tinged with sadness above his forced smile.

"It will be tough for a while," he acknowledged. "I don't know what I'll do without Smoothie Tuesday," she knew he was trying to cheer her.

"There are plenty of places to get a smoothie in Boston," Saffron said, trying to make her voice light.

"Saffron, Smoothie Tuesday was never about the smoothies."

Ginger ale splashed out of the cup onto Saffron's hand as she wrapped her arms around Keahi's waist. He hugged her back, and together they stood embracing.

A racket across the room drew them apart. The bride and groom were leaving, and all the guests went out the front doors and down to the driveway to blow sparkling bubbles into the fresh island air.

As the newlyweds drove away, the rest of the guests began to disperse. Keahi stayed close, holding Saffron's hand as tightly as she was clinging to his. Together, they climbed back up onto the lanai to see the Empress sitting regally in her chair with Mano behind. They were flanked by Rex and Carlo, with Princess nestled happily, pecking at a bubble.

The bubble popped, and Princess let out a satisfied trill.

"This was a beautiful wedding," the Empress said, holding out a hand. Saffron took it, keeping her other one in Keahi's grip. "You did a wonderful job. You're going to be getting some calls for other parties, I think." The Empress leaned close, "Belle Tucker's expecting. We'll have to have a baby shower!"

Saffron couldn't stop the smile that spread across her face. That would be a tropical adventure, for sure.

With his free hand, Keahi reached for Mano's shoulder. "You two keep Saffron busy, will you?" he asked his grandpa, "she's worried she'll be lonely."

Both Mano and the Empress erupted in chiding sounds, "We won't let that happen," Mano said.

"This girl," the Empress squeezed Saffron's hand, "is our ohana now."

Ohana. Family. Saffron soaked in that word for a moment, and the sound of it lifted her gloom a bit. She looked down the long lanai, to the satin ocean spreading away from the island. She wasn't alone, and Keahi, no matter how far away he was, was part of this ohana, too. She felt sure that, like the 'aumakua, when his family needed him, he too, would return.

In the meantime, she had Mano. And the Empress. And the Tuckers. And Bernadette. And Curry and Tikka and all her chickens. In Maika'i, she had found a home.

Handsome or not, he was a stranger. Saffron Skye saw him standing on the beach, looking entirely out of place in a loose-fitting suit, black wingtips, and a fedora. His face looked as if it had been hewn from oak—a strong jaw, angular cheekbones, and narrow temples. He was crouched down, letting Saffron's rooster, Curry, peck at something in his hand. But between glances down at the chicken, the man was clearly staring at Saffron's house.

Saffron's house—a blue bungalow with a wide lanai wrapped all the way around it—was charming, but it held no interest next to what was behind the stranger: a golden beach and the wide sweep of the turquoise Pacific. In her six months here in Hawaii, Saffron had seen dozens of people wandering up and down her beach, and few of them even glanced in the direction of the house.

The stranger was riveted, though. He seemed to be memorizing the place. Or casing it, she supposed. But he would be surprised if he broke in. There were no expensive electronics and not much cash. All he'd find was a cottage full of chicken decor and two refrigerators full of eggs.

Saffron had inherited this place from her uncle, and though it looked like most other vacation houses, it was a working egg farm. Named Ha'oli ka Moa Egg Farm, The Happy Chicken Egg Farm, long before her time, it was a modest operation with more than a hundred birds and a beautiful, spacious egg house consisting of pens with indoor and outdoor runs where the hens could wander about in the tall grass, foraging and flipping sand up on themselves for their favorite activity: dirt bathing.

And the three little cottages behind the farmhouse were mostly empty except for cozy furniture and a few pieces of decor. Saffron had recently finished cleaning them out, re-painting, and renovating them so she could rent them out to tourists. She had two of them rented right now—one to a couple on their anniversary trip and one to a fifty-something single woman who was trying to write a novel. She spent a fair amount of time sitting on her cottage's little lanai, gazing at her laptop in deep concentration.

The three cottages were painted bright colors: banana yellow, Pacific teal, and coral pink. All had white trim, and each had a little white lanai jutting from the front. They'd originally housed the few workers who her grandparents had employed on the egg farm in its heyday, but they'd been filled with junk since her grandparents' death. She'd just recently finished cleaning them out, renovating, and redecorating them, and she'd been able to start renting them the day after they were finished.

The thought of the renovations brought a pang of sadness. Her boyfriend, Keahi, had helped her. They'd worked together on the project for weeks: plumbing and wiring and scouring the places so that she could use them as vacation rentals and bring in a little more money to supplement her egg income.

Keahi was wonderful at fixing things, at seeing problems and addressing them, at laughing and joking even after a long day of wading through years of accumulated junk. He'd made sure everything was addressed: the roofs, the electricity. The only thing Saffron had to be mindful of was a leaky bathroom sink in the Banana Cottage. He thought it was fixed, but had told her to keep checking in on it just in case. He'd checked on it himself during the week before he left.

But now he was gone. Thousands of miles away, in Boston, and Saffron's longing for his company was sharp and constant.

"You ready for the rush?" The voice of Keahi's grandfather, Mano, made Saffron jump.

Mano was missing his grandson, too, and he and Saffron spent a lot of time together these days. Each of them understood, without saying, the hole left in the other's life.

Saffron didn't blame Keahi. He was a trained surgeon, a gifted physician from all accounts. He had fled his work at a top hospital in Boston two years ago, after losing a young patient, but the hospital had long wanted him to come back, and just a few months ago, he had decided that he needed to.

Saffron had tried, in the ensuing weeks, to let him go. Not just to Boston, but to let him go from her heart, from her life.

But Keahi was a rare mix of humor and compassion, of

strength and gentleness. His presence made any situation better, and their connection made him impossible to forget. Instead of sending him off with a smile, as she'd wanted to, she'd ended up sobbing into his shoulder at the Daniel K. Inouye International Airport. When she'd pulled back, tears were running down his warm brown cheeks. Keahi's skin was exactly the color of the sand just at the edge of the wide Hawaiian beaches, where the retreating surf left curves of tawny topaz next to the brighter gold of the dry sand. She'd kissed him then, tasting salt, and let him go.

She and Mano had ridden back to the little town of Maika'i with a melancholy cloud hanging above them. It had taken two weeks and a lot of distraction to lift it.

Now, though, Saffron's loneliness for Keahi was a background melody in the bustle of the day. She had an event to pull off. Her new business, Brightblossom Events, was coordinating an annual benefit for the Friends of Hens, a nonprofit organization. It was to be held on the Coronation Lawn at Iolani Palace. Saffron had planned for them a beautiful celebration in gold and black, two of the colors on their logo, which featured a pair of chickens like she'd seen all over the island.

Wild chickens were a feature of Hawaii. Though Saffron's hundred and twenty hens and her single rooster lived in the spacious Egg House, with wide indoor and outdoor runs, automatic water, roosts, and nest boxes, there were as many as 20,000 chickens that roamed the island free and feral. Friends of Hens worked tirelessly to help control those numbers in a humane way by catching chickens and shipping them to their rescue farm on the mainland. They were a well-respected organization, and sympathetic donors attended the benefit in droves.

During her first meeting with Friends of Hens, Saffron had revealed that she owned a chicken farm, and the passionate staff had insisted coming up from Honolulu for a tour. Once there they found that Saffron's uncle, Beau, had assembled a varied and beautiful flock, of all different colors and shapes.

It was then, in the heat of their delight, that Saffron had agreed to showcase some of her birds at their event.

"The guests can see then what real, cared-for chickens look like!" The director of the organization, fittingly named Birdie Bromley, had clapped her hands with delight. She was a small woman, middle-aged, with enormous round glasses and a way of cocking her head to the side that made her look very much like her namesakes.

Saffron had tried to explain that her chickens were free-range birds that spent their days wandering in and out of the egg house, scratching and roosting and slurping up centipedes in the tall grass of their outdoor runs. Recently, several of her commercial egg customers—the Oceanside Cafe and the Paradise Market, for example, had been sending produce clippings and unsold fruits and vegetables out to the hens, and they'd been scratching and pecking at tomatoes and peas and lettuce, standing atop big mounds of produce. They were not, she emphasized, show birds with proper manners for such an event.

But Birdie insisted that the event could not go on without them. "People see so many feral chickens," Birdie had pleaded, "and they think that all chickens are scrawny and unwanted. But these girls," she'd waved her hand down the row of pens, "could give them another view of chickens. They could be ambassadors for their species!" She had personally selected five of Saffron's most beautiful birds, and Saffron had gotten the distinct feeling that if she refused, Birdie would find herself another event planner. Mano was here to help her catch them, get them ready for their four hours of fame, and attend the event with Saffron.

Back in Washington DC, Saffron had run an event planning business with two full-time assistants and several part-time staff. But she hadn't quite got Brightblossom up and running to that extent yet, so she had no employees. She and Mano did everything necessary to arrange the event. Though she insisted on paying Mano, he wouldn't take cash and generally "forgot" to cash her checks.

Saffron tore herself away from the window even though the stranger was still standing like a stone on the beach, staring at the bungalow. Something told her she would see him again.

"You are an ambassador," Saffron hissed at the fluffy hen in her arms, "stop flapping!"

When she came to Hawaii less than a year ago, Saffron had expected beautiful flowers, beach bungalows, and the ocean. What she had not expected was a grand and elegant palace like the one she was standing in front of. Iolani Palace, in the heart of Honolulu, stood as regal as the emerald mountains.

Luna, the chicken in Saffron's arms, didn't seem to care that they were in such a regal setting. She flailed about for two more full seconds before trilling her annoyance and settling down into Saffron's arms. Saffron tried to smile at the stern, suited attendant eying her and the bird.

"This is the next animal on the permit?" The man asked.

"Yes. Yes. Luna," Saffron raised the chicken a little in greeting. "She's a lavender orpington." Saffron raised a hand to stroke the hen's soft feathers. They were a shade that Saffron had seen only in the early morning sky, before the oranges and yellows of sunrise. Soft, cloud-gray feathers that Luna kept preened and fluffed. She was a big chicken, a round and fluffy hen that waddled around her pen back at Ha'oli Ka Moa egg farm, which Saffron had inherited from her uncle.

The attendant scanned the paperwork. He was a big man,

bald and intimidating, with a mainland—maybe Californian—accent and a firm set to his pale jaw. Saffron could see why he was employed here. Nobody would want to break the rules with his narrowed gaze on them.

"The chicken will be contained at all times." He said forcefully. "You will be responsible for any damage the chicken does to the grounds of the palace. We assume no liability."

"Right," Saffron said, glad that Friends of Hens had signed all the paperwork for hosting the hens here at their event.

She carried Luna to her appointed place. Friends of Hens had supplied beautiful chromed show pens. Saffron had set them atop chest-high pedestal tables with flowing black or gold tablecloths, depending on which color best showcased the color of the bird. Friends of Hens had offered to put soft shavings down on the bottom for the hens, but Saffron knew that the minute she set her girls on shavings they would scratch right to the floor of the pen and toss those shavings out onto the tablecloths and any admiring onlookers. She'd opted for long shreds of colorful paper in coordinating shades. As Luna settled into the springy bedding, Saffron worried she may not ever be happy on anything less elegant.

The hen was round and fluffy, a beautiful example of one of Saffron's biggest breeds. A high voice at Saffron's shoulder drew her attention.

"Oh, aren't they stunning?!" It was Birdie, rushing across the wide lawn. Behind her slouched a skinny teen in khakis and a white shirt. Birdie's hands were clasped together in ecstasy. "This is the perfect event!" She indicated the sweeping lawn, dotted with high tables and careful seating arrangements.

Saffron was proud of it. From the scattered chickens to the delicate toasted-seed cakes, it was an event fit for chicken-lovers.

Birdie grasped Saffron's arm. "Tell me again what kinds they are, so I can answer when people ask me!"

Saffron started to tell her that each chicken was identified with a card on its cage, but Birdie looked up at her so imploringly that Saffron realized she just wanted to talk about chickens. So Saffron indulged her.

"Luna here is a Lavender Orpington. Tikka, over there, with the gold feathers laced with black, is a Gold-Laced Wyandotte. Blossom," Saffron waved a hand at a beautiful hen covered with tan, black, and white speckles, graced with a fluffy crest atop her head, "is a Swedish Flower hen."

Birdie made a joyous sound, "She looks like she's wearing a crown!"

Saffron couldn't help but smile. "She does." They walked over to Curry's cage, and he switched from his anxious tuk-tuk-tuk sound to his a contented rattle that he saved for his friends. It amazed Saffron that he remembered Birdie after only visiting Ha'oli Ka Moa once. "Curry here is kind of special."

"Because he's the rooster!" Birdie jumped in.

"Well, that, and his special color. See how his feathers are edged with blue?" Birdie nodded, "That's because he's a Blue-Laced Red Wyandotte."

"Like Tikka?" Birdie asked.

Saffron was impressed that she remembered that Tikka was a Wyandotte, "Yes, but different coloration. And over there we have Cleo, she's the huge fluffy buff one with the black collar."

"A Brahma?" Birdie was clearly pleased to know this breed.

"Right."

"Oh aren't they fantastic? Birdie clapped a little, making Luna jump a little in her cage.

The teen looked through Birdie to Saffron. "My mom is crazy about chickens."

Saffron detected the emphasis on the crazy. Saffron felt the need to defend his mom. After all, she appreciated Birdie's enthusiasm and activism in a world that was too often cynical and complacent.

"Chickens are fascinating creatures," she said, looking the kid in the eye. "Did you know they are the closest living relatives to Tyrannosaurus Rex?"

The kid leveled a half-lidded gaze at Saffron. "That would be fascinating," he said, "if I was four."

Saffron blinked. She realized that she was used to the relaxed, cheerful, live-and-let live island attitude of her neighbors in Maika'i. This bitter banter was jolting. But Saffron had lived most of her life in Washington, DC. She could remember how to be sharp and cold.

"Oh, you aren't?" she asked, "I'm sorry. You were just acting so childish, I assumed you'd find that interesting."

The kid pressed his lips together.

Birdie jumped in. "Oh, don't mind Jake," she said brightly. "He's just being a teenager."

Saffron looked to see how this assessment affected him. If it did, she couldn't tell by his closed expression.

"How about this chicken fact?" she asked, dredging up everything she could remember from her favorite chicken handbook: The Rewarding Art of Chicken Keeping. "Did you know that chickens can tell the difference between over a hundred different people and animals? That's way more than dogs or horses. Curry here remembers that he's met your mom before, even though she just came by once." He looked mildly interested, so Saffron went on. "And did you know that they are the most common birds on the planet? There are over twenty-five billion of them!"

"I believe that," Jake said, sniffing. "There are ten billion at our house right now."

Saffron couldn't help but smile. Despite his nastiness, the kid had a sense of humor that Saffron understood.

"Not that many!" Birdie scolded. She gazed at a spot above her and to her right. Her tiny eyes blinked rapidly as she calculated. "Six in the crate, fifteen in the coop, seven in the shed, three in the bathtub," Saffron exchanged a look with Jake, who seemed to be saying I told you. "About thirty-ish," Birdie finished. "Only thirty-ish."

Saffron knew chickens. She spent several days a week cleaning out big, roomy pens with twenty-ish chickens in them each, and she knew what a mess they could make. And Birdie lived here in Honolulu, where Saffron was sure she had much less space. She tried to smile. "That's a good-sized flock."

"Oh, they're not permanent," Birdie fluttered a hand, "they're our rescues. They'll be headed out to the Ranch out in Kentucky at the end of the week." Saffron had seen pictures of the Friends of Hens Rescue Ranch: rolling acres of green, dotted with little ponds and roosting trees, where hundreds of rescued Hawaiian chickens wandered free and happy. Funded by wealthy chicken lovers around the world who had visited Hawaii and been moved to charity by seeing the feral chickens in the street, the ranch provided the best food, the most modern buildings, and two veterinarians on staff full-time. The chickens in Birdie's bathtub were about to strike it rich.

"There will be more the day after that," Jake said.

Birdie, seeming to miss the bitterness in his voice, gushed, "That's true. There are so many that need our help. So many roaming and wandering chickens—both hens and roosters—that need our care."

Jake rolled his eyes and turned abruptly, cutting through the tall tables to stand sullenly on the edge of the lawn with Iolani Palace rising elegantly behind him.

Birdie didn't seem to notice. "Sometimes I think we should change our name to Friends of Chickens so that we could be more inclusive of roosters, but it's a lot of work to change the name when you're a non-profit, and frankly, between my fundraising efforts and rescuing feral birds, I just don't have the time."

Saffron understood. Taking care of livestock was a lot of

work. But Birdie seemed to enjoy it. Jake, on the other hand, did not. He scoffed again.

"Not a fan of the feathered friends, eh, Jake?" Saffron challenged. She always found it useful to be direct, especially with young people. They were adept at spotting hypocrites.

The boy was about to answer when his gaze suddenly shifted past her and she saw him unconsciously straighten. He mumbled a response, "Not really," and his earlier sharp wit was noticeably lacking. Saffron swiveled her head to follow his gaze.

Into the party had walked a lovely girl in her teens. She had long, black hair, and perfect skin that was exactly the same color as the sunlit bark of the banyan trees behind her. Saffron smiled. She'd met the girl, who worked for the caterers.

"Would you like me to introduce you?" Saffron asked.

Jake's eyes widened and his gaze snapped back to Saffron. There was horror in his voice when he spoke. "No!" Then, with great effort evident in his bobbing Adam's apple and his set jaw, he said, "I don't know what you're talking about." Then, to his mother, he said, "I'm going to the car. I'll be back when there's food." He turned and walked stiffly across the lawn, cutting through the tables. Saffron suppressed a smile.

"I'm sorry," Birdie sighed. "That was rude. He's been a bit of a handful since his father left."

The words hit Saffron like a gut punch. Her own father had left when she was just a baby, and there was still a dad-shaped hole in her heart. She understood the kid a little more now.

"It's okay," she said, "I can just tell he likes Savannah over there."

Birdie blinked and looked around, "Oh," she said blankly. Saffron realized that the woman really was single-minded. She had seemingly missed Jake's obvious attraction to the girl. It made Saffron wonder what else Birdie didn't know about her son.

***

Join Saffron and the hens on their next adventure in Hard Boiled: Book 3 in the Aloha Chicken Mysteries!

DEAR READER,

Thank you for visiting Maika'i and the Hau'oli ka Moa Egg Farm! I hope you enjoyed Hen Party, and I hope you'll read more of Saffron's adventures in Book 3: Hard Boiled. If you did enjoy the book, please consider writing a review on Amazon and Goodreads. I love hearing from my readers and your reviews help other readers find my novels! I truly appreciate every review and every reader who spends time with Saffron, the hens, and me!

-Josi Avari

Made in the USA
Columbia, SC
19 September 2023

23065063R00155